I0638403

Dead Storm Rising

by

Shane Gries

All works © 2023 Cannon Publishing LLC & Shane Gries

Chapter 1

3 August, 2016
Kansas City, Missouri
0147 Hours Local

The two Humvees crept their way through the labyrinth of abandoned cars and trucks, occasionally ducking through ditches when necessary. They crawled along never exceeding ten miles per hour, taking great care to avoid bungling into an obstacle which might hang them up on some random bit of wreckage or debris. The light trucks were four-wheel drives, but that didn't mean they couldn't get stuck, and getting stuck out here at night in the middle of the Hot Zone was a nightmare scenario.

The temperature felt almost cool, at least compared to the brutal heat of midday. Mark Foley sat in the "shotgun" position of the vehicle with a bandana wrapped tightly around his face, vainly trying to keep out the stink of rotting bodies that hung heavily in the thick, summer air.

He peered through the monocular tube suspended in front of his right eye, the soft, green glow allowing him to see outside, if just barely. While the stars twinkled brightly, there was no moon, which blanketed the world in inky blackness. The night vision goggles merely amplified the ambient light and since there was scant little to be had, they could barely see a thing, making the drive particularly challenging.

The infrared beams on their headlights provided light straight ahead of them, but it helped them not one bit to their flanks or rear. The gunners up top behind the machine guns had their own IR illuminators which assisted them, but the passengers inside could not use theirs. They easily could have if the windows were rolled down, but nobody dared do that sort of thing anymore. Not with the undead running around. The infected had a tendency to reach through open windows and drag the occupants out kicking and screaming, at the most inopportune times. So they always rode with the windows rolled up, making for a stuffy, uncomfortable ride.

Off on their right flank they heard the beating of rotor blades, even through the earphones secured to their helmets. Somewhere, four hundred meters distant, a pair of Apache attack helicopters covered their movement. The choppers hovered out there, invisible in the darkness, tracking their movement and giving reports.

"White One, this is Tango One Six. Over." The radio crackled in Mark's ear, giving him a start.

"Tango One Six, White One. Send your traffic. Over."

"Yeah, roger. You might want to hold up. We've got movement down on the deck just to your 12 o'clock. Over." The Apache pilot's voice came in clear as a bell over the radio, even with the high-pitched hum from the turbine engine running in the background.

"Okay, hold up," Mark said to his driver. The vehicle eased to a stop while he hit the transmit key again. "White Two, did you monitor? Over."

"One, this is Two. I monitored. Pulling up right behind you. Over." Specialist Burbey's voice came over the radio slightly high in pitch, with a quick cadence. When they left the safety of the Forward Operating Base earlier in the evening, he'd sounded sluggish and exhausted. Now the adrenaline rushed through their veins.

Out front in the distance, just past the limits of their infrared headlights, stood the blackened silhouette of a large building next to a sprawling parking lot. Mark felt his arms turn to gooseflesh and the hairs on the back of his neck stand up when it came into view. There was no mistaking the shape of the casino they'd fought their way through the month before. The thought of what transpired there turned his stomach and he could immediately sense the unease in the others as well.

God, I hope we don't see any of them, Mark thought to himself, the idea of finding any of their former comrades turned seemed more terrifying than anything else. The rotting, animated husks of the dead were bad enough. It would be even more unsettling if they recognized any of them, and all too many of their platoon had succumbed to the snapping jaws of the dead and the contagion right there, in that terrible place looming in front of them.

"Why couldn't they send someone else on this mission, Sarn't?" Private James Johnson had a death-grip with one hand on the steering wheel, while using the other to toggle the intercom. He did not take his attention away from the movement out in front of them, staring straight ahead through his own set of NVGs.

"Because we're the only ones that know exactly where the track is located, dipshit," growled the machine gunner, Private Lauren Gray, from her position up in the cupola. "It'd take some other patrol a ton of time to locate it, and the more time someone lingers out here, the more fucking dangerous it is."

"Gray's right. Plus, it's our equipment and therefore our job to recover it." Mark turned to the driver and put his hand on the man's shoulder. "Listen, I feel the same way you do about this, but we can do it. Roger?"

"Roger, Sarn't." Johnson didn't sound convinced, his voice phlegmy.

"I'm right here with ya, Battle. Nothing's gonna go wrong. We got this," chimed in Johnson's best friend, Private Dante Dubois, from the back seat right behind him. The two of them were inseparable since the day they were assigned to the same squad back at Fort Riley. "This reminds of that time when we got cornered in that keep by a coven of vampires."

"Oh my god, you two aren't going to start up with your Dungeons and Dragons shit again, are you?" Gray's voice dripped with contempt.

"Okay, knock it off, all of you," Mark interjected. He toggled the switch forward, transmitting over the radio. "Tango One Six, White One. Can you paint me a picture? Over."

"*Yeah, roger, White One. Looks like we stirred up a hornet's nest down there. We've got beaucoup movement headed our way. I think the last of them are coming out of the casino and the herd is thinning somewhat. I'd give it another three mikes or so. I'll call when you're clear to move. Over.*"

"Sarn't Matthews, do you think this is actually going to work?" Johson asked, still staring at the moving shadows scurrying across the parking lot several hundred yards distant. Some moved with incredible speed while others shambled along. "Sarn't?"

"Um, what? Oh, yeah. Yes, this is going to work." Mark caught himself once again. Whenever he got tired, he'd sometimes forget he'd taken on a new identity. At least he did now, ever since he escaped from the Fort Leavenworth Disciplinary Barracks, wearing the uniform of the MP he dispatched after being turned by the undead. On occasion, people called him by the assumed name and he'd be slow to respond. While it didn't happen often, it still happened regularly enough to elicit strange looks from the soldiers in the company.

"It's simple, Battle. The zeds can't see any better than we can in the dark, so they rely on smell and sound. We move on the ground in the dark, while the helicopters and their noisy rotors draw them away from us. It's a proven tactic that's been perfected over the last few weeks." Dubois explained it calmly and convincingly to his friend, though none of them were completely confident in the plan. They all had seen things go wrong before while operating in the city since the dead never seemed to follow their well-laid plans. Like they always say in the Army, the enemy gets a vote.

"Wish we had a few of those helicopters during the outbreak. There might be a few more of us still alive." Gray said out loud what the rest of them were thinking.

"Yeah, well we all had to learn a lot of things the hard way over the last few weeks." Mark checked his GPS tracker, noting they had just over a kilometer to go before they reached their objective. They couldn't see it out there in the pitch blackness, but they all knew that just beyond the casino and its sprawling parking lot sat the piece of equipment they were after. It was a Bradley Infantry Fighting Vehicle with the name "*BOHICA*" stenciled on the side. The same vehicle they had to abandon during the initial outbreak. It was an invaluable and irreplaceable bit of gear they desperately needed to secure the railyards and highways running through Kansas City.

"*White One, this is Tango One Six. Time to move. Over.*"

"Tango One Six, this is White One. Roger, moving." Mark nervously clenched his fists and took a deep breath. "Two, this is One. Follow us in."

"*I'll be right on your tail, One.*"

Mark swallowed hard before turning to his driver. "Johnson, move out."

The two Humvees crawled along slowly, their engines barely revving above idle. They transited the open asphalt, taking care to avoid the light poles spaced evenly throughout the massive parking lot. Gray scanned a sector to the front, while Private McDermott in the trail vehicle covered the rear. Off to the left they passed by the massive building dedicated to games of chance, which now lay darkened and silent. It was now the site of a tomb, which held the remains of several of their fallen comrades.

The lead truck ran over a rotting corpse, suddenly lurching and forcing the passengers to reach out to steady themselves, startling them all.

"Damnit, Johnson, be careful. Watch where you're driving." Mark braced himself against the dashboard and the radio stack next to him. He knew Gray wanted to start yelling at the driver, but she knew better than to make any excessive noise while they were out here and held her tongue.

After a few minutes they came upon an offramp from the highway and followed it up to where they found a vehicle pile-up, and right next to it rested *BOHICA* in all her martial glory. Like the wrecks, she sat motionless and silent.

Johnson pulled their Humvee up as close to the Infantry Fighting Vehicle as possible before putting it in park. They all quickly dismounted the vehicle and set to work, while Burbey moved off to the side. Only the two machine gunners up top behind their crew-served weapons remained on the trucks, peering down their barrels, keeping watch.

The six of them on the ground opened doors and compartments as quietly as possible, taking care not to slam doors shut, securing things gently in place. They retrieved a tool bag and gingerly removed the contents next to the armored behemoth.

The IFV had "thrown track" while negotiating a steep incline next to the wreck on the onramp, stranding it in place. It became immobile when the weight of the vehicle put too much stress on the steel tracks, separating them from the road wheels. The track was now separated from the grooves in the wheels and bound up under the vehicle itself.

Back in their Forward Operating Base, the lot of them

practiced fixing this problem over and over again until Mark was satisfied with their time. Then he drilled them in the dark so they could literally do it with their eyes closed. They'd have to be quick, because the process involved using heavy steel hammers banging on equally hard steel pins. It would also require them to drive off the track once it was separated, before driving it back on once everything got realigned. Then they'd have to bang the pins back in place. They'd wrapped their hammer in cloth along with some of the other tools to silence them somewhat, but no matter what they did to mitigate the sound, it was still going to be noisy, and noise attracted the dead.

That meant they needed to move fast.

Mark unholstered the M9 pistol attached to his Fighting Load Carrier vest before retrieving a small flashlight. He took a deep breath to calm himself, then climbed up on the IFV, shining the light inside through the open hatches, with pistol pointed and at the ready. To his relief, he found nothing inside and he motioned to the others, indicating it was clear.

"Bags" Bagdasarian, the platoon's medic, scrambled up the front slope of the Bradley, struggling with a heavy jerry can of fuel. Burbey grabbed a heavy set of jumper cables known colloquially as "slave cables," first hooking them up near the battery pack on the Humvee, then running them through the drivers hatch of the track. While the two of them did that, Hong, Dubois and Johnson readied their tools to begin "breaking track."

While they worked, the steady hum of the hovering helicopters echoed against the blacked-out buildings, holding their position nearly a quarter mile away. The howls and screeches of the undead pierced the night and while Mark couldn't see them, he could clearly picture them in his mind crowded beneath the Apaches, reaching upwards toward them like primitives worshiping one of their ancient gods.

"We're ready, Sarn't," whispered Burbey, sitting in the driver's seat of the armored vehicle.

"Got it." Mark reached into his Humvee and grabbed one of the handmikes, looking off into the direction of the choppers before transmitting. "Tango One Six, this is White One we're set. Time to execute. Over."

"Roger, executing now."

The pitch of the rotor blades changed and the two attack helicopters backed off from the mass of animated flesh-eaters, before piercing the night with their 30 millimeter auto-cannons. Each of them took a turn firing a three-round burst, which thundered with a massive *"thump, thump, thump."* Tracers lanced the darkness and slammed into the mob of assembled monsters, flashing, sparking and blasting bodies into shattered chunks of rotted flesh and bone.

Without waiting to be told, the soldiers instantly set to work. The three working on the track began working a breaker-bar to loosen a nut while Burbey fired up the ignition. The nut came loose with little trouble and they began pounding out the pin holding a section of steel track shoes together while the driver tried to turn over the engine.

While they did that, Mark hit the illumination button on his G-Shock, watching the seconds tick by. His heart rate picked up as the sledge hammer pounded away at the pin, driving it out of the track shoe while Burbey continued to crank on the starter without any success. "Come on, damnit. Come on."

Finally, the pin came free and the engine coughed to life.

Mark signaled to Burbey to back up once the rest were clear. Moving along its one good track the IFV backed up, sloughing off the disconnected set on the right-hand side of the vehicle. Bags stood behind and to the rear, guiding it up the offramp and onto the asphalt. They worked feverishly, just as they'd practiced dozens of times before, all while the Apaches took turns in predetermined timed intervals, firing on the dead, drawing even more of them away from the recovery team.

They hooked the unlimbered track up to one of the Humvees and dragged it up the onramp and the group of them man-handled them into place until they lined up properly with the road wheels. All the while, McDermott and Gray stood watch behind their M-240B machine guns, nervously scanning their sectors, trying to pick out any movement in the poor illumination.

Finally, they got the track back on and worked with a set of clamps to get the shoes lined up, struggling in the dark with their night vision goggles on. It would have been much easier to use headlamps or flashlights, but it would have only served to draw in the ravenous flesh-eaters.

Bags stood on top of the Bradley, pouring the contents of the jerry can into the fuel tank when she felt something with a vice-like grip latch onto her ankle. She looked down through her NVGs and the infrared beam lit up a decayed and twisted face looking back up at her. It gave a quick yank and she immediately lost her footing, tumbling over the side of the vehicle, landing on the ground with an audible thump. The thing descended on her and she let out a shrill scream.

All of their heads snapped up at the sound and Mark bolted around the side of the IFV to find the beast straddling Bags, both of them locked in a deadly struggle. The thing's flesh was badly mangled and deteriorated, with bits of gore torn and hanging from bone and gristle. Its jaws snapped at the medic while she pushed it back, trying to keep a distance between herself and those awful teeth.

Mark came running, snatching his sidearm from its holster. He closed the distance in seconds, pressing the muzzle against the monster's head, ensuring that it was pointed away from Bags before pulling the trigger. The opposite side of the head exploded, sending chunks of rancid brain and skull flying, before the limp carcass collapsed on the soldier.

He quickly grabbed the body and rolled it off before untying the cravat wrapped around his face. "Hold on, don't get up," he said to her, using the rag to wipe black goop from her face. He took care to wipe it away from her eyes, nose and mouth, so the infected fluids didn't get into her bloodstream. "You got any baby wipes?"

"Yeah," she said. "I've got some in my cargo pocket.

"Good, I think I got most of it off, but you need to thoroughly clean your face." He did a quick inspection of her, looking for cuts or scratches. "You okay?"

"I think so."

"Alright then, get up and..." Mark got interrupted by a loud hiss. He looked up to see three more of the creatures hunched over and skulking toward them. "*Shit!*" He brought the pistol to bear and snapped off three rounds in quick succession, dropping them in their tracks.

A machine gun thundered from behind them.

"*We've got company!*" Shouted Gray. She leaned into her crew-served weapon and loosed another burst, sending tracers flying off into the night.

Mark helped Bags get back onto her feet. "Get on the truck, we're rolling." She nodded and he bolted. When he came back around McDermott lit something up as well, with both automatic weapons firing in wide arcs in opposite directions at targets he could not see. "It's game time," he said to himself before climbing up *BOHICA*'s front slope.

Dubois swung the hammer as fast as he could, trying to get the track pin set in place. Even with the head of it wrapped in cloth, it made an audible "ting, ting, ting."

Mark leaned over the side. "How much longer? We're out of time!"

"Almost there!" Hong answered back, while the M-240 Bravo machine guns barked in the background.

"Message for you on the command net!" Gray called out before engaging another target.

"Right, give me a second!" Mark jumped up onto the turret, then lowered himself inside the open commander's hatch. He did a quick check and ensured the turret power was on before turning to the radios behind him. He feverishly worked the buttons on them before eventually programming in the right frequency. Since they weren't operating against living human enemies, they didn't bother using comsec or crypto, sending transmissions "in the clear." That saved him a ton of time. He slipped on the Combat Vehicle Crewman's helmet and adjusted the boom mike before transmitting. "Tango One Six, this is White One. Over."

"*Yeah, White One, you've a large number of zeds headed your way. You need to get out of there, now. Over.*"

Mark looked over the lip of the hatch and saw the tracers from the Apache chain guns engaging targets on the ground. They were backing off deliberately, trying to draw the herd away. "Tango One Six, can you keep 'em off our backs for a bit longer? Over."

"*Negative. We've tied up the majority of them over here and if we shift fire to give you direct support, it'll take the pressure off and you'll have a million of 'em on your heads in a matter of minutes. Recommend we keep doing what we're doing and you un-ass the AO. Break.*" There was a pause in the transmission before the chopper pilot went on. "*Also, we're 'red' on ammo and will be 'Winchester' in a few minutes. It's time to fish or cut bait, partner. Over.*"

Mark knew the runners would be on them in no time,

followed up by legions of walkers and shamblers. "Roger, understood." He stood up and leaned over the side of the turret so he could get a look at the crew reassembling the track shoes. They'd stopped hammering and it looked like they were working like mad with a big ratchet. "Hey, are you guys done yet? We gotta go!"

"Almost, Sarn't. Practically there!"

Something caught his eye in the gloom. A runner came out of nowhere, coming straight at the three on the ground. "*Look out!*" Mark pulled out the 9 millimeter sidearm and started popping off rounds in rapid succession, not hitting a thing. It simply moved too fast.

Dubois kept cranking on the ratchet while Johnson and Hong turned to face the threat. The thing hit Johnson mid-section, hitting him like a linebacker and slamming him into the armored skirts of the Bradley. Mark lost sight of them, trying to lean over the turret to see if he could get a shot. He started to climb out of the turret when a rifle cracked.

"All clear!"

Johnson came stumbling back out into view, reaching down the open collar of his shirt and retrieving the small Mjölnir pendant he wore on a chain around his neck. He kissed it and stuffed it back inside his shirt before looking up at Mark and giving the "thumbs up." Hong did as well, still holding the M-4 carbine he'd used to dispatch the runner.

"Done!" Dubois shouted.

"No time for a PMCS fellas, it's time to roll. Mount up!" The three on the ground scooped up the tools and their weapons, beating feet for the Humvees. Mark dropped down inside, closing the commander's hatch behind him. Inside the turret, he quickly checked the coaxial machine gun and the ammo boxes right next to it. They were partially full and the gun was charged, ready to fire. Just like he'd left it a month ago. He shifted over to the gunner's station and made some adjustments before flipping on the night sights, then toggled the intercom. "Burbey, close your hatch. We're rollin'."

"Roger, Sarn't." Burbey pulled down the driver's hatch with an audible "thunk."

"White One, Tango One Six. We are 'Winchester' ammo. We'll continue hovering and try to draw as many away as we can. We'll also give you recon reports on anything up ahead you might run into. Recommend you haul ass, they'll be on you anytime now. Over."

Mark slewed the turret and scanned his surroundings. Gray and McDermott were hammering away in short bursts while the last of his people jumped aboard the Humvees. When he dialed up the magnification he nearly gasped, seeing scores of runners nearly on top of them. He knew that was only the tip of the iceberg and the rest were following behind. He hit the transmit key on their platoon internal frequency. "Guidons, White One. Follow us. We'll take the lead." He then switched to the intercom to speak with his driver. "Okay, dude, pivot steer right then take us down the slope nose first. Don't take it on an angle like last time."

"Wilco."

The Bradley spun to the right with tracks moving in opposite directions and when it was oriented properly, it moved forward, down the overgrown grassy slope of the onramp. When they got to flat ground the engine began to whine as it picked up speed. Both Humvees moved out and fell into formation behind the IFV, easily keeping up.

"You see what I'm seeing, Sarn't?" Burbey's voice sounded tinny and crackled some. The humidity and weather affected the internal communications systems while sitting outside with open hatches over the previous month.

Through the Bradley's Independent Sight Unit Mark

clearly saw what the driver saw and much more. "If you're talking about the thousand zeds coming at us across the parking lot, then yes, I see it." He armed the coax machine gun and took aim at the runners leading the pack, but thought better of it. There weren't enough rounds in the hopper to deal with this and besides that, shooting them wasn't necessary.

"You gonna light 'em up then?"

"No need, just keep moving forward. We'll grease the tracks with them."

"Roger."

Burbey gently applied more pressure to the accelerator and *BOHICA* gradually picked up speed with the two Humvees following close behind. The armored vehicle hit the onrushing dead without slowing down, plowing through them as the bow of a ship would through heavy surf. Many got tossed aside while others fell under the tracks, mashed to a pulp under the IFV's tremendous weight, but at that speed, a few rolled up onto the front slope, relatively intact. A few of them regained their footing and scurried up onto the turret.

Gray watched one step off over the side and fall off the vehicle harmlessly, while a few others climbed up on top. She couldn't help but notice the gunner and cargo hatches were still wide open. "*White One, this is White Two. You've got zeds up on top of the track. Over!*"

"What?" Mark looked straight up from the gunner's position to the open hatch above his head to find the contorted look of horror staring straight back at him. One of the dead sniffed at the air and immediately began coming through only inches away from him.

He whipped the pistol out and pressed it against the creature's forehead while he covered his face with the crook of his left elbow. Black goop splattered all over, covering everything and he once again found himself thankful for wearing the ballistic eyewear, which was now completely coated in a layer of slimy, infected fluid.

The sound of the report inside the turret made his ears ring, even though they were covered by the headset. There were more transmissions coming over the radio but the ringing in his ears made it impossible to hear.

He stood and struggled to push the body back up and out of the hatch, grunting the whole time. The nasty thing may have been decomposing, but it didn't make it much lighter. It was still heavy and unwieldy.

Eventually he shoved it out. He took off the glasses and tossed them aside so he could see, standing up to unlatch the combat locks when he saw another terrible face looking down at him. In a flash he reached up and pulled the armored hatch down, securing it tightly. He plopped back down in the gunner's seat and breathed a sigh of relief. Then, the ringing in his ears subsided enough that he could understand the incoming transmissions once again.

"…*White One, do you read me? White One, come in. Over!*" Gray shouted over the radio.

"White Two, this is White One. I'm here. Over."

"*Roger. Your cargo hatch on the back deck is still open, they're getting inside your track. Over!*"

Electric shocks went down his spine. Mark shot a glance down at the turret access door and found it to be securely in place, so even if they got into the back troop compartment, he was safe, but the driver on the other hand… *shit!* There was a small gap between the turret housing connecting the troop compartment to the driver. If they managed to squeeze through it—and there was no reason why they couldn't—they'd be on him in no time.

"Ummm, Sergeant?" Burbey's voice trembled. He'd heard Gray's report too.

"Don't worry, I'm coming, buddy!" He grabbed his flashlight, rolled over and crouched down on all fours before disengaging the lock and sliding open the sheet-metal door.

He shined his light through and saw several pairs of legs, clad in filthy, tattered trousers. *Fuck me*, he thought to himself. He twisted and contorted himself so he could get an angle up to try for a headshot. They saw the light dancing around and suddenly he became the center of attention. The nearest one lunged and Mark put a round between its eyes, dropping it to the diamond-plate floorboards.

He pointed the weapon at the next nearest one only then realizing that the slide was locked to the rear on an empty magazine. *Dear God!* From his position crouched down and peering through the small door with flashlight in one hand and gun in the other, he couldn't reach for a spare mag to reload.

Mark wormed his way back into the turret, followed by a couple of flesh-eaters. The two of them tried coming through the small opening at the same time and jammed themselves up, but their arms reached out for their victim. Sitting on the floor with his back against the gun shield, he kicked at them with the heels of his boots, trying to push them back.

Without warning the vehicle came to an abrupt stop and the back of Mark's helmet slammed into the main weapons control panel. He continued kicking frantically while reaching for a spare magazine when a series of shots exploded inside the tightly enclosed space. Outside the machine guns erupted, going full cyclic with no discipline to the rate of fire.

Mark dropped the empty mag and slammed a fresh one home before releasing the slide lock. He leaned forward and shielded his eyes before pumping a couple of FMJs into the faces of the living nightmares. The hands reaching out for him went limp and he sat back breathing heavily with the sound of his heart thumping in his ears so loudly, it even drowned out the ringing.

Then he heard a loud "Ka-chunk." Someone had closed the open cargo hatch in the back.

"Clear!" Shouted Burbey. "Are you okay in there, Sarn't?"

Still breathing heavily, he said nothing for a moment.

"Sarn't are you alright?"

He snapped himself out of it. "Yeah, brother, I'm good. The muffled sounds of the machine guns outside were getting desperate. "You need to get back up front and we gotta get moving again, pronto. Those Humvees outside are going to get swarmed if we don't get out of here."

"You don't need to tell me twice!"

Mark sat there unmoving with the smell of burnt gunpowder and rotted flesh hanging in the air. There came a jostling sound as Burbey squeezed his way past the turret through the "hell hole" and back into the driver's seat. He felt the vehicles' transmission shift back into gear and the track started moving again.

He shined his light on the crumpled figures in the back and the splattered mess coating the inside of the turret. *Well, we've got a hell of a mess to clean up once we get back to the FOB.*

Chapter 2

Mark found himself riding high in the commander's position of a Bradley Fighting Vehicle. The further they got from immediate danger, the more fatigue set in and he used the stinking breeze blowing in his face to help keep him awake. His eyelids hung heavily and he found himself nodding off from time to time, fighting to stay alert.

He'd shifted from the gunner's position to the other side of the turret since it was covered in infected shit and he didn't want to risk getting any in his eyes, nose or mouth. He'd seen many times what happened to a person when that occurred and the outcome was never good. The lucky ones simply died, while the rest... just sort of died.

After a time his mind began to wander, thinking back over major events of his life, particularly those of the last month. He thought about how before the outbreak he counted down the days, praying for an early release from his prison sentence at Fort Leavenworth. He remembered all the hard work it took to get on that work-release program, cutting hair at the barber shop on the main post next to the Lewis and Clark building. As bad a hand as life had dealt him, there had been a light at the end of the tunnel and he'd dreamed of a life of freedom after his incarceration.

Right up until the dead decided to walk the Earth.

Many of the memories of that terrible day were nothing more than a blur anymore. He recalled bolting from the barber shop to assist his guard who'd been attacked on a sidewalk across the street. Mark couldn't shake the images of that woman's contorted face and those awful eyes as she clawed and bit the nearly helpless MP. Worse, he remembered bashing the woman's head in with a nightstick and then turning it on the infected prison guard right after that. Though at the time he didn't know they were infected. He just knew they were out of their minds and he'd managed to kill a couple of people with his bare hands.

The rest of it was nothing more than flashes of images. He recalled stripping off the MP's uniform and grabbing the man's car keys before making his escape. He clearly pictured the old retiree in the barber shop watching him through the window, shaking his head and mouthing the word "no."

His escape didn't last very long and he soon found himself pressed into service with an infantry platoon manning a checkpoint in Kansas City. His stolen uniform had become both a blessing and a curse at the same time. The soldiers never suspected that he'd taken it from a dead MP and only knew him as "Sergeant Matthews," giving him the perfect assumed identity, but that same uniform that protected him from suspicion also dragged him back into an Army he was desperately trying to escape from. He'd spent nearly every minute of every day back then trying to figure out how to get away, until it seemed nearly pointless. The world had been overrun and the safest place to be was surrounded by a bunch of people with guns, so he decided to stay. At least for the time being. At least until he could figure out how to get the hell out of there and make his way to his family in Ohio.

"White One, Tango One Six. Over."

"Send it." They were close to their base camp and Mark could barely make it out just up ahead.

"It's been a long night and you're clear the rest of the way in. Good job back there. Over." The pilot's voice croaked when he spoke, the adrenaline worn off and crushing fatigue settling in.

"Tango One Six, roger, you too. Thanks for all the help tonight. We'd have been dead meat back there if it weren't for you guys. Over."

"De nada. You take it easy and be safe out there. One Six. Out." The two Apache gunships peeled off from their protective positions on the flanks of the small convoy and roared off to the southwest. They'd done a tremendous job and once they got back to the FARP site, the birds would get rearmed, refueled and the crews would get some much-needed rest before heading back out again to support some other suicidal op in the city.

Mark switched frequencies to the company command net. "Battle Axe Six, this is White One. Over."

"White One, Battle Axe Six. Welcome back. Over." Their company commander, Lieutenant Baker sounded far too cheerful and awake for this time of night.

Battle Axe Six, I've got the package. All personnel, weapons and equipment accounted for. No casualties. We are 400 meters out and should be there in two mikes. Over." Mark felt his energy crashing as they neared the outer perimeter of their Forward Operating Base.

"Sounds good, White One. Anything else to report? Over."

"Yeah roger. My driver, myself and a couple of others came in close contact. We're going to need to hit the showers and spend some time in monitored quarantine. Plus, we'll also need a CBRN team to do a deliberate decon of the track. This thing is a fucking mess. Over."

"Understood. Everything is set up and ready for you. I look forward to your debrief. Battle Axe Six. Out."

Up ahead an infrared strobe flashed, marking the entrance to the FOB. The three vehicles flashed their IR countersign and headed straight for it, passing on through the gate and into their safe refuge.

***

11 July , 2015
Fort Riley, Kansas
One Year Before the Outbreak

"That was a nice dinner tonight dear, we haven't eaten out in ages," said Barbara Williams, pulling her shoes off and opening up the front closet.

"Yes, it's been a long time since we ate at the Tap House. I really like how they expanded on the menu, we'll definitely have to go back soon to try out some of the other options." Colonel Dane Williams was in the adjoining room and raised his voice just a bit to carry on the conversation. "Would you care for a nightcap, Sweetie?"

"I'm dying for one," Barbara said while settling into a chair in the living room.

A few minutes later Dane came into the living room holding two gin and tonics. He carefully handed one to his wife before settling in the La Z Boy just across from her, with only an end table separating the two of them. He pulled out a coaster and placed it on the table top before setting his drink down.

The two of them lived in a beautiful, rented home just outside of the Manhattan town limits. It was located in a small development clustered among other attractive single-family homes built in a modern, trendy style. The people that lived there were not wealthy, but they weren't poor either, coming from upper middle-class backgrounds. Due to its proximity to the US Army base, many of the homes were occupied by families whose households were headed by the senior officers stationed there.

While many of their neighbors had children living at home, the Williams' did not. Their two kids were now grown and moved out. One an officer himself in the Army and the other still in college. Barbara decorated the place liberally with photos of the kids and there were plenty of family photos of them all over the world, smiling and posing for the camera in all sorts of exotic locales. Just like many families, the photos made the impression that they were much happier than they actually were, and Barbara preferred to keep the illusion alive that theirs had been an enchanted and exceptional one. She often ignored the reality that her husband Dane was basically an absentee father and the kids barely had a relationship with him. Barbara found it much easier to forget about that when she was drinking, which she often did.

"We're all out of Henrick's so I had to use Beefeater. I hope you don't mind," Dane said, looking at the Army-issued laptop computer sitting on the nearby desk.

Barbara caught him looking at the computer. "Don't you dare even think about checking e-mails tonight. If they have something important for you, they'll call. They always do."

"Okay, okay... fair enough," he said in an unconvincing tone.

"So what was it you wanted to tell me in the car?" Barbara took a long pull from her drink before setting it down. Admiring how the ice-filled glass was beginning to sweat.

"Ah yes. You remember Jimmy Miller?" He picked up his glass and swirled it a bit, staring at it with a distant look in his eye.

"Jimmy from Fort Carson?"

"Yeah, that's right. He just got confirmed and he'll be pinning on his first star here in the very near future." Dane took a drink and swallowed hard before placing it back down on the coaster. "He's in the same year group as me, you know."

"Good for him. I'm sure Dianne is excited," she said, taking another drink and not making eye contact with her husband.

"I'm sure she is. Anyway, the general officer selection boards are convening again soon."

"You don't say." Barbara's voice was devoid of emotion.

"I swear to god, I better get picked up for promotion soon or else it's going to be too late." His jaw muscles clenched. "I've worked hard in this career and succeeded where most others didn't. Hell, I'm an infantry officer without a Ranger Tab and I still got selected for a brigade command. Do you know how hard that is?"

She said nothing. She had heard all of this before.

"I've had an extraordinarily successful command too so far, but none of that means anything. Only 3% of colonels make brigadier general, it's the toughest cut yet." Dane leaned forward, staring off into space.

"Yes dear." She took another drink, draining it this time. "Would you like another? I'm going to have another one."

"No thank you. I'm fine." He watched her get up and go to the kitchen to make herself a drink. "Do you know how the pre-screening for the selection boards work?"

"I have no idea," she lied. He had probably told her how this worked at least a hundred times already.

"It's like this. Before your file even goes in front of the promotion board there is a pre-screening. A bunch of generals get together in a locked room with cigars and glasses of bourbon and look through every eligible colonel's records. They basically hold each file up and ask if anyone knows that person."

Barbara came back to the living room holding two fresh gin and tonics.

"Sweetie, I told you I didn't need another drink. I'm still working on this one," Dane said.

"Oh, my mistake, I thought you wanted another," she lied again. Fully intending to drink both herself. She wanted to dull her wits if she was going to suffer through another session of her husband scheming a way to get promoted again. "You were saying?"

"Right, so like I said, they hold up the files in a room full of generals and ask if anyone's heard of this particular colonel."

"And if they don't?" She said, pretending to be engaged with the conversation.

"Then they toss the colonel's file into the waste bin and it never even goes in front of the promotion board for consideration. It doesn't matter how well he performed. Doesn't matter how good of a job he did. If none of the generals knows him, then he's not even looked at for promotion." He picked up his glass and took a sip before setting it back down. "My problem is that not enough generals know me, so I've been working extra hard to get my name and face out there. Writing for professional journals, going to important meetings and briefings, hosting training events here. All of it."

"Well, it sounds like you're doing everything you can do then." When she was in the kitchen making another round, she made her drinks much stronger than Dane would have. She only used a splash of tonic for flavor. It burned just a touch while she gulped some more down, rewarded with a nice warm sensation in her belly.

"Clearly I'm not. My peers are getting promoted and I'm not and I *know* I'm a more capable officer than they are." He stood up from the La Z Boy and started pacing back and forth on the carpet. "The Army needs many serious reforms and changes and I have ideas on how to do it, but I can't affect any change as a measly colonel. I need to be a general to bring about any real change."

"I thought you had to serve time as a G-3 or Chief of Staff

after command first, before they'd consider selecting you." The gin began to kick in and she felt the gentle buzz take hold.

"I don't have time for that, it'll take years."

"So, what then? What else can you do?"

"I don't know yet, but I need to find something. Something that will get me noticed by the senior leaders. Something where I can make a name for myself and get my promotion file in front of the board. Once it gets there, I know I'll have a shot," he said as he walked over to the laptop, opening it up and logging on.

Barbara didn't bother to protest when he pulled up his e-mails and started working. She merely reached over and grabbed his barely touched gin and tonic before finishing it off for him. "Okay, dear. I'm off to bed then."

Dane Williams only grunted and never even turned from his work as she got up and left himself alone to his work.

***

3 August, 2016
Argentine Rail Yard
Forward Operating Base "Jayhawk"
0535 Hours Local

Colonel Dane Williams stretched, reaching his arms wide and yawning loudly before focusing on the maps and tracking charts displayed on the various screens in front of him. He liked to get up early and get his briefings from the night shift before getting something to eat and beginning his "battlefield circulation" at sunrise. At this time of year that was the most pleasant time to be out and about anyway, since the heat would be stifling by noon. That and the smell of death wafting in from the city.

The command post was quieter in the morning too which also appealed to him. The staff working there were tired as they neared the end of their shift and they carried on with their drudgery until the relief arrived for change-over. Still, they worked with a silent efficiency that he appreciated.

Dane had been scheduled to relinquish command of his brigade in mid-July when his two years in command finished up. Those plans were put on hold when the outbreak occurred and he got deployment orders to send 2nd Brigade into Kansas City. The division commander even insisted on changing him out in the middle of all the unfolding madness because the general wanted him to be the Division Chief of Staff. That never happened because his replacement and successor, Colonel Tony Collins, disappeared along with the rest of his family during the limited outbreak at Fort Riley and the surrounding communities. Publicly, Dane expressed remorse and sadness for Colonel Collins and his family. Secretly, he felt happy he didn't have to give up command and General Napier hadn't mentioned it in weeks. There were simply more pressing matters at hand.

His Deputy Commander stood close by, waiting for him to absorb the current operational graphics and updates to the charts. Lieutenant Colonel Ben Laughlin graduated from Norwich and spoke like a Southie. Built like a fireplug, he was bald and had a perpetual five-o'clock shadow, though he shaved two or three times a day. "Do you have any questions, sir?"

"I see the battalions have been wrapping up their recovery missions, anything of significance left to get?"

"No, sir. We've managed to bring back all the rolling stock and pacing items that were still out there."

Command Sergeant Major McMahon joined the two officers, studying the maps himself. "Any casualties from last night's ops?"

"Negative, Sergeant Major. We had a clean run last night. We managed to get the equipment without losing anyone. Though Vanguard reports they had four personnel come in close contact." Laughlin scratched the stubble on his chin before using his laser pointer, shining it on *FOB Chiefs*. "They are in quarantine as per SOP."

"Excellent. Any updates on the retrograde operations to the *Cascadia Redoubt*?"

"The 757th Rail Battalion has been busy and they've kept shipments of units and equipment moving west. The Acting-President put out a press release and announced that the government was now officially setting up in the Pacific Northwest with Seattle as the temporary capital." Laughlin had the Night Ops Officer In Charge switch images on the projector to focus on a large map of the United States. There were lines and unit boundaries depicted everywhere, with NATO symbols for different formations scattered about. "Most of the surviving active-duty units are displacing and moving toward the *Cascadia Redoubt* now. It's been a giant clusterfuck getting everything moving, but things are finally in motion."

"He's not the 'Acting-President,' Ben. He's been officially sworn into office." Dane gave his XO a stern look.

"Yes, sir. You are of course correct." Laughlin's face flushed red and he cleared his throat before going on. "Anyway, while our active units are moving westward, we're still having issues with the Reserve Component."

"Are they still not complying? What's NORTHCOM doing about it?" Dane motioned to one of the intelligence analysts huddled behind a computer to go get him a cup of coffee. The young captain nodded and scurried off.

"Basically General Turner is beating his head against a

wall. The governors have universally ignored mobilization orders and kept their National Guard units under their own commands. The... umm... President keeps ordering them to comply but most aren't even taking his phone calls anymore. The only governors playing ball are the ones from the Pacific Northwest located inside of the consolidated federal footprint. They have been unsurprisingly cooperative."

"And the Reserves? They're federal and not controlled by the Governors."

"We've been seeing selective compliance there. Some of them dropped off the net, taking their weapons and equipment to secure their local communities. Others obeyed their mobilization orders. Most of the units that did report, did so badly under strength. While the commanders may have complied, many of the soldiers in those units simply deserted. A lot of them deserted after they got issued their weapons first. People don't like the idea of abandoning their families and local communities in the middle of this pandemic."

"There are going to be a whole lot of court martials when this thing is over with." The young captain brought a cup of steaming-hot coffee over and Dane took it from him without acknowledging the officer's presence. He blew on the hot liquid before taking his first sip, grunting in satisfaction.

"I think we have a lot of work to do before we have the luxury to do that." Laughlin's jaw muscles flexed and the Sergeant Major gave him a concerned look.

"And the civilian populace?"

"No change. The urban areas east of the Mississippi are almost all completely overrun. The bigger cities in the Midwest are just as bad. The rural areas are largely uninfected to varying degrees. Things are beginning to stabilize somewhat.

"There are hold-outs of large military units who can't

move themselves, setting up bastions where they can. One of the bigger ones is being fortified by 10th Mountain Division in upstate New York. There are a few others of notable size as well."

Dane held the Styrofoam cup in his hand, wishing he had some of the good coffee he used to make back at his headquarters at Riley. Barbara used to pick up a certain roasted blend that he was particularly fond of. That got him wondering for the first time in days how she was doing. "Any word on our families back at Riley?"

Laughlin visibly relaxed some and the redness faded a bit from his face. "The midnight update indicated that all remains well. They said that we should expect a load of mail from them on the next logistical package."

"That's good." Dane got word that his wife survived and was in good health, residing with the other rescued families in a tent city set up in the middle of one of Fort Riley's remote training areas, well away from any populated communities. The Division Commander tasked 1st Brigade with the mission of securing and protecting them after the limited outbreak on the Army installation in the opening days of the pandemic. Though several hundred family members succumbed to the virus and its spread, the units on post managed to keep things from spreading any further and got the vast majority of their dependents to safety. "How's your wife and kids doing? Did you get any messages from them?"

"They're doing well, sir. The kids think living in the tent city is like one big camping trip and Tina is adapting like all the other spouses."

"That's good to hear." Dane took another sip before looking at some of the tracking charts. General Napier knew that the only way to keep his combat units intact and in the field was if they knew their families were safe, so that became the highest priority. He was just glad that the mission to secure the dependents fell on the 1st Brigade and not his own. He'd rather be out commanding his people in battle rather than babysitting the civilians. It might have been important, but it wasn't the mission that was going to get him noticed by his superiors. No, this outbreak presented a once-in-a-lifetime opportunity for him and he aimed to take advantage of it.

"Well, unless there's anything else, I'm going to grab some chow before heading out on my battlefield circulation."

"Yes, sir. We'll give you a call if there are any issues."

"Very good. Carry on."

***

FOB Chiefs
0735 Hours Local

Mark stretched out flat on his back on the cot, hat draped over his eyes, quietly dozing. He slept uneasily, haunted by the dreams that he never seemed to shake. His fitful slumber was suddenly interrupted by a few voices in the haze.

"Sarn't, you awake?"

Mark grumbled and pulled the cap from his eyes, squinting in the early daylight. He felt somewhat annoyed at being woken during one of the coolest parts of the day, because later it would be hot as an oven and impossible to sleep. "Yeah, I'm awake."

"We thought we'd bring you some chow." Gray stood there with a paper plate loaded with food balanced in one hand, while holding a cup of steaming coffee in the other. On either side of her stood Harris and Donahue, both of whom wore shit-eating grins.

"What's so funny?" Mark sat up on the cot, slipping on his

boots.

"We never thought we'd see an MP in jail." Donahue balanced himself with a pair of crutches tucked under each armpit. His leg wound from the fight inside the casino still hadn't completely healed up yet, but it seemed to be doing well.

Mark looked at the steel cage he was being held in and frowned. It didn't exactly bring back good memories, though he sure couldn't share them with this bunch. "Hardy-fuckin' har har, but the joke's on you guys."

"Why's that?" Harris asked, still taking joy in seeing the NCO behind bars.

"Because after getting slopped with rotting goop we had to go through a thorough decon. It was the best shower I've had in weeks. Then they issued us clean uniforms too. Can't say it's all bad. We sure as hell smell better than you."

"You better dig in before it gets cold." Gray walked toward the front of the cage and set the food down on a shelf with a slot between the bars, fabricated for that purpose.

"Thanks." Mark took the plastic utensils and dug in right there, eating while standing up. The eggs and bacon weren't all that great, but under the circumstances it was a feast fit for a king. They hadn't received any white bread with their hot meals in a couple of weeks and nobody wanted to think about when all the meat, powdered eggs and canned vegetables would run out. They were told if they kept the trains running, then the supplies would keep flowing. So that was motivation in and of itself to stay focused on the mission.

Around them the area bustled with activity. The quarantine area was offset from the rest of the railyard, near the eastern perimeter. Humvees and trucks moved about, while soldiers offloaded supplies and equipment. Railroad box cars and engines stretched out as far as the eye could see, with some pulling out to make way for others coming in. It all appeared orderly somehow in all its randomness, like some director teasing a melody out of his symphony.

The quarantine area itself consisted of fifty cages crudely welded together with minimum accommodation made for comfort. Other than a cot, the engineers did fabricate sheet-metal roofs over the tops to keep the sun and the rain out, but other than that they were open to the air. A bucket in the corner served as the latrine for them to relieve themselves, with no thought given to a modesty curtain. They said it was so the soldiers in quarantine could be monitored all the time, but most suspected that it was simply more bother than it was worth for the engineers who slapped them together. Besides, nobody cared if you shit in a bucket in front of the rest of the world.

In the cage next to his, Hong and McDermott spent time with Burbey after bringing his breakfast. The three of them laughed about something particularly funny, likely at someone else's expense. Further down the line Bags sat in another cage on her cot, eating her food, while Johnson and Dubois sat on the ground nearby, dealing out some cards through the bars.

"How does the track look, Sarn't?" Donahue leaned heavily into the crutches while taking the pressure off his injured leg.

"It was pretty dark when we recovered it, but it looked much the same as when we left it out there last month. Though we did smoke a few zeds during the exfil." Mark shoved a piece of greasy bacon into his mouth and chewed noisily.

"I didn't think they were going to make it. They plowed through a sizable herd of them and a bunch got on top. Before I knew it, they started climbing inside." Gray shook her head while she spoke. "Then they stopped and we almost slammed into them. I didn't see what happened after that because we halted in the middle of hundreds of 'em and we started to get swarmed. I nearly ran out of '240 rounds trying to keep the fuckers off the truck." She mimed with her hands as if she were still behind the gun, hammering away at the dead.

"Jesus," Harris said, pulling out a cigarette and lighting it. Donahue looked at him longingly and Harris noticed, but didn't offer him one. "I heard that's how those guys from Alpha Company bought it last week."

"So, how's my favorite Platoon Leader doing?" The group turned to see Lieutenant Baker approaching.

"Group, atten-shun!" Mark called out, whipping out a crisp salute. The others locked their heels together and did the same.

Baker walked up in his Nomex coveralls, tanker boots and patrol cap while shouldering an assault pack. He had a leather G.I. holster strapped across his torso with an issue M9 pistol secured inside. He casually returned the salute from the enlisted while approaching Mark's cage. "Carry on. As you were. I thought I'd stop by and check up on you all."

They all dropped their salutes and relaxed. Dubois and Johnson wasted no time taking a seat and getting back to their game of *Magic: The Gathering*.

"Sir, I'm just a Sergeant. I'm no Platoon Leader." Mark picked up the paper cup and gulped down some cold coffee to wash the bacon down.

"Could have fooled me. You're the senior ranking member of the platoon, that makes you Platoon Leader." Baker rested his hands on his hips and surveyed the other cages. The only ones occupied were by Mark, Burbey, Johnson and Bags. The rest sat empty. "I see your people brought you some chow, you need anything else?"

"No, sir. We're good. How's the track?" Mark shoved a spoonful of eggs in his mouth, doing his best to ignore their green-ish hue.

"The Chemical Company finished up a short while ago. The crews in the hazmat suits went in first to clear out the bodies, then they did a deliberate decon. It took them nearly an hour to hose the whole thing out, but now it looks like it just got out of a carwash." Baker smiled broadly. "You know what that means, right?"

The junior enlisted soldiers looked at each other in confusion, not knowing the answer to the lieutenant's question. Mark knew however, and he smirked. "Time for maintenance, right, sir?"

"That's right, Sergeant. It's time for Preventative Maintenance Checks and Services. Better known as 'PMCS.' And there's no time like the present." He cocked the patrol cap back, exposing his forehead. "But you four are stuck here in quarantine for a full seventy-two hours, so you're going to have to put someone else in charge."

"You're right, sir. I hereby nominate the senior member of the 'E-4 Mafia.' Harris, you're in charge. Time to get hot."

Harris looked crestfallen. "But, Sarn't, I'm still recovering from wounds."

"You ain't hurt that bad. Now get moving, time to get after it." Mark popped in another piece of bacon, chewing with his mouth open. "And take the rest of these degenerates with you."

"Roger, Sarn't." Harris's shoulders sagged. "Come on guys, let's go."

"Oh, and Donahue. Make sure you clear the coax before you start messing around in the turret. The weapon is still hot. I don't want a negligent discharge in the motor pool."

Donahue gave Mark a quizzical look. "No problem, Sarn't." He leaned over to face his buddy, Burbey in the neighboring cage. "See you later, Battle."

"Have fun in the motorpool, pole-smoker." Burbey waved goodbye while sitting on his bare cot, finishing his breakfast.

Mark finished his food and set the paper plate aside before draining the dregs of his cup. "So, sir, what's the word from Battalion? Any news?"

"Yeah, it sounds like things are finally stabilizing a bit here locally, but that ain't saying much. The entire city center is one giant infected zone and they say there are probably more than half-million people turned in there. The suburbs are more spread out, so things are somewhat better." Baker scratched the back of his neck and looked up at the sky. It was already starting to get warm. "But between us, the National Guard and organized groups of armed civilians, the outbreaks stopped spreading for the most part."

"Does that mean what I think it means?"

"If you think it means we're going to begin clearing the city block by block, then yes."

Mark shook his head. "We'd be better off if they just fucking nuked the place. We lost a ton of people already, there's no way we have enough manpower to do that."

"Believe me, a couple of weeks ago up at headquarters the rumors were flying and they were talking about doing just that. A ten-megaton warhead would wipe the slate clean, but now the conversation is how we are going to move on from this. There's too much expensive, largely-intact infrastructure here and it's too valuable to blow up. They want to clear the dead out and re-use the place once we're done."

"That's why they've been having us police up all our lost equipment? So we can go on the offensive?"

"That's what my sources at Battalion are telling me." Baker wore a smile on his face that never reached the eyes.

"Remind me to write my congressman when I get out of quarantine."

"You know every member of congress is dead, right? At least, dead-ish."

"Sir, you are a ray of sunshine. Got any other good news?"

"Not right now. I'll have someone drop by and give you guys some poncho liners, books and whatever else you need to pass the time comfortably for the next few days." He unshouldered the assault pack, unzipped it, revealing the contents. Inside was a bottle of Jim Beam. "I'm going to leave you with this for now. Be sure to share it with the others."

Mark's eyes lit up at the sight. "Now, sir, this is how you raise morale!"

"Consider a reward for a job well-done." He looked over at Burbey, Johnson and Bags. "You two need anything?"

They responded with a respectful "No, sir," before returning their attention back to their breakfasts.

"Thanks again, Lieutenant."

"Don't mention it. Now get some rest over the next few days. Because after Doc clears you from quarantine, we're going to have a lot of work to do and it's going to be balls to the wall."

Chapter 3

7 August, 2016
0555 Hours Local
"Operation Toe Cutter"

Mark leaned forward in the commander's hatch, hitting the illumination button on his watch. *Nearly LD time*, he thought to himself before switching on his red-lens flashlight and taking one last look at the map board laid out in front of him. He'd taken two pieces of plexiglass and sandwiched a map between them before taping up the sides with the military green duct tape. He secured a third sheet on one edge, using the tape as a hinge so he could flip it up and down. That third sheet is where he drew his operational graphics with an alcohol marker. If the graphics got too busy, he could simply flip up the sheet for a clearer look at the map whenever he desired. Donahue had given him another strange look when he brought the self-fabricated map board on the vehicle, but Mark ignored him.

The faint orange glow of the impending sunrise fought its way through the gloom while the engines of the vehicles idled calmly. The entire battalion had lined up on the road next to the *Charles B. Wheeler Downtown Airport,* just inside the perimeter. The smell of exhaust hung in the air as the entire unit sat, patiently awaiting the word.

Due to recent combat losses and maintenance issues, they could only muster thirty-nine combat vehicles, but it would be enough. They task-organized themselves into "company teams," which were a mixture of mechanized infantry and tank platoons. The battalion also brought along its complement of heavy-armored recovery vehicles and some attached engineers. The scout platoon deployed at dusk the night before with their Humvees and were already distributed on the ground throughout the zone, providing a set of "eyes" and timely reports.

Off to their right on the airfield came the steady hum of rotor blades as elements of the Combat Aviation Brigade spooled up their engines. The high-pitched lawnmower sound temporarily drowned them out when the RQ-7 Shadow drones took off, headed southward. The unmanned aerial vehicles would get set over the target area and loiter, giving perfect real-time reconnaissance throughout critical portions of the operation.

The command net crackled to life. "All stations this net, this is Battle Axe Six. Report REDCON status in sequence. Over."

Mark toggled the intercom. "Driver, you up?"

"Ready to rock this bitch," Burbey responded.

Mark shook his head with a smirk before speaking into the handmike. "Battle Axe Six, this is White One. REDCON One. Over." He switched back over to the intercom again. "How you feelin' Donahue? You good?"

"I'm good, Sarn't. My leg is still a bit sore, but I won't be doing much walking here in the gunner's seat."

"Harris, how are you all doing back there?"

"We're all set, Sarn't."

"Good, you stay buttoned up back there until I tell you." Mark shined the light on the map again, checking their route. It was redundant to do so since his GPS worked perfectly, but he liked to have an analog back-up solution, just in case.

"Guidons, this is Battle Axe Six. LD, time now. Over."

At the head of the column, soldiers manning the gate opened it up and the first of the combat vehicles rolled out. One after the other, the Bradleys and tanks followed along on the road right behind a couple of M-88 recovery vehicles who led the way with their scraper-blades lowered, clearing abandoned cars and trucks out of the way. The going was meant to be slow and deliberate, with no attempt at noise discipline.

The battalion proceeded steadily, crossing the US-169 bridge southbound, over the Missouri River. To their left the orange glow grew in intensity, bringing the first light of the day to the blacked-out city. The grid had been down since the first day of the outbreak, so the only artificial light for miles was that created by the units, operating from the safety of their heavily fortified FOBs.

Before the lead element got half-way across the bridge, the helicopters took flight from the airfield, passing overhead with a roar. They tried to stay as low as possible, making their way south. This too constituted part of the plan, the low-flying aircraft generating a lot of noise. Noise that would surely attract the dead.

"Sarn't, I'm not sure I like this." Burbey sounded more annoyed than frightened, though it was difficult to tell over the sound of the engine.

"Like what?"

"Rolling out in the daylight. Those fuckers see better during the day. At least at night we've got night vision equipment which gives us an edge. This seems like taking on an unnecessary risk."

"Battle, you worry too much," Donahue interjected.

"The only thing I worry about, is throwing out my back humping your mom," Burbey shot back.

The column crossed the bridge slowing down occasionally while the M-88s plowed the obstacles from the road where necessary. While they did this, Blackhawks and Apaches worked the flanks, providing a sort of screening force while the mechanized ground element moved forward.

After a short while they crossed I-70 and then headed due south. They intentionally avoided I-35 off to their west when the recon element the night before reported the highway completely choked off with wrecks and abandoned civilian vehicles. Before long they found themselves passing through a heavily built-up area with businesses on both sides of the road.

Blackhawk helicopters hovering off to the sides were no longer visible, obscured by the buildings. Though they couldn't see them, they heard the door gunners firing long bursts from their machine guns over the thumping of the rotor blades.

The armored vehicles did their best to cover the flanks with their primary weapon systems, orienting turrets alternatively left and right. They would have to slew gun barrels to the front to avoid light poles, stationary trucks and other obstacles, making it difficult to scan. That forced the vehicle commanders, gunners and loaders to stay perched outside their hatches with eyes peeled and rifles at the ready.

The whole avenue was covered in detritus. Windows were smashed and doors hung ajar by hinges with some structures burned to the ground. Seemingly everywhere, decayed corpses littered the streets, sidewalks and parking lots. They were in a horrible state, some torn apart by animals and most covered in maggots. In the early days the soldiers would have turned to look away, but they had become numb to such things now, hardly fazed by any of it anymore. Those that couldn't deal with it had already stuck a gun barrel in their mouths and pulled the triggers long ago.

Rifle shots started to crack while they weaved through the remains of a once-thriving metropolis. Soon thereafter, loaders on the tanks joined in with their automatic weapons. What started off randomly picked up all up and down the line of the column.

"Guidons, Battle Axe Six. We've got runners. Watch your lanes. Over."

"Watch your lanes he says. What are we? On a rifle range?" Donahue's voice was thick with mockery, then changed as if a switch had been flipped. "Oh shit. Identified!"

"Where?"

Forehead resting on the brow-pad, peering through the sight, Donahue opened up on a creature emerging from the broken window of a nearby hardware store. The coax machine gun barked, sending three long streams of slugs crashing into it. The brick storefront erupted into a cloud of red dust and the jacketed slugs slammed into the creature's body. One of the dozen solid hits found its mark, crashing through the thing's mouth and blowing the brainstem out the back of the head, sending it tumbling back inside.

Out of the corner of his eye Mark spotted a half-dozen more racing toward them from the right. He rotated the selector-switch of his M-4 carbine and shouldered it. "Hang on gang, things are about to get sporty."

***

2nd Brigade Tactical Operations Center
FOB Jayhawk
0615 Hours Local

The UAV feeds streamed in, displayed prominently on one of the screens at the front of the command post. Nicknamed "Kill TV," it gave commanders and staffs excellent situational awareness of unfolding combat operations in real time. Colonel Dane Williams stood with arms akimbo, watching events play out.

On the screen the staff saw the black-and-white images of the National World War I Museum and Memorial. On the ground Blackhawk helicopters inserted the last of the combat engineers, while CH-47 Chinooks, the heavy lift choppers, brought in massive pallets of barrier materials, dropping them on the extreme edges of the museum's grounds.

The soldiers of the 82nd Brigade Engineer Battalion worked like mad, unpacking the pallets and emplacing hasty obstacles in critical locations throughout the area. Security teams in overwatch positions dispatched the occasional flesh-eater emerging from the surrounding buildings, allowing them to work. In a flurry of activity they pounded steel pickets into the ground while tying in row after row of concertina wire. Apaches from the "1st Attack" Battalion flew in close support just outside the hasty perimeter, laying waste with their 30mm chain guns.

The museum grounds were open fields which under normal circumstances would have been neatly trimmed and groomed, but were now overgrown in tall grass. Still, it presented the best option for them. It was the largest piece of open terrain located in the middle of a heavily urbanized section of the city. The grounds themselves were cigar-shaped, running north to south. To the west and southwest were public parks with baseball diamonds.

The engineers frantically emplaced a series of razor-wire barriers in the area. Some were designed to disrupt and slow movement forward, while others had the purpose of channeling foot traffic into open areas supportable with good fields of fire. The last layer constituted a final protective ring where the men and women of 2nd Battalion would establish their defensive positions. Meanwhile, as they pounded in stakes and unraveled and extended bundles of wire, a team from the Division Artillery group raced to the top of the 217-

foot "Liberty Memorial Tower" that dominated the museum grounds, giving the observers unobscured visibility of their surroundings.

"What's Vanguard's status?" Williams pulled out a folding chair from beneath one of the field tables and sat down, his gaze fixed to the screens. Around him, dozens of staffers worked behind their laptop computers while communicating over headsets connected to radio remotes. Still early in the morning, the sun hadn't started to bake the tent yet, so the air conditioners remained idle and the place smelled of burnt coffee and body odor.

The Brigade Operations Officer, Major Watts, turned on a laser pointer and oriented it on the center screen. It was a map displaying the Brigade operational graphics, along with dozens of icons indicating unit locations. "Sir, Vanguard reports crossing Phase Line *Chiefs* and continuing to push south."

"That's awfully slow-going isn't it? Shouldn't they be crossing *Vikings* by now?"

"The streets are a mess in there, sir. The sappers have had to execute one in-stride breach already and they're getting ready to do another." Watts turned to face his commander, standing near the displays in the center of the room as if he were giving a formal briefing. Dane picked him to be the "Brigade 3" only after his first choice came down with appendicitis. Colonel Williams disliked having an Armor officer in this position, but he didn't have many other options. All the best infantry officers were unavailable.

"Fine. Tell them to keep moving as fast as they can." Williams sighed before scratching his chin. "Is my chopper ready?"

"Yes, sir. It's ready to go when you are," chimed the Deputy Commander from the corner of the room.

"Alright then. Ben, you've got the fight until I get over the Battle Position. Any questions?"

There weren't any, so Dane got up, plopped the helmet on his head and left the command post, headed toward his awaiting chopper.

***

The command net gradually picked up with each passing minute. Reports came in hot and heavy as the dead started working their way out of the woodwork. Lieutenant Baker rotated the cupola to the right, orienting his .50 caliber machine gun toward a bridal shop. A few runners emerged from behind the building followed up by a couple dozen walkers. He got a bead on them and squeezed the trigger, sending forth a burst of massive slugs. When they made contact, the bodies blew apart from the impact. He didn't need to make head-shots with the fifty; once the dead were blown in half they weren't much of a threat anymore. At least not while they were in the tank.

While Baker worked the western side to the right, most of the contacts came flooding in from the left side to the east. Yokey, the loader, stood in the loader's hatch behind the M-240B, laying it on thick, while Gomez, the gunner, engaged with the coaxial machine gun.

"Hey, El Tee, everything good on your side?" The crew-served weapon thundered over the intercom while Yokey spoke.

"Yeah, Yokey, I'm good. Why do you ask?"

"You know what this reminds me of?"

Baker paused before answering. "I'm afraid to even ask. What?"

Yokey immediately broke out in song.

"The armored shell corroded from blood that now is dry
Markings left to signify the deaths of many lives
Through many years of silence breaks a horrifying sound
You turn to look in disbelief he's come to hunt you down!
The Hate Tank
The Hate Tank
The Hate Tank
HATE TAAAAAANK!!!"

"Yokey?"

"Yeah, El Tee?"

"Remind me when we get back to formally requisition another loader. You fucking suck."

***

Battle Position Gibraltar
National World War I Museum and Memorial
0751 Hours Local

The last two Humvees from the Scout Platoon came screaming in with the trail vehicle erratically shooting their .50 caliber over the back deck. They came at the south-side entrance driving as fast as they could, stomping on the brakes at the last minute when signaled by the engineers to stop. They quickly opened up a gap in the wire, then guided them inside, emplacing them at pre-arranged positions on the perimeter. A detail snatched up pre-positioned cans of ammunition and handed them up to the gunners as the truck crews settled in, with vehicle commanders going over their assigned fire lanes.

Squads of engineers continued engaging the ever-increasing number of the dead appearing out of nowhere all around the perimeter while their buddies continued pounding pickets and stringing wire. Rifles cracked and grenade launchers thumped while the picket-pounders worked in a rhythmic "ting, ting, ting." The noise of the construction, along with the small arms fire only continued to attract more of them, with their numbers growing exponentially with each passing minute.

Moments later the low-pitched grumble of the diesels engines aboard the M-88s grew steadily louder until they became a roar. The lead vehicles of the column belched thick, black smoke from their exhaust manifolds, leading the way with the rest of the armored battalion task force following up close behind. The column emerged from the built-up area on the northwest side of the perimeter along Broadway Boulevard, then headed straight toward the designated entrance on the southern side. Hot on their tails came hundreds of the dead.

The Apaches, working in concert with the Blackhawks, raked the surface over and over again, hovering mere feet above the task force. They kept up the pressure until they ran out of ammunition, working in relays as some aircrews rotated out back to the FARP site to rearm and refuel.

The Abrams tanks and Bradley Fighting Vehicles shot their machine guns, but their main guns remained silent. They did not have proper range or fields of fire to work with, so they held back on the big guns for the time being.

The entire force came at the pre-arranged entry point, moving toward guides on the ground waving brightly-colored marker panels. The battalion rolled in a single file, like a giant constrictor, taking shelter inside the inner protective barrier of concertina wire. The razor wire itself was made up of two rows on the ground with one row stacked on top in between. It didn't appear all that formidable, but it was staked and properly tied in with barbed wire, making it difficult to breach.

Guides on the ground set to work identifying their units and linking up with them, setting each platoon and individual vehicle into their assigned position, facing outward. The M1 tanks and the M2 IFVs all had pre-planned spots on the perimeter, giving them interlocking fields of fire, optimizing the capabilities of the weapon systems they possessed. The tanks focused on areas covering large flat open areas, while the Bradleys covered dips in the ground and other defiles, where their high-arcing, high-explosive rounds could affect.

As the last platoon of Bradleys entered the battle position they peeled off by section to the left and right, spinning their turrets around and laying it on as thick as they could. For the first time they unleashed their 25mm Bushmaster autocannons. They fired in three-round bursts in a deafening "thump, thump, thump." They let fly with high-explosive anti-personnel rounds that landed among a mass of the dead, blowing them into scraps of rotted meat.

The engineers closed the gap and the helicopters suddenly peeled away, headed due west. With the pressure off, the undead came on unimpeded, streaming in from the surrounding streets and alleyways, pouring in by the hundreds.

"Burbey, pull us through this small grove of trees. Pull us up on the right side of the lieutenant's tank."

"Roger, Sarn't." Burbey pulled the Bradley over to the right side of Lieutenant Baker's tank, spaced about twenty meters away. They set in on the southeast portion of the perimeter facing the Federal Reserve Bank of Kansas City.

"Drop ramp!"

Burbey unlocked the latches and hit the switch, lowering the ramp, gunning the engine as he did so. The ramp yawned open and lowered until it slammed to the earth with a resounding "clunk." The dismount squad poured out the back, pushed on by Harris. Gray, Hong and McDermott. They took off, going to ground behind some trees off to the right of *BOHICA*, while Harris, Johnson and Dubois went to the left, filling the gap between themselves and the tank.

"Do not get in front of that tank! *You hear?*" Mark shouted over the noise to his dismounts on the ground. Harris and the others nodded and gave him a thumbs-up before focusing their attention on the wave of creatures rolling in at them through the gaps between the buildings to their front.

"Gunner, HE, troops, 400 meters!" Mark said over the intercom, giving the standard fire command as if rehearsed a thousand times.

"Identified!" came Donahue's conditioned response.

"*Fire!*"

"On the way!"

Thump, thump, thump…

Thump, thump, thump…

Six rounds of High Explosive Incendiary Tracer arced out, landing in and among a charging mass, to devastating effect. To the left and right the dismounted infantry joined in, adding to the fray at long range as the threat closed the distance. All along the line, vehicles, infantry and engineers let fly with everything they had, sending in waves of tracers and ball, scything through the charging dead, cutting them to shreds.

Then, a series of detonations shook the very ground, rattling the fillings in their teeth loose. On the extreme north end and off to the west, artillery came raining down, unleashing utter carnage. The rounds came in "danger close" making the armored vehicle crews button up and forcing the dismounted infantry and engineers to ground.

Donahue stopped waiting for the next fire command and went to work with the coax, sweeping the killing field with jacketed slugs. The undead jerked and twitched with the hits, sometimes falling to the ground under shattered femurs or the random headshot. The runners tumbled and the walkers collapsed, their bodies collecting in heaps. Eventually, their numbers overwhelmed the ability to hold them back and they started to get close, tangling themselves in the protective wire.

More and more closed in on the razor wire, thrashing about and shredding their own flesh. The more they struggled, the more trapped they became. They squirmed and lashed out, completely stuck in the mess, even as more came in and joined them. The soldiers initially ignored them when they realized they were immobilized, but that began to change. The more of the animated dead that fell upon the obstacles, the more they stacked up on one another. Eventually there were so many, they began to flatten the wire, and the more the dismounts and crews killed them in the wire, the more it contributed to weakening their protective obstacle.

"Guidons, this is Battle Axe Six. I want everyone to shift fire and engage targets deep. Do not engage the ones hung up in the obstacles. All stations acknowledge. Over."

Their 3rd Platoon acknowledged the order but Mark had a hard time believing his ears. "Axe Six, White One. If we don't do something about those zeds, they are going to simply walk over the backs of the ones caught in the wire and come right at us unimpeded. We need to stop them. Over."

"Just do what I say, Sergeant Matthews. Shift your fire. Acknowledge."

"Roger, shifting fire." Mark shook his head and toggled the intercom. "You heard the man, Donahue. Focus on the ones further out."

"Got it, Sarn't. *On the way!*"

The Bushmaster barked again, temporarily blinding Mark with puffs of white smoke from the muzzle brake. The rounds sailed forth, landing among another tight cluster over 400 meters distant, blowing them to pieces.

Mark watched uncomfortably as the mass of the dead piled up on the concertina wire. It began to sag inward toward the defenders right in front of them, while more came up from behind, walking over the back of those caught in the tangled mess.

Just as it was about to give way two deafening thunderclaps went off nearby, making Mark wince. Lieutenant Baker and his wingman opened up in a volley fire, shooting a pair of 120mm canister anti-personnel rounds straight into the mass. They sent a cloud of tungsten balls into them, blasting rotten meat, bone and viscera in a shotgun pattern for nearly half a mile. When the smoke cleared, there remained nothing to their front that resembled the human shape, dead or otherwise.

Even with all the commotion going on, Mark could hear Yokey howling with joy from inside the lieutenant's tank.

***

Colonel Williams sat in the back of the Blackhawk helicopter, strapped into his four-point harness, listening to the traffic coming over the Brigade command net. They were focusing all fires on pre-planned targets surrounding *Gibraltar*, putting a wall of steel up on certain portions of the perimeter where there was sufficient stand-off range. Where there was inadequate range to fire artillery, they relied upon the heavier ground units employing their direct-fire systems. By the reports rolling in, the tank crews were doing an impressive job.

They flew high above the city several miles from the action, allowing Williams to observe through the window. He raised a pair of binoculars, peered through them and whistled.

The sun had fully risen above the horizon now, but even with the full light of day, the light show down there was impressive. Tracers zipped outward from the encircled troops in every direction while puffs of smoke blossomed on the northern and western edges from the artillery shells. A few of the surrounding buildings had caught fire and were beginning to rage.

Williams slammed a fist onto his thigh in excitement. "By God, look at that! *It's beautiful!*" He set the binoculars down with the twinkle in his eye before toggling the transmit key on the radio. "Dagger CP, this is actual. Check fire on all indirect, I want to get on the ground. Over."

"Dagger Six, this is Dagger CP, WILCO. Over."

The Brigade Commander continued to watch impatiently while the fighting continued to rage down below. His knee bobbed up and down in nervous anticipation, waiting for the last artillery round to leave its tube and make the trip to one of the engagement areas on the battlefield. After waiting for what seemed like an eternity, the last round impacted on the surface.

"Dagger Six, this is Dagger CP. All fires are suspended. You are clear to go. Over."

"We monitored, sir," said the pilot, nosing the aircraft forward, diving toward the center of the conflagration. Within seconds they were over the center of the Battle Position, hovering thirty feet above the surface.

Running through the center of the grounds lay a sidewalk leading to the museum. It sat recessed, lower than the surrounding grounds which made it impossible to land the helicopter. While they hovered, the crew chief slid open the passenger door and tossed out a thick rope, unfurling it to the ground, then gave his Brigade Commander a "thumbs up" signal.

Williams nodded, unsecuring his harness before grasping

onto the rope. He grabbed it tight with thick, tan, leather work gloves, then wrapped his legs around it. He slid down the rope like a fireman's pole, reaching the ground in seconds. He took a look around to orient himself, suddenly aware of the deafening noise around him. He'd never heard such a racket in his entire life, even though he'd been on countless live-fire ranges and even in combat.

He looked around for a few seconds, trying to get his bearings when an engineer officer flagged him down, standing near the entrance to the museum. Williams ran over, eventually recognizing the soldier as the Battalion Operations Officer from the engineer battalion.

As soon as the crew chief in the helicopter saw that the colonel was clear, he unfastened the thick rope and dropped it to the ground while sliding the door shut again. The pilot nosed the aircraft over and headed off to the west while the crew chief climbed back into his seat and opened up with his M-240B going full cyclic, Vietnam door gunner-style.

Williams followed the engineer officer through the main entrance and he quickly closed the doors behind them, cutting the noise somewhat, making it possible to speak. Inside the foyer stood an older man with disheveled gray hair and an unkempt beard. His cheeks were drawn and he looked like he'd been sleeping in his clothes for quite some time.

"Colonel, this is Mr. Bock. He's the curator here at the museum." The engineer major still had to raise his voice in order to be heard clearly.

"Is there a reason you're introducing me to this gentleman? There are clearly other, more pressing matters at hand." Williams barely kept his annoyance in check. He needed to get into the fight, not sit around meeting inconsequential civilians.

The old man pulled out a large ring of keys. "I'm going to take you to the quickest entrance to the tower. That's where you want to go, isn't it?"

"Mr. Bock knows this place better than anyone, sir." The major put his hand on the old man's bony shoulder. "We've had a team in communication with him for over a week now, using his knowledge to help plan the op."

"I've been locked up in here since the outbreak began, living off the food left in the café." He jangled the keys in front of Williams. "Now, I know you're in a bit of a hurry, so please follow me."

"Sir, I'll leave in Mr. Bock's capable hands. I have to get back outside and help out my commander." The major wasn't asking permission to be excused and darted off, heading back outside.

The old man turned on his heel and took off as quickly as he could. Williams grimaced and followed the curator, easily keeping up.

They went deeper inside the facility, ignoring the exhibits, displaying the tools of destruction that helped extinguish an entire generation a century beforehand. The two of them went to the extreme end of the facility and up some stairs, emerging over top of the museum and back out in the sunshine, staring straight ahead at the massive tower.

Mr. Bock pointed over at the art deco monstrosity, yelling as loud as he could. "The entrance is over there! The spiral staircase will take you to the top! My old legs can't keep up, so you're on your own! Best of luck, Colonel!"

Williams turned didn't have a chance to answer the old man before he disappeared back inside and the relative safety of the museum. Shells exploded nearby with shrapnel sizzling overhead, forcing him to crouch. Staying low, he made off for the entrance to the tower suddenly realizing how exposed he was.

Inside he found the elevator, but with no power it would

do him no good. Access to the staircase was unlocked so he began the leg-burning climb, not enjoying it one bit dressed in full kit. He preferred to carry a rifle and no pistol, armed the same as the typical line-infantryman and the chest rig full of loaded magazines suddenly felt very heavy.

With chest heaving and sweat pouring, he eventually emerged up top. He found a Fire Support Team from 2nd Battalion huddled behind the protected concrete guardrails speaking into their radios, with their antennas sticking out the tops of day-packs. Roughly ten feet away kneeled a pair of Air Force Joint Terminal Attack Controllers who also busied themselves talking into handmikes.

The Fire Support Officer peeked over the top of the concrete rail, just enough to use his binoculars. The shells kept pouring in from the brigade's artillery battalion and the occasional hot steel fragment smacked off the tower, reminding them all just how close they had brought the onslaught in. One sliver of metal hit nearby with such force it forced Williams to duck and wince.

Williams, crouching once again, approached the officer from behind and tapped the man on his shoulder.

The young man turned with a scowl, "What? *Can't you see I'm busy?*" When he realized he was staring face to face with his Brigade Commander his facial expression instantly changed. "Oh, sir, I didn't realize it was you. My apologies. Can I help you with something?"

"Yes, Captain…"

"Captain Hadrian, sir. Captain Yves Hadrian, I'm the Battalion Fire Support Officer for 1-18 Infantry."

"Okay, Yves, give me a SITREP."

"Yes, sir. The perimeter is established and from what I can tell, the infantry and engineers are holding back packs of runners and the large herd coming in from the southeast. We are firing our pre-planned targets and slaughtering them wholesale, but, I'm getting word that I need to shut the fires off for a bit."

"Why would you do that?" Williams raised an eyebrow and kneeled on the cool concrete while steadying himself with his left hand. It was terribly uncomfortable and certainly not as easy as it was when he was a much younger man.

"They need to bring in more ammo on the Chinooks. Those boys and girls down there are burning through Class V like it's going out of style. We gotta put a temporary halt on the artillery so the choppers can safely fly in here, but I hope the resupply doesn't take too long."

"Why's that?"

"Take a look, sir. Just be careful and keep your head low. Those shells are coming in awfully close."

Williams nodded and peaked over the concrete parapet. He raised his own pair of binoculars while the captain did the same next to him.

To the extreme northern edge of the property thousands of the dead stormed in, scurrying through a cratered no-man's land, undeterred by the soul-wrenching explosions from the 155mm high explosive shells. These worked with devastating effect, tearing and rendering them into mangled heaps of flesh. Those that made it through the bottleneck relatively unscathed got quickly dispatched by the dismounts and vehicle crews.

To the west a similar scene played out, only with a deeper kill zone. The trees that once dotted the happy little public park had been blown into slivers, leaving nothing to obstruct the views of the tank and Bradley crews. They happily poured on a criss-cross of ball and tracer fire into the inferno.

Williams scooted around the tower to get a look in the other direction. The southwest approach looked like the school-house engagement areas they taught at the professional military schools in legendary places like Fort Benning or Fort Leonard Wood. The only difference being that these enemies did not shoot back, which made things quite a lot easier. The numbers coming at them in these human-wave attacks rivaled anything seen since the great battles on the Western Front in France during the First World War, or even in Korea a generation later, but in neither of those wars did the attackers yearn for the taste of human flesh.

To the east and southeast were a vast parking lot and a cemetery which also gave the soldiers excellent stand-off. Between the artillery and the armored vehicles on the ground, nothing was getting through. They had established an impenetrable wall of steel around their battle position and the infected could not breach it.

Then Williams looked down and saw the sobering reality. The pallets of ammunition brought in earlier were nearly expended. Details of soldiers ran back and forth, hauling heavy cans and tank shells back and forth. Many of the Bradley Fighting Vehicles along the line had pulled back to go through their laborious and time-consuming reloading procedures.

What made things even stickier was the fact that the incredible noise they made had kicked over the anthill and the dead came streaming in from all directions. As far as the eye could see they continued coming on, crowding the streets and alleyways, drawn like a moth to the flame to their well-established killing fields. The moment they shut down that artillery, those things would be on them in very little time, but with the ammo nearly running out, they desperately needed that resupply. Particularly if they had any hopes of shooting their way out of there.

"Hey, Captain. I got somethin' for ya." One of the Air Force JTACs smiled up at him while huddled around his radio pack. He was a Technical Sergeant and his partner a Staff Sergeant. Both of them sported long sideburns, wore non-regulation baseball caps and had their sleeves rolled half-way up their forearms. They also had non-issue jackets and trousers, with un-tucked Merrell hiking shoes on their feet to complete the ensemble. At least they had plate carriers on, but somehow managed to squeeze in some profane morale patches which they stuck to the Velcro. They appeared to have looked up every uniform regulation in the Air Force and intentionally violated every single one of them. It made Colonel Williams bristle just to look at them.

"What's up, Jiggy?"

"Got F-15s on station. You want 'em now?" The Tech Sergeant smirked.

"Is that a rhetorical question?" Hadrian smiled broadly back at him. "Bring the heat, baby."

"Copy that!" He turned to his partner. "Okay, Sanchez. Bring out 'The Gimp.'"

Williams cocked an eyebrow. The Staff Sergeant's name tape on his body armor read "Hamer" and not "Sanchez" which confused the Colonel. "Sanchez?"

"It's short for 'Dirty Sanchez.' It's a long story, sir," explained the Tech Sergeant.

"Sanchez" grabbed the laser designator with "The Gimp" stenciled on the side and propped it on top of the railing while Captain Hadrian pointed out the targets. The Air Force NCO nodded and put the invisible laser on a huge mob of the dead while his supervisor talked to the pilots running racetracks in the sky.

The Tech Sergeant nicknamed "Jiggy" finally said the words "Cleared hot" into his handset and Captain Hadrian ducked down, looking up at the Colonel. "Sir, you might want to get down. Things are about to get spicy."

Williams got low about the same time Sanchez snatched up his kit and took cover. Within a matter of seconds came a series of detonations that would have given Krakatoa a run for its money. Debris fell from the sky and chunks of airborne detritus slammed into the tower with an unnerving "smack."

After the bone-jarring experience Jiggy put the handset to his head, nodding along to the conversation between him and the aircrews, then gave the others a "thumbs up." Almost in unison, the Army Forward Observers and the Air Force JTACs popped their heads up like a bunch of meerkats emerging from their burrows, trying to get a look. Williams took a cue from them and took a peek as well.

The fighter jets dropped JDAMs right where Sanchez had designated, flattening thousands of animated corpses, putting their lights out permanently. The fire from the armored vehicles and dismounts slackened off some, finishing off the remaining ones hung up in the wire. The bombs bought them a little time, but only a little. From their vantage point up as high as they were, they could see thousands more flowing in like water from every direction.

In the distance the CH-47 Chinooks came into view, all of them carrying heavy loads of ammunition attached by sling-load underneath, swinging in the breeze. The fat, dual rotor cargo choppers moved at a brisk pace but the Apache attack helicopters blasted past them, heading toward the Battle Position at full speed.

They swooped in and began unleashing a torrent of rockets from wing-mounted hardpoints. While the Apaches set up an outer cordon, engaging with guns and rockets, the large cargo birds came in. They hovered carefully above the museum grounds, taking direction from pathfinders down below, carefully detaching their precious cargoes.

As intense as the attack from the helicopters, there weren't nearly enough of them to stem the tide. Hordes of infected came through, oblivious to the murderous fire from above. The runners came in at full speed with the rest close behind, hitting the outer ring of obstacles. They came on hard, rushing over wire flattened under countless bodies, or coming through gaps blasted into it from the artillery barrage. Some appeared to avoid the wire altogether, seeking breaches in the defensive belt.

On top of that the defensive small arms fire reduced in volume as the ammunition ran out.

Things were beginning to go critical.

***

Donahue pressed the trigger on his hand-control station and sent another burst downrange, dropping a few more climbing over the bodies of the fallen. He cut loose again when the weapon suddenly stopped. "Misfire!"

Mark leaned over to confirm what he already knew. The ammo cans were empty. "Not a misfire, we're out." He peered through the reflex sight mounted to the top of his M4 carbine and put the red dot on another one, squeezing the trigger with a burst. Individual shots at this range were too inaccurate and he had to engage this way, even though it tended to empty magazines far too quickly.

Donahue popped up through the gunner's hatch next to him in the Bradley turret, bringing his own personal weapon to bear, popping off several rounds in rapid succession. He glanced over the side of the track and found no one there. Lieutenant Baker's tank still positioned itself next to them, but the dismounts were gone. "Sarn't, is the rest of the squad over on your side?"

Mark looked over to the right and didn't see any dismounts

on the ground either. "No. Nobody's there." He turned around, craning his neck to see over the back deck to find all six of their infantry running away.

Baker's tank fired its main gun, shredding hundreds of flesh-eaters to their front. The lieutenant hammered away on the .50 cal while Yokey popped his head out of the loader's hatch and started working it with the '240. The giant turret swept left and right while the coax coughed to life, spitting hot death.

When the dust settled from the main gun, not only had it blown scores of the dead to pieces, but it also punched a nice, big hole in their protective wire. Within seconds they began to pour in.

Mark fired his carbine again and the bolt locked to the rear. He dropped the empty mag and felt around the pouches attached to his belt. They were empty too. All along the line weapons went silent at the same time the infected started coming through in large numbers.

"Battle Axe Six, this is White One. We're out of ammo and my infantry has displaced to the rear." Mark couldn't make himself say that his dismounts were retreating. "What are your orders? Over."

Lieutenant Baker, sitting in the tank next to them, looked over, doing his best impression of "Iron Mike" with his arm raised, the iconic statue at Fort Benning. *Follow me!*"

The tank lurched forward, its tracks churning up chunks of grass and topsoil, flinging them from the back of the vehicle. It raced forward while the lieutenant and Yokey dropped down inside, closing the hatches as they did so. The Company Commander's wingman followed close behind, launching into the fray and within seconds the two armored behemoths were at the wire, running circuits back and forth, mashing the dead under their tracks, grinding the decomposing attackers into the earth.

Mark looked over at Donahue who simply shrugged his shoulders. "Okay then, driver, move out!"

Tracked vehicles all throughout the perimeter broke from their pre-planned fighting positions and joined in, engaged in a form of mounted hand-to-hand combat. Meanwhile, the dismounted engineers and infantry descended on the pallets of ammunition, tearing them apart and desperately breaking down the contents.

***

"Come on you guys, let's go!" shouted Specialist Harris. He, along with dozens of other soldiers tore the tie-down straps from the boxes and crates of ammunition stacked on the wooden pallets. They worked feverishly with their personal weapons slug across their backs, liberating small arms ammunition first, then the bigger items for the vehicles. Some ripped open cans, while others worked with stripper clips, refilling rifle magazines. The NCOs and other junior leaders organized themselves instead of allowing a "free for all." They worked as fast as they could with one on the perimeter, watching the infected come storming in.

While they toiled away, a M-113 armored personnel carrier pulled up with the vehicle commander waving his hands over his head up in the cupola, trying to get their attention. Harris noticed it was Sergeant Medina, their company clerk and standing behind him in the open cargo hatch was Staff Sergeant Packard, the Company First Sergeant. Packard got bumped up from 3rd Platoon after 1st Sergeant Landreau went AWOL over a month prior, never to be seen again.

"You guys throw that shit in the back of the track!" The

ramp dropped and Packard darted out, coming up beside the rest of them, scooping up whatever ammo he could grab, hauling it into the back of the M-113. There were dismounts from 3rd Platoon intermingled with the crowd and they wasted no time bringing cans and crates over, tossing them roughly inside the APC. They were not getting graded for finesse or neatness.

When they filled it as much as they could, Packard climbed on top of the pile and slapped Medina on the shoulder. *"Let's go!"*

Specialist Beltran mashed the accelerator to the floor and the track took off, headed back toward the perimeter where Bravo Company hung on by the skin of their teeth.

Harris looked at the others. "You all good?"

Everyone checked to make sure they carried as many mags and belts as they could carry, then nodded to the Squad Leader.

"Okay, let's do this!"

***

Burbey knocked down walkers like bowling pins, the unlucky ones falling underneath his tracks, their bones snapping like twigs. The Bradley Fighting Vehicle wasn't anywhere near as heavy as the Abrams, but it was more than enough to dispatch their foe, buttoned up inside, the three of them could see very little, peering through the periscopes, but it was enough to get around.

Mark couldn't tell if the undead had completely made it through, so they continued working a pattern in the field to their front, running over and crushing the things. Over near the three o'clock position of the perimeter two of 3rd Platoon's Bradleys crashed into one another. It rang the crew's bells, causing a few cuts and bruises, but otherwise everything turned out fine. The crews were alive, the vehicles could still move and they got back into action right away after the collision.

"Guidons, this is Battle Axe Six. Get ready, we got incoming."

No sooner had Lieutenant Baker ended his transmission than they got hit with a massive shockwave and blast. The three of them painfully bounced around inside the IFV, suddenly wishing the thing were padded with feather pillows.

"Damn, that was close!" Donahue said, holding his ribs.

"I think I knocked a tooth loose," replied Burbey, sounding somewhat worse for wear.

"Those rounds are coming in on pre-planned targets. Entirely too close. Burbey, get us out of here!" Mark grasped the bridge of his nose. He'd slammed into the commander's sight unit and he wasn't sure if it was broken.

Machine guns and small arms barked outside while the artillery came smashing in again. The armored vehicles quickly fell back to their original positions to find the dismounts back in place, tossing crates and cans of munitions from the back of the First Sergeant's M-113.

While the artillery thundered along the outer perimeter, the infantry and engineer squads laid down a blanket of fire within the Battle Position, clearing out the leakers that managed to get through. Once the vehicles got back into position, crew members began leaping from tanks and tracks, racing for the caches of ammo, grabbing arm-loads and handing them to crewmates. Meanwhile it appeared that the whole city had emptied out and were headed toward the museum for a visit.

***

Colonel Williams peered over the ledge through his

binoculars with mouth hanging agape. It just didn't seem possible. They'd cut down thousands of them, easily, but the undead kept coming on. Only now the concentration of them seemed utterly unbelievable. They hadn't put a dent in the numbers out there and not only hadn't the volume tapered off any, it seemed to be growing exponentially.

They were going to be overrun and they were all going to die.

Coming out here today was a bad idea.

"Colonel?"

No response.

"*Colonel!*"

Williams snapped out of it to see Hadrian sticking a radio handset in his face. "Sir, it's Vanguard Six. He says things are getting untenable. He recommends that we withdraw. With your permission, he is going to give the order to pull out of here."

All along the perimeter ramps of Bradleys were lowered and infantry squads mounted up as fast as their legs could carry them. Teams of medics loaded wounded on stretchers into the backs of M-113 ambulances and the engineers clambered atop the tanks and anything else that could roll under its own power. It became clear that Vanguard Six had already given the order to retreat, but he called his Brigade Commander as an afterthought out of courtesy.

The JTACs and FOs were already shrugging on their packs and gathering up their weapons before waiting for an order from Williams. They were packing up and moving out, with or without him.

Dane Williams collected himself and cleared his throat. "Yes, Captain, call Vanguard Actual back and tell him that I approve the retrograde. I will be joining him shortly."

He followed the rest of the men as they raced back

downstairs to the base of the tower.

***

Soldiers held on tight to the tops of vehicles of every shape and size. The M-88 recovery vehicles, the ambulances, the Bradleys, tanks and even the Scout Humvees. If there was available space to pile on, someone occupied it.

Alpha Company led the charge, not bothering to run the serpentine entrance at the south side of the perimeter. Instead, they charged off straight to the west, running over the piles of bodies that swamped and buried the wire obstacles. It was a grisly affair, but effective enough, shaving valuable time off their exit from the Battle Position named *Gibraltar*. Once they hit Broadway Boulevard they hooked north, headlong into a thoroughfare crowded with the dead.

The tanks in the lead fired canister shot in rapid succession, laying waste to their front, while the Apaches worked the flanks to the best of their ability. Engineers and infantry piled on top fired small arms in every direction, while 25mm auto-cannons and coax machine guns spat a steady stream of hot death. Fires burned in the buildings all around them and the air stunk of burning plastic, rubber and decomposing flesh.

"Okay, Burbey, we're 'Tail-end Charlie.' Follow the others." Mark fired his M-4 wildly at the charging masses coming at them from all sides. The column moved swiftly out of the area, but they came out last, contending with the massive surge swallowing up the museum grounds. Up ahead an engineer got grabbed by the ankle and pulled down from a tank straight into the gnashing teeth of a dozen of the infected. As many times as he'd seen it before he still couldn't bear to watch and looked away.

"Donahue, swing the turret to the six o'clock position." Mark continued shooting, barely bothering to aim anymore. The things were everywhere, making it nearly impossible to miss.

"What do you want me to engage, Sarn't?"

"Anything, damnit! Weapons free! Just kill shit!"

"Roger that." Donahue hit the 'coax' button on the control panel then cut loose. He didn't need to adjust for range, the targets filling his reticle.

"Sarn't look out! They're coming up over the front slope of the track!" Burbey cried over the intercom.

As the turret came around, facing to the rear, Mark swiveled 180 degrees and saw three coming up the front slope, headed straight at him. Startled, he fired the first burst wide, but then leveled it on the nearest one blowing its head apart. He swung the weapon to the left and did it again, sending another tumbling off the side of the IFV. The bolt locked to the rear and he struggled to free his pistol before the last one was upon him, barely drawing it in time and shooting it in the mouth, sending a 9mm FMJ smashing through the brainstem.

Jesus, that was close, he thought to himself, reaching for another rifle magazine and slapping it into the mag well of his M-4.

"Sarn't, you okay?" Burbey asked, his voice tinged with concern.

"Yeah, dude, I'm alright." Mark's hands shook and his mouth grew cottony. "Just keep up with the rest of the column. Keep the formation tight."

"Roger!"

Mark shot his rifle over the front deck of *BOHICA*, keeping it clear of the occasional climber that managed to get lucky and not fall under their steel track shoes. Donahue kept the turret over the back deck for a while, hosing away until they built up enough speed to outrun even the fastest ones. He still oriented the main gun backwards, though he didn't engage anything unless it became a real threat, doing his best to conserve their dwindling supply of 7.62 FMJ.

Rolling down the street the animated corpses continued emerging from side streets and the occasional doorway, lunging at them from sidewalks to no avail. After a while the armor to their front had opened up a pretty effective path, like tire tracks in freshly fallen snow. Only this was no snow.

It went on like that for a long time, with concentrated fire emanating all up and down the line from the vehicles and dismounts sitting atop, unprotected on the outside. The Apaches flying support rotated in and out in relays, rearming and refueling, while Blackhawks took turns as well, with crew-chief door-gunners slinging hot lead.

At some point in the middle of it all, Lieutenant Baker came over the net. *"Guidons, there's a breakdown in the center of the road up ahead. One of the tanks from Charlie Company blew a pack and is stuck. They are attempting a recovery. All elements pass on the left-hand side. Break. White One, you and I will hang back with them to provide security. How copy? Over."*

"Battle Axe Six, this is White One. WILCO. Over." Mark took a deep breath before toggling the intercom. "You heard the man, Burbey. Get ready to stop. Donahue, keep scanning and stay frosty."

"I got a bad feeling about this," Donahue said, adjusting his seat and repositioning himself. "This is no time to be slowing down. We've got half the city's former residents right on our ass."

"You don't have to like it, dude. You just gotta do it." Mark hoped he sounded more confident than he felt. He grabbed the loosely-hanging olive drab bandana hanging around his neck and pulled it up to cover his mouth and nose. It had become standard procedure to cover eyes, noses and mouths if one expected close combat with the dead. In the early days many had tried wearing their Army-issued gas masks, but that had fallen out of fashion fairly quickly. It was terribly hard to see and breathe with one of those on, making it much more difficult to shoot an fight, so practically everyone elected to wear something, anything, else to cover the face to protect against infectious splatter.

Up ahead he saw the M-88 recovery vehicle backing up to a tank, sitting stationary in the middle of the street. A blown pack meant that the engine on the vehicle suffered a catastrophic failure. The only way to recover a vehicle in that state was to drag it with another vehicle, which is what the recovery crew on the M-88 intended to do.

The column passed to the left and right of the breakdown, hammering away at the infected emerging from the side streets and parking lots. None of them slowed down, executing a perfect L.A.-style "drive by," shredding them to pieces and moving on.

The crews from the M-88 and the broken down tank boiled out of their hatches, unlimbering heavy steel tow bars and shackles, working as quickly as they could to hook the vehicles up. The commanders of both armored vehicles remained behind their .50 caliber machine guns, letting fly with the occasional burst whenever a runner or cluster of other stragglers got too close.

Bringing up the extreme rear of the column, Lieutenant Baker pulled his Abrams off to the right, stopping where he had a decent field of fire covering a parking lot, while Burbey did the same with *BOHICA* off to the left.

"Donahue, gun to the nine o'clock position. Harris, pop the cargo hatch. Everyone up and scanning."

The turret swiveled and the 25mm Bushmaster autocannon pointed off to the left, covering the western avenue of approach. No sooner did it get into position when the coax spat its first burst, sending tracers flying. The cargo hatch creaked open and landed in the open position with an audible "thunk." All six dismounts stood in the back, tightly crowded together in the small rectangular opening, facing outward with their small arms in hand. Gray flipped the bipod down on her SAW and set it on the open hatch, pointing it to their rear, oriented south. Harris grabbed a couple of wooden ammo crates and set them on the diamond-plate flooring. With her short legs, she needed to stand on them to see and bring her weapon into action properly.

No sooner did they stop when Broadway Boulevard to the south began filling up with hundreds of the dead and they were coming after the column as fast as their rotted legs would carry them. Machine guns hammered away at the threats to their left and right, hitting the handful coming in from the flanks. The crews did not see the massive horde coalescing right behind them. Even over the noise of the automatic weapons Harris and the rest of the squad could clearly hear their howls and shrieks, their pace quickening as the sights and smells of the living grew stronger for them.

"We got Zulus! Twelve o'clock, 300 meters and they're coming fast!" Gray leaned into the weapon and opened up. She cut loose a rapid succession of bursts, sprinkling empty shell casings from the bottom of the SAW's receiver onto the open cargo hatch.

Johnson and Hong crowded in next to her, joining in as well. Hong brought his own light machine gun to bear, while Johnson put his M-320 grenade launcher into action, making a loud "boomp" every time he fired it. The LMGs sent hot lead zinging into the screaming mass, while the grenades lazily arced in, landing among them, blasting satisfying holes into the crowd.

Still, they came on with a singular purpose. To consume the living.

Harris, Dubois and McDermott climbed up precariously onto the top of the Bradley, carefully balancing themselves while they joined in the fusillade.

Mark looked on with grave concern, watching how fast the mob down the street was closing in on them. He turned to see the tankers and mechanics racing around and fumbling with towing hardware, trying to get it assembled, while the rate of fire from the .50 cals picked up. He keyed the transmit key. "Lieutenant, you need to tell the tank crew to abandon that hunk of shit. Just get on the M-88 and haul ass. They'll never get it hooked up in time. Over!"

Off to the right on the east side past Lieutenant Baker's tank was a tavern next door to a burger joint. Both places had broken windows and wreckage strewn everywhere, and the walls pocked with bullet holes. Before the officer could answer Mark caught sight of movement behind him, only thirty yards distant. Coming around the bar came dozens of runners, the lead ones pointing at the stationary vehicles, screaming at the top of their rancid lungs.

"Lieutenant look out!" Mark pointed at the emerging threat, coming on at speed.

"Oh, fu…." Baker's transmission ended abruptly as he and his loader Yokey ducked down inside of their tank, pulling the hatches down shut behind them.

Mark turned to his dismount squad. "Everybody, inside and button up! *Now!*"

A mob of them crashed into Baker's tank like a wave hitting the surf, with dozens climbing up and onto the Abrams. Like water, the rest flowed around running directly into the tank crew and mechanics trying to hook up the stranded vehicle. They were overwhelmed in a matter of seconds, with no way to escape.

The commander and gunner ducked inside, hastily closing hatches behind them, as did the two mechanics fortunate to still be aboard the M-88. The creatures with their spider-webbed, varicose skin and evil, red eyes swarmed the two armored behemoths like ants on a giant grub. The men caught outside trying to attach the crow bar shrieked high-pitched screams as the dead sank their teeth into warm flesh.

Mark attempted to shoot the men to put them out of their misery, but there was no time. The tsunami of infected swarmed them as well, but the crew and dismounts aboard *BOHICA* managed to get inside and secure their hatches just in time.

He sat down on the padded leather seat with forearms resting on knees, his hands visibly shaking. It would have been completely dark inside the turret except for the daylight coming in through the periscopes and the blue dome light, emanating its cool glow.

Mark took a deep breath and looked over to find Donahue staring back at him. Neither said a word, sitting in complete silence, listening to the animal howls outside until a radio transmission cut through like a knife. *"White One, Axe Six. You guys okay over there? Over."*

Mark toggled the intercom. "Harris, you all good back there?"

"Roger, Sarn't. I monitored. We're all good."

"Battle Axe Six, White One. We're up. No casualties. Over." Mark's stomach turned and the saliva filled his mouth. He fought the urge to vomit, swallowing hard.

"Good. Let's get out of here. Fall in behind me and cover the rear."

"WILCO."

Mark forced himself to sit up and look through the periscope, over to the two tanks and the M-88. He tried not to look at the group of creatures crouched over and feeding on the soldiers like a pack of wolves tearing an elk apart. Instead he watched the recovery vehicle belch smoke from its exhaust, giving off a rumbling roar when the diesel engines kicked in, plowing over the walkers and shamblers to its front, greasing its tracks with their guts. Once it got moving, Lieutenant Baker's tank with the word *CARNAGE* stenciled on the main gun barrel followed close behind.

"Driver, move out."

Burbey said nothing, putting the Bradley's transmission into gear and pressing his foot on the accelerator, gradually accelerating to catch up with the rest of the column.

Chapter 4

FOB Chiefs
1548 Hours Local

The entire battalion lined up their vehicles in neat rows, marshaled forward by guides from the Chemical Decontamination unit. These specialized troops wore full chemical protective suits and protective masks, running a site next to the Missouri River that functioned like a giant car wash.

While the decontamination teams hosed gunk and infected biological material off the vehicles, the soldiers themselves lined up for inspections and showers. There were multiple medical teams set up on the far side of the Quartermaster shower facility, all supervised by the Brigade Surgeon and the battalion's Physician Assistant. Bags and the other medics did exhaustive checks on the troops, while guards escorted "close contact" cases off to the quarantine cages.

Mark and the rest of 2nd Platoon waited patiently for medical clearance while trying to ignore the four soldiers being marched off to an awaiting cargo Humvee, escorted by armed MPs. The four of them were stripped of any equipment and had hands zip-tied behind them. Their heads hung limply and shoulders sagged while one of them bawled like a baby. The Battalion Chaplain walked alongside them, clutching a bible and doing his best to console them. They all tested positive for the virus and were being taken to a private area on the edge of the FOB where they would be quietly euthanized. The security detail tried to move them away in the most dignified manner possible, but there was only so much one could do. A few religious types crossed themselves and others said a silent prayer, but most looked away. Nobody said a word until they had been loaded up and driven out of sight.

When they were gone, Bags announced the verdict to the group of them with a subdued smile. "Sergeant Matthews, you all have passed your health screenings, but as per SOP, everyone is restricted to the company area for the next seventy-two hours. You are all going to be subject to hourly health checks during that period as well. If anyone is feeling unwell, they need to immediately self-declare so we can put them in quarantine and further observation."

"Restricted to the company area for the next three days? That sounds great if you ask me. It's not like we can go out clubbing or anything like that anyway and restriction means no work details." Harris couldn't resist chiming in. Being the senior member of the "E-4 Mafia," he felt it was his duty to demonstrate how clever he was all the time.

"Thanks, Bags. What about Burbey and Donahue?" Mark pointed over to the decontamination station near the river with all the heavy tracked vehicles lined up. Tracks, road wheels and skirts were covered in ocher-colored gunk. All of it highly toxic to the living. Like the others, *BOHICA* was coated in the vile stuff, waiting to get hosed off.

"As soon as they are done helping out the decon teams, I'll personally check them out after the showers."

"Awesome. Let me know if there are any issues." Mark turned to the others while picking up his weapons and gear. "Come on you reprobates, let's get back to the tent city. They're actually delivering room service and hot chow is supposed to get delivered in a couple of hours."

***

When they arrived at their tent, Dubois tossed open the flaps and loudly announced their presence, taking on the tone and mannerism of a gaudy, Victorian-era thespian. "Hearken thee, fellow knaves. Your fellow party-members have returned after a long and arduous quest, filled with many adventures and tales of bravery!"

"You're back!" Bailey Roberts, the blonde-haired teenage girl, burst from her cot and wrapped her arms around Dubois, squeezing him so hard it hurt his ribs. "I'm so glad you're okay!"

The other members of the platoon came into the tent, walking around the immobilized pair near the entrance. McDermott got hit with the next hug, this one from the other teenage girl, Consuela, who planted a wet kiss on his cheek. She then did the same for the others while her boyfriend, Angel, came forward smiling broadly and shaking everyone's hand. Angel and Consuela said some things in rapid-fire Spanish to them, words they couldn't understand, but the sentiment was clear, the two of them were happy to see the soldiers return. Clay Roberts and his wife Cynthia came forward as well, shaking hands and slapping people on the backs and shoulders.

"Everybody back off and give me some space!" shouted Angela Carnegie. She still wore her sheriff's uniform, though the body armor and gun belt lay resting on her nearby bunk. She held the leash of her Alsatian named Saxon, who looked up at her, awaiting a command.

"It's okay, Angie, we got checked out at the med station and we're all good to go," said Private Jimmy Hong, casually holding his M-249 Squad Automatic Weapon by the carrying handle.

"There's only one test I give a shit about. You know the docs sometimes miss stuff. That's why they have quarantines. Saxon has a 100% proven track record." Angie's eyes were hard as flints and she stiffened up as if she were ready to go to blows. The woman had the build of a mixed-martial arts fighter and everyone knew she could hold her own, so nobody felt eager to call her bluff.

Mark sighed and shook his head. "It's fine. Everybody line up. This isn't going to kill you." He approached first, offering his hand to the dog.

The rest of them did the same and Saxon went down the queue, giving each soldier a good sniff. Satisfied, the dog's jaw slackened and his long tongue hung out, casually panting.

"Alright, you can come in then," Carnegie said, relaxing somewhat and returning to her corner of the tent with the German Shepherd. They settled down next to Darin Jefferson, the other sheriff's deputy who didn't get up from his cot, still recovering from a nasty leg wound. The two law enforcement officers picked their cards back up and got back to their game of gin rummy.

Swanson, Weber and Devons, all still recovering from their wounds as well, made their way over as best they could. Before long, the returning heroes were completely surrounded by smiling comrades, all laughing and joking until Clay Roberts noticed someone missing. "Wait, where's Donahue and Burbey?"

The warm atmosphere instantly cooled a little when everyone realized they weren't standing there with the rest.

Mark raised his hand consolingly. "Listen, they're fine. *BOHICA* came back covered in zombie guts and they are outside with the decon teams from the Chem Battalion, washing it and giving the track a proper detail job. The two of them will be back in a little while."

Everyone in the tent relaxed when they heard the news, letting out a collective sigh of relief that everyone from 2nd Platoon made it back safe and sound. Even Angela Carnegie seemed to soften somewhat, while Saxon curled up next to her feet.

"It's a little early in the day yet, why's everyone back here in the tent?" Mark looked around and saw all of his people gathered there, minus his driver and gunner. All of 2nd Platoon were present, including their adopted members of the group as well.

"Work parties supporting 2nd Battalion got the day off today. Instead of going out on the work details, they let us listen to the radios to see how you guys were doing out there. The lieutenant over in the Distro Platoon let us listen to one of theirs." Clay Roberts being easily the oldest one of the group quickly became a sort of father figure to them. He may have been a banker in his previous life, but he'd also been a marathon-runner with his wife Cynthia. He also enjoyed firearms and shooting in his free time. Both of those hobbies paid off great dividends during the opening days of the outbreak. "We heard a lot of the radio traffic, but didn't get a feel for the big picture. How did things ultimately work out?"

"If you don't mind, it's been a long day," Mark said, pointing with his chin at all the gear he still carried in his hands.

"Oh, sorry. Please relax," Clay responded politely.

Mark excused himself and walked past, setting his kit down on his cot before taking a seat and untying his boots. He pulled them off and sighed deeply while closing his eyes. When he opened them, he watched Clay settle in on the bunk across from him with an eager look on his face. "Yeah, the lieutenant said that the mission overall went well."

The rest of the platoon broke up and dispersed themselves to their own corners of the tent, buddies doubling up, while a few of the loners stretched out and relaxed. The sound of the generator outside and the hum of the air conditioner in the background brought on a sudden sense of serenity to them all.

"So, everything went okay? It sounded pretty crazy when we listened in." Clay lowered his voice and looked around to make sure their discussion was reasonably private. The rest of the group had gone on to doing their own things, carrying on separate conversations or taking care of important chores like weapons maintenance.

"Yeah, it got a little close for comfort out there. Let's just put it that way." He peeled off his socks and laid them out carefully so they'd dry properly. He leaned over to the rucksack at the head of his cot, rummaging around in it for a fresh pair. They might not have been clean, but at least they'd be dry.

"What was the butcher's bill on this little outing?"

"They said that the battalion lost a dozen people on this one. Twice as many as that wounded. The artillery was coming in so close you could've shaved with the shrapnel. Lots of people got hit during those 'danger close' missions. We managed to get all the injured out though, but God knows if any more will develop symptoms in quarantine. I guess we'll have to wait and see." He found a Ziplock bag with socks in it and pulled it free from the backpack. "Bingo!"

"How many Zulus did you all kill?"

"Not sure. Thousands at least. Battalion S-2 said that we might have taken out between ten and twenty-thousand, but they can't be sure until the recon birds get some better imagery and the analysts get some time to study it." He leaned over again and retrieved a rifle cleaning kit and opened it up, spreading the components out. Mark popped the rear retaining pin of his M-4 before pulling the charging handle and dropping the bolt-carrier group out onto his lap. The inner components of the weapon were coated in a thick layer of carbon, the result of firing hundreds of rounds in the middle of a running gunfight.

"I wouldn't want that job, but it sounds like it was a big win to me." Clay offered the younger man a rag to wipe down the parts.

"Thanks." Mark accepted the rag and wiped down the carrier-group before disassembling it into several smaller pieces. "We lost at least a dozen people today taking down thousands of zeds. If we managed to take out the top-end of the estimate, we'll need to do this mission again another twenty-five times to clear out the city and secure it. Except that it won't be that easy. Once we thin them out a bit, we'll have to start clearing the neighborhoods house by house, room by room, and while our casualties weren't huge, we'll still keep getting whittled down and the house-clearing shit will be the most dangerous and costly part of this whole operation."

"Jesus, that could take months."

"Yeah, and in case the geniuses up at Division haven't noticed yet, we aren't getting any replacements for our losses, and well, our 'enemy' is." He dabbed a bit of oil on a tiny cloth patch and affixed it to the end of a cleaning rod to run down the barrel of his rifle.

"What are you trying to say?"

Mark leaned in closer to Clay and kept his voice low so the others couldn't hear. "I don't have no degree in military science or anything like that and they sure as shit didn't send me to West Point, but I know what a 'war of attrition' is, and if that's what we're fighting, I'm not sure we're going to win." He ran the patch through the barrel, removing it and prepping another one.

Clay sat up straighter with a thoughtful look while rubbing his chin. He looked over at his wife Cynthia and his daughter Bailey who sat on either side of Angel and Consuela, giving them their daily English lesson. Then he locked his gaze with Mark. "So, all of this is for nothing then?" It wasn't a question.

Mark looked away without responding, running another patch through the barrel.

"Listen to me, there has to be some purpose to all of this or else we all might as well just end it right now." He leaned in closer once again and softened his tone. "You don't talk much about yourself, but you must have someone out there you care about. A partner, some family maybe?"

Images of his parents and brother suddenly ran through his mind. He'd been trying to get to them when the world fell apart, stranding him with these people. He had no idea if any of his family were still alive, but he hoped they were. There were survivors all over the country, lots of them, so there was a good chance they were still out there too, hanging on like the rest of them. "It's possible, I guess. I haven't heard any news about them."

"Then you have to stay focused. These people in this platoon need you. We need you. You have to stay positive and believe that this will all work out or else the end will be predetermined. If you believe we will lose then it will become a self-fulfilling prophecy. Do you understand?"

Mark looked up and met his gaze again. "Yeah, I guess so. I suppose you're right."

"You're the leader of this group and we all look to you for strength. If you are filled with doubt everyone will see it. There's no way to cover it up, we'll know." Clay wasn't talking down to him, he was mentoring. The man's salt-and-pepper hair and wisdom lines on his forehead, lent some credence to his words.

"You ever serve in the military, Clay?"

"Not that I recall. Why do you ask?"

"You seem to know a lot about leadership for a guy who never served."

"Well, I may have learned a few things over the years." He

smiled warmly, accentuating the wrinkles from the corners of his eyes. "You want to tell me about those loved ones of yours?"

Mark didn't want to reveal too much. The less he told them the better. If they found out he was an escaped felon from prison, who knows what might happen to him. The prisons and jails weren't exactly running at the moment, so the Army might elect to line him up against a wall and shoot him, rather than bother with incarceration. "Maybe later, when we have some time."

Clay nodded, then gently slapped Mark on the knee before getting up and wandering back over to his family.

***

FOB Chiefs
1615 Hours Local
Decon Site

The UH-60 Blackhawk swept in and flared prior to landing, kicking up a cloud of dust while taking direction from the Pathfinder on the ground. The sleek-looking chopper put down on its wheeled landing gear and settled in, easing down on the Landing Zone. The crew chief hopped out with the extra-long coiled cable attached to his helmet and helped slide open the large door, allowing the passengers to disembark. Colonel Dane Williams and Lieutenant Colonel Jerry Hamilton stood by waiting along with their Sergeants Major to receive them.

The Division Commander, Major General Randall "Bud" Napier, hopped out first, followed by his own Command Sergeant Major. After that emerged two colonels and the aide de camp who stayed close, but at a respectful distance.

Williams and Hamilton rendered salutes, standing at the rigid position of "attention." The general casually returned them and offered his hand with a big, toothy smile. "Gentlemen, It's good to see you both again."

The officers shook hands and headed off while the sergeants major did this same thing, only in a more subdued manner. The senior NCOs followed the commanders, with the staff officers trailing a bit further behind the rest of the group.

"Thank you, sir. I'm glad you could break away and make the trip out here." Dane Williams gently guided them toward the Chemical Decontamination stations set up near the river. Some of the vehicles had been thoroughly cleaned and were emerging from the far end, their crews preparing to drive them off to the battalion motor pool.

"It's no trouble at all. I'm glad to see us finally on the offensive in this war and wanted to come out and congratulate some of the soldiers in person." Out of range of the helicopter's rotor wash, the general motioned to his aide who came jogging up, handing the commanding officer his patrol cap with two large black stars sewn on the front. Napier stood there with hands on his hips for a moment, looking at the site. He did not wear body armor or any other equipment, electing to wear the leather general-officer's belt and issue sidearm. While not authorized, the commanding general and his sergeant major both wore starched uniforms, though it was anyone's guess where they found the starch or anyone to press them. "This operation was a smashing success. You should be very proud. With more victories like this, we'll be taking the country back in no time!"

Commander of 2nd Battalion, Lieutenant Colonel Jerry Hamilton, looked over to his Brigade Commander to gauge his reaction. During the initial outbreak Hamilton had ordered his people to exercise restraint and only fire on the infected in self-defense, believing that there would be a cure found soon and he wanted to minimize civilian fatalities. That decision cost his unit scores of casualties in the first day alone, a decision that would haunt him every single day since. Before then he'd been an officer of quick wit and humor. Now he carried out his duties with grim determination, always wrapped in a shroud of melancholy.

Dane Williams saw the look on Hamilton's face and ignored it, turning his attention to the commanding general. "Yes, sir, I agree. We effectively leveraged our forces at echelon to maximize kinetic effect. 'Operation Toe Cutter' represents the first of a series of planned, named operations which will reduce concentrations of zulus, which ultimately will allow us to transition to the next phase in our campaign plan."

"That's excellent news." General Napier watched the teams of soldiers dressed in hazmat suits with hoses meticulously spraying down the vehicles of 2nd Battalion, standing back on the high ground at a very safe distance. Pumps took water directly from the river, while run-off flowed downstream. "Will you be ready to execute the next one on schedule?"

"Oh, absolutely, General. As you know, it'll take a few days to reset the Brigade with ammunition and fuel brought in by rail, then we'll be ready to go again. We'll rotate the battalions within the Brigade, so they'll take turns and each one will go out on another op similar to this on average about every ten days or so." Dane Williams stole a glance over at Hamilton again, watching the color drain from his face. It looked like his subordinate commander was going to be sick.

Napier turned to the two colonels he'd brought with him on the chopper from Fort Riley. They were his Division Chief of Staff and the Operations Officer, the men who made the

"Big Red One" function from day to day. They had their notepads out, ready to write down anything important the general had to say. "Guys, make sure we are getting the supporting enablers to 2nd Brigade so they can continue on seamlessly. Comms, ISR, fires, you name it."

"Yes, sir," said the Chief of Staff, who quietly leaned over to the Operations Officer, whispering something in his ear. The Ops Officer, or G-3, simply nodded, never looking up from his small notebook, scribbling down the details.

Napier noticed Hamilton standing there silently, his face turning a shade of green. "You okay, Jerry? You don't look so good."

"I'm fine, General. I didn't get much sleep last night and it's been a long day, that's all."

The Division Commander slapped him on the shoulder. "You did a great job today and you should be proud. Now, get your people cleaned up and fed. I am looking forward to you doing this again in a few days!"

***

Division Main Command Post
Fort Riley, Kansas
8 August, 2016

The Division's primary staff officers crowded around a few field tables while seated on folding chairs. They dressed in their camouflage field uniforms, carrying their Army-issued sidearms worn in various styles of holsters each of them had procured from different "tactical" companies and websites prior to the beginning of the current unpleasantness. All of them wore the mask of fatigue, working around the clock to keep the unit running, sometimes in the face of impossible odds.

Lieutenant Colonel Rich Sullivan served as the Division Logistics Officer, or G-4 for short. He'd been assigned to that position earlier in the summer after relinquishing command of a battalion, a job he dearly loved. As a career logistician, he'd spent the vast majority of his career on staffs at different levels, and when he got selected to be the 1st Division's G-4 he threw himself into his new duties just as he always had in every previous assignment. Now he found himself managing the "beans and bullets" for an entire "heavy" division. He'd been deployed on combat assignments before, but he never dreamed he'd be supporting combat operations in the continental United States. Against an army of the dead.

The Chief of Staff convened the meeting with them and had asked for routine updates before turning it over to the G-3 for the current operational overview. Rich still couldn't believe that they were engaging in such ambitious endeavors, particularly since their supply lifelines were so tenuous. It appeared to him that they were accepting an irresponsible level of risk.

"That concludes my portion of the briefing. Are there any questions?" The Chief of Current Operations or "CHOPS" stood at the head of the field tables next to the screen with the operational picture projected on it. He'd been using it to discuss the plans for the coming weeks.

"Yeah, I do." Rich shifted in his chair, pulling out a laser pointer to highlight particular areas on the large map in the center of the screen. "We only just got rail running reliably a week ago and we're moving enormous volumes of personnel and equipment, most of it still heading west which is taking up most of the capacity. Right?"

The G-3 nodded to the CHOPS, indicating it was okay for him to have a seat, before standing up at the head of the table himself. "Yes, Rich, that's correct. After the current government evacuated from Washington DC and relocated to Seattle, they ordered a consolidation of military forces in the Pacific Northwest, so most of the rail capacity is supporting those troop movements."

"Okay, and why isn't TRANSCOM helping with strategic airlift to move some of this?" Rich already knew the answer to this, but he was getting ready to make his point.

"Well, Rich, as you know, the President ordered all troops stationed abroad to be brought back to the Continental United States. Most strategic air and sealift is currently allocated to bringing our men and women back home from Europe and Asia. NORTHCOM has been having a hell of a time balancing the requirements of getting our people home with force protection concerns." The G-3 pointed to the laptop sitting in front of his CHOPS. "Pull up the slides from this morning's Battlefield Update Brief."

"Yes, sir." The CHOPS clicked a couple of buttons and opened up some PowerPoint slides showing the global strategic situation.

"Outbreaks are out of control nearly everywhere, except in the British Isles, Japan, Australia and New Zealand as best we can tell. The Brits, Japanese, Aussies and Kiwis managed to lock down their countries and keep the virus out, but everyone else in the world is suffering just as badly, if not worse than we are." He nodded to the major again. "Next slide."

The slide changed and icons appeared over multiple flashpoints covering the globe.

"Korea is in a total meltdown right now and is already going kinetic all along the DMZ. The ROK government is losing their minds because we're pulling US Forces Korea out right when they need help dealing with both the Zulus and the Norks. The Japanese are perfectly happy to see us go, while the Europeans are begging us to stay to try and get things under control, because their own police and military forces are completely unable to do the job. We don't even know what's going on in most of Asia, Africa or the rest of the Americas right now, since the Intelligence Community shifted all its assets to focus on the domestic emergency in CONUS. The situation across the globe is one giant soup-sandwich and we're just trying to redeploy our people back home before it's too late."

Rich slouched in his chair, ignoring the other staffers in the room watching the exchange between himself and the G-3. "Well, that brings us to our problem then."

"Spit it out, man. I know you're dying to tell us what's on your mind." The Chief of Staff didn't have a reputation for patience and liked to keep these meetings moving.

"The issue, gentlemen, is that we can't sustain major operations of this scale. Just getting the various classes of supply to Kansas City is problematic. Getting them there in the volume required to keep this up will be impossible. Not unless we give everything to 2nd Brigade at the expense of the rest of the Division." Rich crossed his arms and waited for the response he knew would be coming.

The Chief of Staff shook his head. "It's not impossible because that's precisely what we intend to do." He looked up at the G-3. "Right?"

The G-3 nodded in agreement. "That's correct. We make 2nd Brigade our Main Effort and shift all available resources to them. The Kansas National Guard made it clear they don't want our help clearing and securing Topeka, so our principal focus is getting Kansas City under control."

"That's all fine, but the expenditure rates of critical classes of supply such as fuel and ammunition during these operations are off the charts. We're emptying out our war stockages everywhere and zeroing out our strategic fuel reserves. Then there's the bottleneck in moving it. Even using the rail system, we're barely able to move adequate amounts of that stuff, and don't get me started on the storage requirements. 'Just in time logistics' isn't really a thing right now, which means we have to do it the old fashioned way and stockpile everything. The FOBs aren't all that large and we're going to have to shoehorn this mountain of supply in there unless we expand the perimeters."

"You know we can't make the FOB footprints any larger. The bigger the perimeters, the more people you need to guard and secure them. We're already stretched to the limit in that regard. If we bleed off more personnel to guard the fence lines, walls and protective barriers, then we have fewer available for offensive operations." The G-3 looked tired. He'd gone over this point many times in the last couple of weeks and the argument about the physical size of the FOBs grew exhausting. It was a math problem. The bigger the FOB, the more people you needed to guard it and the Commanding General was not interested in hunkering down in permanent armed camps. He'd made that quite clear.

Rich shook his head in frustration. "I'm going to have to discuss this with the Deputy Commanding General for Sustainment and let her know."

The Chief of Staff held up a hand. "There's no need to discuss it with her. The 'S' already spoke with the Commander about this very subject."

Rich looked confused. "And?"

The Chief's brow furrowed. "And, the CG shut her down. He told her that he was willing to accept the risk. It's a deliberate decision and we're going to execute."

"So, General Napier told her to 'shut up and color'?"

"Pretty much."

Rich slouched some more in his folding chair. "Fucking wonderful."

***

FOB Chiefs
8 August, 2016
1630 Hours Local

The temperature outside lingered in the upper 80's with oppressive humidity. It'd rained earlier in the day which made it somewhat cooler, but once the clouds moved on and the sun came back out, it turned into a steam bath. Luckily, 2nd Platoon was in their second day of restriction to the company area so they didn't have to participate in any work details, which allowed them to hang out in the air-conditioned tent, killing time. It wasn't all bad, things tended to get a little boring, but they all preferred "boring" to the alternative.

Just as they'd been told earlier in the day, the tent flap flipped open and the Brigade Surgeon came in, accompanied by the Brigade Assistant Operations Officer. They were making the rounds from unit to unit, conducting After Action Reviews with the soldiers who participated in "Operation Toe Cutter." They spent the time getting first-hand reports in order to gather lessons learned in order to improve performance in the future and to gain efficiencies. They'd learned a lot over the course of the previous month and these AARs shaped their ever-evolving tactics fighting the dead.

Mark set his paperback novel down and got up from his bunk to welcome the officers. "Gentlemen, good afternoon." He turned to the rest of the platoon also hanging out in the tent, some playing board games, others talking or napping. "Alright you guys, it's time for the AAR."

Lieutenant Baker came in last, trailing the other two, more senior officers. "Sergeant Matthews, you got all your people?"

"Affirmative, sir. Everybody's here." Mark motioned to the rest of them as they gathered in closer. The civilians they had with them that they now considered part of the team were still off on their work details, downloading equipment at the railhead from the train cars.

"Good, let's get started then." The Brigade Assistant Operations Officer was a young infantry captain who wasn't much older than Lieutenant Baker. He may have been twenty-seven years old, but he looked a lot younger. Rumor on the street was that this captain was on the short list to take command of Bravo Company, which hardly inspired much confidence in any of them. Not that they got a vote in the matter. "Everybody pull it in and gather round."

They all came in closer and sat down on a couple of cots directly across from the officers, every single one of them clutching their personal weapons. They'd been trained since Basic to never leave their weapon more than an arm's-reach away and the zombie apocalypse had done a fine job of hammering that lesson home, the hard way.

The captain looked at Harris settling down right in front of him. "Are you Korean?"

Harris hadn't heard that question in a while and got taken aback for a moment. "Um... ah, yes, sir. I am."

"I did my PL time in Korea. Anyeonghaseyo." The young officer wore a genuinely friendly look on his face, trying to make a connection with the enlisted soldier.

"Ah, sorry, sir. I was adopted by American parents. I don't speak the language." Harris wasn't trying to be a jerk, but the exchange was awkward.

"I see." The captain immediately shifted gears, trying to change the subject. "Anyway, we're wrapping up our debriefs and only have a few more left after we finish up with you. I think we've got some really great information, but we did have a few questions for you."

"Yes, sir. We're happy to help." Lieutenant Baker sat next to the captain and the Brigade Surgeon, pulling out a small notebook and a pen. He wore his Nomex fire-retardant coveralls, soaked around the neck and armpits with sweat.

"Sounds good. We got some excellent feedback already on the fight and had the opportunity to look at video footage from the UAVs too. One thing we weren't able to ascertain so far was whether or not you had seen or experienced all the known classes of Zulus during the fight." The captain opened up a laptop computer and began typing while he spoke.

"I'm not sure I know what you mean, sir." Mark shifted his weight on the cot, making himself more comfortable. He noticed Johnson and Dubois goofing off, acting like a couple of kids and he gave them a hard look, which got them acting serious again.

"What the captain is trying to say is, did you see any 'Alphas' out there during the op?" The Brigade Surgeon was a large man wearing the rank of Major. He wore glasses and his hair was long, definitely not within regulations. He probably did it intentionally to make some sort of statement against Army conformity. It was pretty normal for Army doctors to act that way, they all thought they were channeling Hawkeye Pierce or something. "We're specifically trying to gather more data on that class of Zulu."

If anyone in the tent still felt any levity or lightheartedness it got suddenly crushed. The mood turned very cool at the very mention of an "Alpha." Those things were walking nightmares that they didn't even like to think about. If there was one thing they all feared, it was that.

"No, sir. I don't know that we positively identified any of

them during the mission. I mean, they could have been intermixed among the thousands we shot up, but there's no way for us to know for sure." Mark turned to the others. "Did any of you guys ID one?"

The rest of the soldiers shook their heads "no," not wanting to speak about them.

McDermott raised his hand but didn't wait to be acknowledged before speaking. "Excuse me, sir, but has anyone figured out what the deal is with them? The 'Alphas,' I mean."

The major grimaced and closed his notebook before scratching his chin. "Well, soldier, it's like this. The 'Revenant Virus' or 'RV' as we like to call it affects its hosts differently. Based upon an individual's immune system, metabolism and other biological factors, the virus manifests in various ways. When infected, some people just die, like being bitten by a highly venomous snake. Some people lose most of their motor function and drag themselves around…"

"The 'Shamblers' you mean?" McDermott interrupted.

"Yes, those would be the 'Shamblers.' 'Walkers' and 'Runners' are less affected and move much better. The 'Alphas' seem to have had the most resistance to the virus, not only maintaining full mobility, but some intelligence and even retaining a basic language function. They have the IQ of chimpanzees or dogs, but that's more than intelligent enough to be extraordinarily dangerous."

"That's why 'Alphas' hunt in packs," Mark interjected. "They are wicked smart."

"Indeed. The one thing they all have in common however is the uncontrollable urge to spread the infection. The 'RV' is elegant in that regard. It will drive the host with singular focus to spread the virus to the uninfected." The Surgeon swept his gaze to see if there were any more questions.

"But we haven't seen many Alphas since the opening days of the outbreak. Are they dying out?" McDermott fidgeted while rubbing the back of his neck.

The young captain shook his head. "No, that's not what we're hearing. The reports from civilian survivors continue describing them. Our analysts believe that the Alphas have learned to avoid military personnel, electing to hunt easier prey, but they are most certainly still out there."

Lieutenant Baker saw the look of discomfort on all of their faces and decided to change the subject. "Captain, at the end of the mission a tank blew its pack and they attempted a recovery but that went sideways. Two tank crewmen managed to lock themselves inside of their vehicle before it got swarmed and we had no choice but to leave them behind. Is somebody going to go back and rescue them?"

Captain Nordstrom nodded. "Yes, it's already been done. They sent in a team last night and got them out."

"That's really good news," Baker said, a smile cracking on his face.

"They lost three men in the rescue operation."

Baker's smile immediately melted away. "Jesus. They lost three guys?"

"Yup. They lost three to save two. Not exactly a great outcome." A silence descended on them all, lasting for an uncomfortable moment. "Anyway, what's done is done. Now, let's get on with the AAR, shall we?"

Chapter 5

FOB Jayhawk
1ˢᵗ Battalion, 7ᵗʰ Artillery
22 August, 2016
1535 Hours Local

Staff Sergeant Victor Hightower had the "Thousand Yard Stare," standing there near the railhead supervising his soldiers. They'd just finished up supporting another one of the Zulu Attrition Ops that had been ongoing for the last couple of weeks. The firing batteries of 1-7 Field Artillery had been working non-stop, shooting fire missions constantly in support of the maneuver battalions in the brigade who took turns in a rotation, deploying in various parts of the city. Today's mission had them supporting 5ᵗʰ Squadron, 4ᵗʰ Cav and now that the op had concluded, the boys and girls from the Cav were down at the decon site washing off their vehicles.

Between the maneuver battalions and the cav squadron, there were four different formations taking turns shooting up the town. There was however, only one artillery battalion to give them supporting fire missions, which meant that they kept plenty busy. There'd been talk early on of using a single firing battery and rotate them as well, but the Zulu population was still too dense and they needed every tube of artillery in the fight. So all the supporting arms, to include the combat aviation units, were running ragged with no letup in sight. They were slaughtering the undead by the tens of thousands, but there seemed to be no shortage of them. Brigade headquarters said that things should begin slacking off in a few weeks, but that seemed like an eternity from now considering how smoked they all were.

Hightower watched one of his crewmen "ground guiding"

their tracked, self-propelled howitzer from the hot refuel point. The other vehicles, including their ammunition carriers, were lined up next to the fuel trucks getting topped off with JP-8 before they parked them in the motorpool for the night. Luckily, Bravo Battery had night duty and would be headed off to their firing points while he and the rest of the men and women from Alpha Battery would lock up the guns, grab some chow and maybe get some rack time.

The FOB itself was crowded and the ground guides had to be particularly careful maneuvering the large armored vehicles around. There were crates of ammunition and blivets of fuel everywhere, neatly arranged next to the rail lines and box cars. The Army rail unit kept those trains moving constantly, never lingering for too long, but they too were manned by human beings that needed to stay on secure FOBs at night for rest. So at the moment the place found itself crowded with locomotives, rail cars and hundreds of Army vehicles of all shapes and sizes. There was barely any space to move at all.

He followed his crew as they carefully weaved the giant M109 Paladin around a pair of stationary cargo trucks and onward toward their battalion motor park. A few of the guns from Alpha Battery were already there and the guides worked with the drivers to pack them in tight, hub to hub. Parked that way it was impossible to do maintenance on the track and road wheels properly, which forced them to do it earlier, right after they'd plussed up with ammunition. Now all they had to do was park the huge beasts, lock them up and throw tarps over the tops, then call it a day.

The artillerymen were already smelling the barn and they worked like mad to put the vehicles in their proper spaces. Once parked, Hightower opened the back and tossed his assault pack inside before his boys secured it. It may have seemed counterintuitive to lock up combat vehicles in the middle of the zombie apocalypse, but soldiers are soldiers and they tend to steal anything that isn't nailed down. Hightower had grown up in the Army partaking of the age-old tradition himself over the years and was no sap. He didn't want his tools and other critical items "walking away" so he had the crew lock everything up tight so it would all be there waiting for them in the morning.

When he and the others finished up, they walked away in a group. A gentle breeze blew in from the city and the group of them grimaced. With the wind hung the thick smell of death, brought on by the thousands of bloating corpses putrefying in the city. It nearly made Hightower retch. The stink was so intense that none of them smelled the smoke emanating from inside their vehicle, caused by a small fire burning leaking fuel from a faulty heater. They didn't notice it at all, nor did the other members of Alpha Battery who were making a hasty retreat from the motorpool, finishing up their duties for the day.

***

The fire from the fuel leak started off small enough, not much bigger than a candle wick, dancing lazily for quite some time, but then as it slowly burned, the puddle of combustible liquid gradually grew and so did the flames. It seeped into the lower deck and the inside of the Paladin, growing thick with smoke. Under normal circumstances it might have choked itself out before getting out of control, but these were hardly anything but routine conditions. The puddle of JP-8 continued to spread out, bringing with it the flames, until it reached the artillery propellent bags stored on the vehicle. Had they been stored correctly, the bags might not have posed any danger, but they weren't. The crew had haphazardly stowed them, knowing they'd be used first thing in the morning.

The propellant charges came in bags that were stuffed in the breach of the cannon during a live fire mission. The crew could adjust the number of bags to load in order to affect how far the 155-millimeter shells flew. Each high-explosive shell weighed ninety-five pounds, so each of the powder bags packed a significant punch. Not only were they very powerful, they were extremely flammable and volatile.

When the small heater fire reached the first exposed propellant bag it ignited in a flash, instantly setting off the others around it. A series of sympathetic detonations went off inside the vehicle in less than a second, until the vehicle itself exploded in a massive fireball. When it did, it sent unexploded artillery shells flying into the air, showering down on the entire motorpool like steel rain.

The Paladin itself then burned furiously, ignited by the accelerants, its now ruptured fuel tanks adding to the inferno. Within moments the blaze became so hot that the aluminum armor itself caught fire, burning furiously. The self-propelled guns parked on either side were mere inches away and quickly started to smoke in the heat, before themselves igniting and adding to the blaze.

Soldiers standing guard nearby came running after the first explosion, looking aghast at the burning vehicles, not quite sure what to do. The sergeant of the guard barked a set of orders and sent a couple running to go get help when the second Paladin blew apart, vomiting its deadly contents skyward as well. High-explosive rounds came falling down all over the FOB, some of them crashing through the roofs of tents, soft-skinned trucks and even the rail cars sitting idle on the tracks.

Troops and refugees all over the base emerged from tents

and vehicles to see what was going on, while the thick, black smoke churned toward the heavens. The second explosion made everyone flinch with some diving for cover, setting most of them into motion, either running away from the conflagration or toward it to help put it out. Groups of them descended on large fire extinguishers mounted on trolleys, while two tried to get the gate open, the chain-link enclosure secured with a heavy padlock. No one could locate the keys and men shouted at one another, desperately trying to get the gate open so they could get inside and try to get the situation under control.

After a few, painfully long minutes a sergeant came sprinting up with a set of bolt-cutters in his hand. Clad only in t-shirt, trousers and boots, he pushed everyone out of the way, putting the steel jaws around the shackle of the padlock before pressing the handles of the bolt cutter together. The blades snapped together and he twisted it, watching the lock fall harmlessly to the ground as the sound of a siren filled their ears.

Two fire engines wormed their way through the overly-crowded rail yard, with the drivers blasting the horn every now and again to get people out of their way. They were manned by National Guard firefighters who'd worked as first-responders full-time before the entire world consumed itself.

Everyone in sight crouched reflexively when another Paladin erupted, some of them covering their heads with arms as shells came showering down all around. The firefighters simply swore and waved at the others to get out of the way, their huge trucks barreling through the now-open gate.

The heat grew with rapid intensity and more vehicles became consumed. The temperature quickly got so hot it drove the unprotected soldiers nearby away, now unable to get close enough to use their portable fire extinguishing equipment.

The engines got as close as they dared and the firefighting teams dismounted, unlimbering hoses and attaching them to pumps. They brought their gear online and sent forth steady streams of water, dousing the vehicles nearest the blaze to keep them from catching. The ones already burning were a lost cause with no point in wasting the water trying to save them.

Then, just as the last of them deployed their equipment, the first of the mobile ammunition carriers parked behind the Paladins began to smoke. These tracked caissons were loaded to the top with propellant and shells, always following the howitzers to give them a steady supply of ammunition. The tenders too were parked in the motorpool and while the guns blazed, they sat idly by. Right up until the first of them went up in a fireball.

The stored ammunition and powder went off with such a concussion, the shockwave flattened nearly half the tents in the FOB. The heat was now so intense that the artillery shells themselves began to cook off, scything the air with steel fragments.

The firefighters themselves never felt a thing when the sympathetic detonations of the parked ammunition tenders vaporized them in the blink of an eye.

***

Main Command Post
1ˢᵗ Infantry Division
Fort Riley, Kansas
23 August, 2016

Major General Bud Napier sat at the head of the conference table looking as dour as anyone had ever seen him. Even during the peak of the outbreak when it seemed as if humanity were about to permanently pass into the abyss, he held a stiff upper lip and held an air of confidence about himself. It had inspired all of those around him in the darkest days, but now, his body language gave off a foreboding feeling which affected them all. He sat quietly after entering the conference room, which consisted of a large annex to the larger field command post. The rest of staff sat without a word as well, with nothing more than the humming of the generators outside to break the silence.

Finally he sighed deeply before nodding to the Division Chief of Staff. "Okay, Chief. Let's hear it."

"Yes, General." Colonel Foster turned to the Division Logistics officer. "Rich, why don't you lead us off."

Lieutenant Colonel Rich Sullivan pushed his glasses up the bridge of his nose before rising from his chair. "Ladies and gentlemen, let me cut to the chase." He approached the large projector screen at the head of the table showing a series of aerial photos. Their time stamps indicated that they were less than an hour old and they showed a scene of total chaos. "FOB *Jayhawk* serves as our central distribution point for all classes of supply supporting our ongoing operations in Kansas City." He spared a glance at the G-3 before clearing his throat. "Due to operational constraints, we had to stockpile our resources both there and at FOB *Chiefs* across the river. We're not sure how the fire broke out yet, but the result is an unmitigated disaster."

Foster's face reddened. "Now, come on, Rich. Don't you think you're being a bit dramatic?"

"Don't interrupt him, Chief," growled the Commanding General. "Continue with your brief, Rich."

"Pull up the live feed please." Rich Sullivan looked at the screen while a streaming video image flickered on, sent in from a UAV flying over the site. Roiling fires raged, generating clouds of thick, black smoke that nearly blotted out the entire FOB. The entire motorpool burned along with hundreds of rail cars parked helplessly in neat rows all throughout Argentine Rail Yard. It looked like Dresden or even Tokyo after the firebombings at the end of World War II. "As you can see here the FOB which surrounded the rail yard is almost completely destroyed. The personnel there spent all night evacuating the survivors by any means necessary to FOB *Chiefs*. The place along with practically all the supplies and equipment stockpiled there have literally gone up in smoke."

Napier nodded grimly. "So, how bad is it?"

"From a Sustainment perspective it's literally the worst-case scenario. We lost over eighty percent of our fuel reserves in the city, along with most of our ammunition. Probably half the brigade's food as well. Not to mention an entire battalion of self-propelled artillery. Luckily we were able to get most of the remaining rolling stock and airframes out of there. I can't speak to the casualties."

The Division G-1 looked almost as grim as the Commanding General. "Over a hundred dead and a similar number injured. We are still trying to get a decent personnel report from 2nd Brigade, but they believe they've got at least fifty missing as well."

They all looked at the live feed video, some shaking their heads. While the fires raged out of control, portions of the perimeter fencing were breached and the dead came in unfettered. The noise and commotion drew them in from all over, but they did not get too close to the blaze. Even they seemed to figure out that fire was bad and kept a healthy distance, much to the soldier's chagrin. The staff officers had hoped that at least the Zulus might have done them a favor and gone into the flames, treating it like a giant bug-zapper, but they had no such luck. Even the infected weren't that dumb and displayed an unsettling instinct for self-preservation.

The Deputy Commanding General for Operations, Brigadier General Hank Mendoza nodded while rubbing his chin. "Well, I suppose this presents us with a bit of a setback. How long until we can reset and get things back on schedule again?"

Sitting directly opposite from him on the other side of the table, Brigadier General Candice Bucher shook her head. "It's not that simple."

"What do you mean?" Mendoza cocked an eyebrow before sparing a glance over to Major General Napier, who sat silently, wearing a mask of granite.

"I don't think I need to remind you that since Day 1 of the outbreak, there has been exactly *zero* industrial production of any kind." Bucher leaned in while pointing at the live video stream. "We can't replace any of that. There aren't any factories manufacturing bullets or artillery shells. No one is working at the fuel refineries and there aren't people packaging MREs anymore. Every bit of that was irreplaceable. We stockpiled those supplies so we could clear Kansas City and now they are gone. Along with an entire rail yard too. Bottom line, any hopes of clearing out the city are over."

Mendoza's jaw muscles clenched. "I'm having trouble believing that. Can't III Corps push us a resupply?"

"No. They stripped out all depots and sent the remaining supplies to the Pacific Northwest. They gave us everything they could spare already and now most of it is gone." Bucher balled her hands up into fists. She'd told the Commanding General that storing everything the way they did at the FOBs was a recipe for disaster, but he'd told her that it was worth the risk. This was the one time where she wished she'd been wrong.

Silence descended on the conference tent again while Rich

stood at the front of the table, shifting his weight uncomfortably.

After a minute, General Napier relaxed his shoulders and leaned back in his folding chair. "All right. Let's wrap this up. I need to call the Corps Commander. We convene an emergency Commander's Update Brief in two hours' time."

***

Napier settled into his chair and stared at the blank screen in front of him, thinking about what he intended to say. It was a secure video-telephone, hooked up to the tactical satellite transceiver parked outside his private office. He needed to call Lieutenant General Jameson, commander of III Corps. He'd talked with the man a half-dozen times over the course of the previous night while the disaster in Kansas City unfolded. Now he had another scheduled update with the man and he wasn't looking forward to it one bit.

He looked at his watch and saw that it was time. He dialed the number and watched the device ring up the other end. Within seconds the image of a stern-looking man appeared, sitting in an empty conference room. General Jameson opened a notebook and clicked an ink pen before adjusting his reading glasses. "What news do you have for me, Bud?"

"More of the same I'm afraid, General. Our 2nd Brigade has consolidated on our remaining FOB in Kansas City with most of its equipment. Most of the supplies stockpiled there are gone and one of the railyards is a complete write-off." Napier shifted uneasily in his chair. "We suffered significant casualties in the incident, but not catastrophically so. I think we can get back up and running within the week if we can get adequately resupplied." He tried not to wince when he said the last part, already knowing what the answer would be.

"Bud, we've been over this. I spoke with NORTHCOM and there is nothing more to give you. Your division was allocated more than enough to accomplish its missions while everything else in war stocks has been shipped off to the *Cascadia Redoubt*." Jameson pointed his ink pen at Napier through the video screen. "This 'incident' as you like to call it is a significant setback."

"Listen, Tony, if we can get some of that diverted back to us I can get the city cleared within two months. We'll have the largest transportation hub in the Midwest open for business soon after that, posturing us to take back the rest of the country." Napier felt a trickle of sweat run down his temple and fought the urge to wipe it away.

"General, this failure is a direct reflection on you and your lack of leadership! NORTHCOM has already denied all requests for reallocation of resources. If you hadn't noticed, most of the world is falling apart and we're dealing with one major emergency after another. Now, we've essentially lost the initiative and the President has started relieving officers left and right. It's a fucking bloodbath right now." Jameson set the pen down and composed himself before going on. "The staff is doing some analysis as we speak and once they get done updating me, I will give you refined guidance. In the meantime, I need you to cease all offensive operations and get yourselves sorted out. Is that clear?"

"Yes, General." Napier struggled to keep the stiff upper lip, maintaining his dignity.

"Good, I will be in contact with you soon. Out here." And with that, the video call ended and the screen winked out, leaving Napier sitting there all by himself, left to his thoughts once again.

***

Rich Sullivan sat on the folding chair in his brown t-shirt, tapping away at his laptop, working his way through the hundred or so e-mails in his inbox. The other officers and NCOs in the Division G-4 Shop carried on with their routine business, careful not to disturb him. They weren't making any attempt to be quiet since Rich had laser-like focus, but they knew better than to interrupt him while he was in the middle of something. While he worked, another e-mail popped into his inbox and he noticed it was from the Division Chief of Operations.

"What the hell is this?" he said to himself, expecting something from one of the Brigade SPOs or even the DCG-S, not the CHOPs. He knew there was only one reason he'd be getting an e-mail from the man and sighed in resignation. He pushed his glasses up the bridge of his nose with an index finger and opened it up. The message itself was blank, with only a subject line that read, "WARNO." That meant there was a new Warning Order published by the Chief of Operations and he needed to check it out.

He clicked a couple of tabs on the Division sharepoint until he found the "CHOPs" page. In there he found the "WARNO" folder and selected it, seeing one labeled "Hot!" all in red. The Knowledge Management dorks would have put little flaming GIFs and skulls next to it if they had their way. Fortunately, the sharepoint lacked the bandwidth to support such frivolities so it remained blissfully generic and business-like.

Rich opened it up and started reading. At first his eyes grew wide and then they narrowed into slits. He slammed a fist down on the plastic folding table and made the laptop jump at least three inches high. "*Goddammit!*"

Major Latesha Adams and Captain Marjorie Taylor stood nearby discussing an unrelated issue when Rich's outburst caught their attention.

"I'll talk to you later," Adams said to the junior officer before approaching Rich. "You okay, Boss?"

"Not anymore. Take a look at this." Rich stood from his chair and turned the computer toward the major.

Major Adams plopped down into the folding chair and scrolled through the Warning Order displayed on the screen. It wasn't very long and it lacked specific details, but it told them enough. "Oh my gosh, are they serious?"

"I was hoping I was reading it wrong." Rich laced his hands behind his neck and looked to the ceiling in their tent, trying to work the fresh stress-headache out. "God, I wish I had some alcohol right about now."

"How is this even possible? I mean, there's no way we can do this." Adams looked up at Rich with a look of shock.

"Yeah, well I guess I'll try to convince the S and the CG of that. In the meantime I need you to get the crew together and figure out the details." He took his hands from behind his neck and planted them on his hips. "I guess we have another long, sleepless night ahead of us."

"Convince the S and the CG of what?"

Rich and Latesha were shocked to find the Deputy Commanding General for Sustainment, aka "The S," standing right behind them, eavesdropping on their conversation. She tended to drift into the G-4 tent like a ghost and everyone found it unsettling.

"Uh, sorry, Ma'am. We didn't realize you were standing there." Rich suddenly felt naked dressed in his brown t-shirt with his camouflage jacket draped over the back of a folding chair. He picked it up and began pulling it on.

"Never mind about that. Talk to me." General Bucher tended to get to the point. Unlike many of her peers in the general officer community, she did not ramble while working problems out in her mind and was not particularly verbose. She preferred to lock onto the salient points like a pitbull.

"Yes, General." Rich turned the computer toward her and punched up a map, then a few other tabs listing an enormous amount of data. To the layman, the acronyms and numbers would have been incomprehensible. For a career logistician, it was simply the language they spoke every day. "CHOPs posted a Warning Order on the Division Sharepoint."

Bucher nodded in understanding, already aware of the Warning Order and what it said. She settled into the chair and leaned into the computer screen while putting on a pair of reading glasses. "Yes, go on."

"They have ordered 2nd Brigade out of Kansas City to fall back to Fort Riley. Then, once the entire Division has consolidated, we are to road march all the way to Yakima in Washington state, where we will link up with other military forces." Rich used an alcohol pen to trace the route on the screen to help her visualize. "That's a drive of approximately 1,700 miles."

Bucher leaned in closer, studying the map closely while rubbing her chin.

"Ma'am, a movement of that length is absolutely unprecedented. Moreover, it's never been attempted without corps-level sustainment support supplying a division with fuel, water and food. We simply don't possess the trucks to carry the supplies we need to get us there. It's impossible."

Bucher looked up at Major Latesha Adams and then back over to Rich. "Okay, understood. We've never tried to move an entire heavy division this far, and we sure as hell haven't tried to do it without support from our integrated logistics enterprise, but surely, we can figure it out. Can't we?"

Rich thought about it for a moment, believing he might be able to come up with a solution until he suddenly realized that the 1st Infantry Division had a unique problem no modern army has had to wrestle with in centuries. "General, normally I'd say yes, but we've got a very big issue that isn't reflected on those consumption tables you're looking at. Those numbers were generated to support the division in the field under combat conditions."

"Yes, so what?"

"Well, Ma'am. We currently are feeding over fifteen thousand family members and other camp followers at Fort Riley, and unless I'm mistaken, the CG will want to take them along with the rest of us. That more than doubles the number of mouths we have to feed." He paused so she could absorb the implications of what he was saying. "That doesn't even take into account how we intend to transport or protect them."

"Dear God." Bucher looked through the numbers, taking it all in. The other staff members, NCOs and officers alike, slowly drifted in closer, all of them listening to the conversation.

"Ma'am, off the top of my head, it would take us over a week under ideal conditions with external support from III Corps to move the division that far. Without external support, we will drain all of our fuel supplies in two or three days. That assumes we are just driving and not doing any fighting. It also doesn't even take into account water and food consumption. That's if we load our trucks with nothing other than food, water and fuel. Don't ask me how we are going to move ammunition, spare parts, barrier material or anything else yet."

Bucher slid the chair back and stood, tonguing an aching tooth while crossing her arms. "This ain't good." She turned to face rich full on while raising the tone of her voice so everyone in the shop could hear. "We've got a big job ahead of us and very little time to prepare for it. I need all of your people to redouble your efforts. I need you all to find a solution to this problem and I need it yesterday. Understood?"

"Yes, Ma'am." Rich's face looked like he'd swallowed a handful of very sour candy.

"Ma'am, I have a question." Latesha Adams didn't normally interrupt when the senior leaders were speaking, so every head turned in her direction the moment she spoke up.

"Yes, Major. What is it?"

"Um, we've got a perfectly good railhead here at Fort Riley. We've used it a million times. Why don't we just load all of our equipment up on the trains and ship the division to Yakima that way instead of trying to drive?" Major Adams' eyes darted back and forth between the DCG-S and the G-4.

Bucher looked over at Rich with a cocked eyebrow. "Shall I explain it to her, or would you like to take a crack at it?"

Rich turned toward his subordinate and the rest of the soldiers in the shop who were starting to crowd in. He also raised his voice just a bit in order for everyone to hear him. "It's like this. The rail networks are a fragile thing, needing lots of people to manage and maintain them under normal conditions.

"It's like an interrelated airport system. When there are disruptions anywhere, it echoes across the entire enterprise creating a cascading series of failures. Right now there is no longer any centralized control of the system nationally and while local lines can be kept clear, the long hauls right now are plagued with abandoned engines and cars on the rails, unmanned spurs, broken switches, no crews clearing fallen trees and so on. We had a few lines cleared and maintained for a short time after the outbreak, until things went sideways in Kansas City. We lost an entire yard, hundreds of pieces of rolling stock, engineers and other personnel who keep things running. We'd barely gotten things running again on a limited scale when the house of cards came tumbling down. Once we lost KC, everything had to be rerouted around the single-most important transportation hub in the midwest.

"If we loaded up the division and made it a third or half-way to Washington and ran into a problem along the way, we might literally be stuck out in the middle of nowhere, with no way to effectively unload our heavy equipment. A washed out bridge, a wreck, fallen trees, broken rails... literally anything could spell disaster for us if we risked it. Then there's the fact that the people who maintain and run the system are either dead or have run off. It's sort of like risking a drive from Kansas City to Yakima without encountering a single traffic jam along the way. Only a traffic jam in our case could mean being marooned out on the plains where we would run out of food, water and fuel with no way to replenish it and that would be a death sentence for us all."

Bucher held up her hand, motioning to Rich that he had said enough. "Everything Colonel Sullivan said is correct, but there's more. Northern Command is working day and night to get the rail system sorted out, but it'll take months before we get any reliable service re-established here in central Kansas, and we don't have months. We have to get to Washington before winter sets in or else we're in big trouble. Like 'Donner Party' trouble. So that's why they told us to move on our own. It's risky, but it's the best option in their assessment." She slowly looked around the room at all the people quietly hanging on her every word. "Now, are there any questions?"

No one said anything.

"Good." The General punched her G-4 lightly on the shoulder. "The logistical planning for this long road march is going to be one of the toughest things you've ever done, but if anyone can do it, it's you and your team. We're all depending on you. Now let's get to it."

***

The company leadership gathered around Lieutenant Baker with a few strap-hangers lingering around to eavesdrop. It was miserably hot outside, but the lieutenant insisted on delivering his Operations Order while briefing it off a sand table located near the perimeter fence about a hundred meters from their sleep tents. Close by were a row of porta-potties that baked in the sun and the smell was pretty ripe. It wasn't nearly as bad as when a breeze blew in from the city, but it wasn't pleasant either.

Mark grabbed the bill of his patrol cap and removed it before running a sleeve across his forehead. He plopped it back on his head and squinted in the bright sunlight. He stood there next to Staff Sergeant Kurtz and Staff Sergeant Pavolovski who represented 1st and 3rd Platoons. Staff Sergeant Packard, the acting First Sergeant, sat in a folding chair next to the lieutenant waving flies away from his face. They all looked miserable.

"So, that's it. Are there any questions?" Baker used a section of radio antenna as an improvised pointer which he used to orient them to the terrain model. He took the olive drab cravat draped around his neck to wipe perspiration from his eyes.

Kurtz hocked up a good bit of phlegm and spit it onto the ground. He commanded Charlie One-Two, the other surviving tank in their understrength company and he wore a set of Nomex coveralls just like Lieutenant Baker. "Yeah, El-Tee. Why are they pulling us out of here all of a sudden? I mean, we still got most of our equipment and we were just starting to turn things around here."

Baker took the tube from his CamelBak hydration system and stuck the nipple in his mouth before taking a long pull of water. "Battalion says that there isn't any more fuel or ammo coming so we gotta leave. That's why the entire brigade is redeploying back to Fort Riley."

Pavolovski kicked at some rocks near his boot, sending them flying toward the chain link fence nearby. "We spent over a month fighting and dying in this city. Are you saying all of that was for nothing?"

"Look, Battalion says that it'll take months before we can get any sort of ammo or fuel shipped here. If any comes at all, and it'll be winter by then and we sure as shit don't want to be stuck out here on short rations with no fuel when the snow starts to fly. Word on the street is we'll spend the winter back at Riley, then maybe we'll refit and come back for a spring offensive."

The NCOs did *not* look convinced.

"I know this is a shit deal. We've fought and bled in this damned city for nearly two months now and things were finally starting to go our way. Then something as simple as a fire completely changed everything. I can't help any of that." Baker took his hat off and scratched his head, his blonde hair darkened by sweat. Like the others, he looked as if he'd aged at least ten years over the last month. "But never forget this. We all managed to survive this long when most of the people around the world haven't. I know more than a few of you wished you were dead, but put that dark shit out of your minds. We are alive now and we will live on to fight another day. We will win in the end, we just can't quit. Do you understand? Failure is bad, but quitting is the worst thing any of us can do."

The junior leaders looked to one another, some with a

skeptical look in their eyes.

"Any more questions?"

There weren't any and no one made eye contact with the lieutenant.

"Okay then, get your people and equipment ready. We roll first thing in the morning and we don't have much time."

***

NW 106th Road
Bremerton, Kansas
27 August, 2016
25 Miles Northwest of Topeka
1645 Hours Local

The Brigade pulled out of FOB *Chiefs* at dawn, spending nearly an hour uncoiling itself and getting on the road. The aviation units left the night prior using their heavy lift assets to move itself back to Fort Riley, running in intervals. Flying overland they'd given detailed reconnaissance reports to both Division Headquarters and Colonel Williams' staff in 2nd Brigade. The reports themselves painted a depressing, though unsurprising picture.

The most direct route from Kansas City overland to Fort Riley would have been over I-70, but they couldn't go that way. The highway itself had been cleared of obstruction so driving was no issue, but a giant obstacle stood in the middle of it.

The governor had taken great pains to deploy the Kansas National Guard into Wichita and Topeka. They managed to save nearly everyone and subsequently treated both cities like giant fortresses, even augmenting their personnel with local home guard militia. The State Adjutant General delivered the message himself to III Corps that no federal troops would be allowed to pass through either one of those population centers for fear of contamination from infected outsiders, and while no shots had yet been exchanged between federal and state troops to date, the leadership at NORTHCOM was disinterested in pushing things too far. Instead, they chose to use the local roads to the north and south of the state capital, giving Topeka wide berth.

This forced the 2nd "Dagger" Brigade to use the country roads to the north of I-70, paralleling the highway, taking a more or less straight shot back toward Riley. The helos, augmented by drones, gave a good picture of what lay ahead of them, only to be confirmed by the ground elements of the brigade's Armored Reconnaissance Squadron. It was all a fairly standard tactical deployment of forces, with security elements riding out on the flanks. None of them wanted to think of America's heartland as a war zone, but it was for all intents and purposes.

As Brigade Commander, Colonel Dane Williams had several different vehicles dedicated solely to him, giving him a variety of choices, but he preferred to ride in a tank. It gave him an adequate command and control suite, a smooth ride and a feeling of power that was unequaled. He stood in the commander's hatch nearly crotch-high feeling the wind in his face, feeling like Irwin Rommel racing across North Africa. The only difference was this wasn't the Afrika Korps and they "raced" along at a whopping fifteen miles per hour. More like a crawl, really. Still, while it wasn't Libya, it reminded him of the "Thunder Run" in Iraq, a much happier time in his life and definitely better than he'd been experiencing lately.

Dane's chest boiled with anger when the order came down from Division to abandon the city and return to Fort Riley. Sure, the fire and loss of supplies and equipment was a setback, but if they'd just delivered more of it, he could have gotten things back on schedule. He even sent patrols out to Cabela's and other sporting goods stores to scavenge for ammo, but they'd all been picked clean. The whole thing stunk of pessimism and they were snatching defeat from the jaws of victory. He sulked in his tent for nearly a day while the staff worked out the redeployment orders and he barely said a word when they briefed it to his battalion commanders, but now that they were moving again, he felt reinvigorated.

They began movement from their Forward Operating Base right at sunup and because they were so tightly packed in there it took quite some time to uncoil. They managed to get everything out that they could, even dragging a few vehicles that couldn't run under their own power to repair later once they arrived at their home base. Naturally, the noise drew the attention of the dead and they came out by the hundreds to "say goodbye." Because they weren't getting any ammunition resupply, Dane ordered that everyone in the brigade refrain from engaging and only fire in extremis. They followed the order and only the occasional rifle pop could be heard while they snaked their way through the suburbs.

The men and women in the brigade witnessed horrible things fighting in the city over the previous six weeks. The psychological impact of it was even too much for some of them to bear, but they carried on, and while the devastation within the city limits was terrible, what they saw in some of the outlying communities may have been even worse. Passing through a few of the towns surrounding Kansas City they saw evidence of marauding bands of looters everywhere. Homes and businesses were gutted by fire with decayed bodies hanging from their necks, tied to tree limbs and lamp posts, many with signs adorning them bearing all sorts of dark messages. Any semblance of law and order had broken down along with anything resembling basic humanity.

The closer to the city the worse it appeared but things gradually got better the further out they got, all of it consistent with the recon reports they were getting from the aviators. The towns themselves were either complete ghost towns, evacuated and abandoned or they were fortified and heavily defended. The organized communities had quite sophisticated defenses established, clearly built under the watchful eye of military veterans. Dane's own combat engineers couldn't have done a more competent job with the resources available if they had tried.

Along the way the brigade spotted the occasional civilian in the distance on foot or bicycle. Drones picked up a pair of dirt bikes racing away from them near the lead elements in the column, headed back to a nearby town. Those had to have been lookouts and scouts reporting back to their friends and neighbors. They hadn't spotted any cars or trucks moving, but that hardly came as a surprise with all the remaining gasoline in those parts having already been hoarded or expended. Other than that, the drive was eerily quiet, with nothing more than the birds to remind them of anything still left alive at all.

They crossed a bridge over Perry Lake near Ozawkie and saw a couple of small sail boats out on the water. The gunners on the tanks and Bradleys reported seeing people on board fishing through their thermal sights. It seemed almost normal, except they all knew that those citizens were gathering food for survival and not out for recreation.

After a few hours the novelty of being on the move began to wear off and things got dull. Dane hadn't authorized any stops along the way for security reasons, so the soldiers made a game out of relieving themselves from the tops of moving vehicles. While some urinated over the side, others took to pissing in empty water bottles and it didn't take long before the first ones were flung at their buddies riding in other vehicles in the column. The officers gave clipped and heated ass-chewings over the radio, but still the juvenile antics continued.

One thing they didn't see were the infected. They also didn't have the sickening smell of rotting flesh hanging in their noses any longer either. The lot of them filled their lungs with the sweet fresh air, tinged slightly with the exhaust from their tracks and trucks.

They passed through mile after mile of country roads and farms. Some of the soldiers themselves grew up in places like this and saw acre after acre of cropland that would not be harvested in the fall. The farmers themselves were out there somewhere, but they wouldn't be bringing in their crops without fuel. As pretty as the greenery was, it reminded many of them that it was going to be a hungry winter ahead of them. It suddenly dawned on more than a few of them why their mission to keep the transportation networks open in Kansas City, it was absolutely critical to keep things moving. Without the roads and the rail, there would be no diesel for the farmers and without the tractors and combines, there would be no food. Many pushed the thought from their minds, while most of the others rode along blissfully ignorant of it.

They kept this going for hours making steady progress and the radio nets grew quiet with only the occasional radio check to break the monotony. Dane checked his electronic maps and their position on the GPS for the thousandth time, getting ever more impatient. Things were going well, more or less, with only a few vehicle break-downs along the way and all of those were recovered without incident.

Dane's staff worked out routes for the brigade that largely avoided populated areas if possible. They didn't want to risk getting near the infected or run-ins with the locals, but it wasn't entirely doable. This proved to be the case with a place called "Bremerton." The road networks up to this point were mostly neat and grid-like, but not here. The terrain basically funneled the unit this way and there was no way to avoid the place unless they took a significant detour which would have likely added several hours to an already painfully-long trip.

Now, the miles-long column began grinding to a halt with the combat vehicles edging off onto the shoulders of the road, staggered and facing outward in a "herringbone" formation. Turrets swept the fields, scanning for targets while leaders impatiently called over the radio networks demanding situation reports. Dane's tank also came to a halt, his anxiety mixed with the late-afternoon heat made him testy.

"Dagger Three, this is Six. What's the hold-up? Why are we stopping? Over." Dane pulled out a standard 1:50,000 scaled military contour map and compared their position to where their GPS had them plotted. They were getting close to Fort Riley, but still a couple hours out at the minimum if they were moving, which they definitely were not.

"*Roger, Six. Our lead elements report that the civilians in the town up ahead have constructed a barricade and are not allowing us to pass through. They are telling us to go around. Over.*"

Dane bristled at the message. He commanded over four thousand American troops, likely far more people served under his command than lived in that town. Probably by an order of magnitude. All he wanted to do was pass through and these people who owed their safety to him were telling him that he wasn't allowed to drive through on the public road.

If they diverted their route not only would it take a lot longer, but fuel was beginning to be a concern, particularly for his tanks. The Abrams tanks had turbine engines in them that burned the same amount of fuel whether they were in motion or sitting still. They didn't measure consumption rates in "miles per gallon," it was more appropriate to measure it in "gallons per hour." It wasn't much help shutting them down and starting them back up again either because the things burned through ten gallons of JP-8 every time they fired up the engine. They had precious little to spare on this one-way trip to Fort Riley and they needed to get there soon.

"Three, this is Six. You tell them we can't detour around their precious, little town. Assure them that we are just passing through and we won't be bothering them. Over." Dane gritted his teeth while he transmitted. He barely kept the volume of his voice under control, though the inflection in it betrayed his true feelings.

"*Roger. Stand by.*"

Dane stared straight ahead, watching the heat shimmer off the pavement. His frustration continued to grow and he spread the map out on top of the turret in front of him, tracing the route ahead of them with his index finger. His stomach rumbled and he realized he hadn't eaten all day. It was just another thing that continued to irritate him.

"*Dagger Six, this is Three. They're saying they want to speak to the person in charge. I will go up and speak to them. Over.*"

Dane shook his head. *If you want to get anything done around here, you need to do it yourself.* "Negative, I'll go up there and handle it myself. Six, out." He toggled the intercom on. "Shut the engine down. I'm going to take the Humvee forward to go see what this is about."

He took off his CVC and replaced it with his ACH helmet before climbing out of the commander's hatch and waving to his Humvee driver who had been following close behind his tank all day. While he climbed down off the side of the tank, the truck pulled up beside. The gunner up top behind the machine gun barely acknowledged the brigade commander, his eyes hidden behind a set of darkened lenses on his ballistic goggles.

The colonel jumped into the front passenger seat and slammed the door shut, still clutching the map in his left hand. "Drive."

"Roger, sir."

The military light truck made its way down the road, straddling the centerline, moving easily along with all the other vehicles in the column pulled off on the shoulders. They passed vehicles of nearly every type, many of them with trailers and all sitting idle. Crews and passengers craned their necks, watching their commander drive past, though Dane did not look up at them, barely acknowledging their existence. He sat in the padded seat and fumed, unhappy with their unscheduled halt.

The column, even with its tight spacing, spread out for miles. It took them a bit of time to reach the front where the lead echelon of the brigade's cavalry squadron was located. As the principle screening and ground reconnaissance element, they usually went first, serving as the "eyes" for the rest of the unit. As they neared the front, the small Kansas town came into view.

Off to the right, they passed a sign with the name "Bremerton" on it. The letters were crossed out with red spray paint and someone affixed another crude sign underneath with the name "Jericho" scrawled on it.

Nearing the front of the column the road itself was blocked with old cars and trucks. In the middle of the thoroughfare sat an ancient school bus that wept streaks of rust down its yellow skin. Next to it, a few soldiers talked with a similar number of civilians. He recognized the soldiers as the senior officers from the Brigade's Cavalry Squadron. A short distance away more civilians stood watch from protected positions and it was impossible not to notice that every single person was armed.

"Stop up there," Dane ordered his driver, as he brought the up-armored Humvee near the group clustered near the roadblock. All eyes were on them when the brigade commander climbed out of the light truck, doing his best to appear "MacArthur-esque." He strode over confidently with his immaculately fitted battle dress, with a 9mm pistol mounted to a chest rig in the center of the ballistic plate of his body armor. "Who's in charge here?"

A man in late middle age faced him. He wore an old sweat-stained baseball cap over brown hair. He stood just north of six feet, with a gray beard and lean build. He wore a Carhartt t-shirt untucked over a pair of dirty blue jeans with a pair of old, but well-maintained Red Wings on his feet. A leather holster hung from the thick belt around his waist, containing a .44 Magnum. The gun hanging there appeared like a natural extension of the man's body. Next to him on either side were a couple of younger men, nervously holding long arms which they wisely pointed in a safe direction. The older man looked Dane up and down with a distrustful look. "I am. My name's Hoffman. I'm the mayor of this town. Who are you?"

Dane bristled at the man's tone, but did his best not to let his annoyance show. "I am Colonel Dane Williams, commander of 2nd Brigade, 1st Infantry Division." As much as he didn't want to, he approached the mayor and extended a gloved hand to shake.

Hoffman did not return the gesture, instead placing his arms akimbo. "Colonel, your men here keep insisting that you be allowed to pass through our town. Are they saying that on your authority?"

"They are indeed, sir." Dane lowered his hand, then looped his thumbs through the armpits of his plate carrier nonchalantly. "We are on our way to Fort Riley and we need to pass through."

"Well, you can go around. Lots of ways to detour and not tear our streets up with the heavy tracks on your vehicles there." The mayor pointed to the Bradleys parked off on the shoulders of the road nearly a hundred meters distant with his chin, not taking his hands from his hips.

"I really wish I could, Mr. Hoffman, but we are on a tight schedule and we need to get to our destination. I assure you, we'll pass on through without disturbing your town and be on our way." Dane looked at the townspeople who peaked through windows and around the corners of buildings to get a look at the soldiers. They all looked to be healthy and well-fed which triggered another loud rumble in his empty stomach. They'd been on short rations since the fire and he was looking forward to a hot meal once they got back to Riley.

"I've heard that story before, Colonel. Ever since the outbreak we've had all sorts of 'visitors' just asking to pass on through. They all approach innocently enough. Some ask for a bit of food or water and then go on their way. Then, later, they come back with friends in great numbers." Hoffman spat on the ground. "We've been raided on four different occasions in the last month. We managed to defend what's ours, but we lost a number of friends and neighbors. So you'll excuse me if I'm a bit distrustful."

"Mayor, we're with the U.S. Army. We are here to protect the people of this country, not to harm them."

"Ha!" Hoffman let out a contemptuous laugh. "You want me to believe that? Where have you and your men been this whole time? They sure as hell weren't here protecting us when we needed them most. Tell me, Colonel, where have you all been?"

"Listen, it's been tough everywhere, but we are going to

take the country back and get things running again. We'll just need a little cooperation and a bit of support."

"If you want to pass through our town, perhaps we can make a deal."

"What do you mean?" Dane didn't like where this was going and began feeling even more uncomfortable.

"It's simple. You give us some fuel and we'll let you pass through the town."

The two officers from the Cavalry Squadron looked at each other nervously. Dane's cheeks began to grow flushed. "Now see here. We will not be bribed. We are on official government business!"

"What government? We haven't seen any government of any kind since this whole thing started. We're out here on our own. Now, we're a farming community and we've got crops in the fields, but without fuel we can't run our equipment to tend to them or harvest, and if we don't harvest, then we starve this winter. It's that simple. If you want to pass through our town, then we are going to charge you a 'fuel tax' so our people don't go hungry when the snow starts to fly. Understand?"

"I can't do that. Even if I were authorized to transfer some over to you, I simply don't have any to spare." He thought about the video images streaming in from the UAVs showing the railcars loaded full of JP-8 back in Kansas City burning out of control, their containers splitting and sending rivers of burning fuel into ditches and gutters. Then he thought about how after a long day of driving, most of his equipment was running on fumes at this point.

"I don't believe you. I was in the Army once. I know that you can't have an outfit like yours without refuelers. They must be tucked into your column down the road back there somewhere."

Dane was quickly losing his patience and didn't feel like discussing the matter with this redneck any longer. They needed to get moving and they needed to do it now, and he wasn't going to be held up by a bunch of farmers. "Mr. Hoffman, I'm done discussing this issue any longer. We aren't going to pay a 'toll' or anything of the sort. You will open up the road and let us pass or we will open it up ourselves. You do not have a choice in the matter." Dane turned to the Cavalry Squadron commander standing there quietly. "Open this road up and get moving. I want to be at Fort Riley before dark."

"Yes, sir."

"You can't do this!" said Hoffman as Williams turned his back on the mayor and walked back to his Humvee, settling back into the passenger-side.

The two other officers ran back to their own vehicles while the civilians stood stubbornly in the middle of the road. After a few short radio transmissions, a couple of M-88 recovery vehicles pulled up from near the head of the stationary column. They were positioned there to move abandoned cars and trucks and had done so many times during the course of the day. The vehicle commanders stood in their hatches behind .50 caliber machine guns, talking over the intercom and directing their drivers forward. The pops and squeaks from the heavy steel tracks were still audible even over the roar of their massive engines moving forward.

The mayor and his companions refused to move an inch so the M-88s drove around them on either side, not slowing their pace a bit. They hit the school bus blocking the road simultaneously with their plows, crumpling the metal skin and pushing it out of the way as if it were made of paper mâché.

A shot rang out and one of the soldiers in the hatch collapsed inside the recovery vehicle. Another went off and ricocheted off the hull of the second one near its track commander as well, sending him diving inside for cover.

"*Contact front!*" someone shouted, before the coax machine guns on the first two Bradley Cavalry Fighting Vehicles opened up, spraying the town with 7.62mm NATO. A nineteeth century building took a pounding, with jacketed slugs spattering the side of the storefront, sending chunks of red brick flying. The rounds stitched up to the second story, smashing out a couple of windows, sending broken glass plummeting to the ground. On the other side of the street, the stream of tracer and ball smashed through the front of a diner, sending debris flying into the street. The civilians onlookers scattered, taking cover where they could, a few of them only making it a few feet before being cut down.

The mayor raised both of his hands, waving them in wide arcs. "Cease fire! Cease fire! *For the love of God stop shooting!*"

The Squadron Commander emerged from his Humvee and waved at the Bradleys in a similar fashion with one arm, while using the other hand to speak into a radio handmike. Then, as suddenly as the shooting started, it stopped.

The mayor and his two bodyguards found themselves standing alone in the middle of the road with a dozen different weapon systems pointed at them, fingers on triggers, with safeties disengaged. He raised his hands into the air and looked to the two younger men with him. "Put your guns down on the ground. Slowly."

"*Medic!*" shouted a mechanic from one of the M-88s.

A woman in town screamed and then wailed uncontrollably. There were a few bodies lying on the sidewalks on either side of Main Street. Friends and neighbors came out to see what they could do for those who were shot, though it became readily apparent there was nothing to be done.

The mayor and his men all carefully placed their weapons on the asphalt before putting their hands in the air. The sound of a Detroit Diesel screamed and a rumbling grew closer as a M-113 armored personnel carrier came forward at speed. Unlike the other tracks in the formation, this one bore a giant red cross on the hull. It raced past and then pulled up next to the M-88 before the ramp dropped and medics came spilling out. One climbed up the recovery vehicle to check the wounded soldier while a couple of others sprinted into Bremerton to lend aid to the civilians.

Dane burst from his truck again and stomped over to the mayor, stopping just short of the man before stabbing a finger in his face. "Hoffman, I hold you responsible for this. If you'd have just let us pass, my people wouldn't have been forced to defend themselves!"

Hoffman's face contorted with rage. "You sonofabitch, we're just a bunch of farmers and you have tanks. I hope you feel like a hero for gunning these people down!"

"Your people shot first, Mr. Mayor." He turned his back to the man and shouted over to his people. "Let's get this brigade moving again. Let's go!"

Engines fired up and the heavy armor started moving again, with the Cavalry Fighting Vehicles taking the lead, their turrets scanning both left and right as they passed down the main thoroughfare. The civilians looked on with hateful expressions as the soldiers drove through their town, uninvited and unopposed.

Dane went back to his up-armored Humvee and reached for the radio handset. "Dagger Three, this is Dagger Six. Over."

"Six, this is Three."

"Three, I need you to call Division. Tell them we were engaged by local militia-types with small arms. We had to defend ourselves and there were casualties. Over."

"*Roger, Six. I'll let them know. Over.*"

Chapter 6

Fort Riley, Kansas
27 August, 2016
2130 Hours Local

"Get off me you dickhead!" Gray pushed Hong off her, his limp head rolling from side to side. He'd fallen asleep and slouched over on top of her. Again.

His eyes peeled open. "Whuh?"

"I said, get off me before I kick your ass." She gave him a sharp shove with her shoulder, knocking him over a few inches.

"Sorry," he said, his voice devoid of any sincerity.

It was hot in the back of the Bradley and they'd been crammed in the back like sardines all day. They hadn't stopped in hours and many of them needed to relieve themselves.

Across from them rode Angie Carnegie with Saxon, his big, furry head resting in her lap. Deputy Jefferson sat next to her, staring straight ahead, holding a rifle between his knees. Angel and Consuela were there too, along with the Roberts family, all of whom looked terribly uncomfortable. In the center the troop compartment remained open, locked in place to allow some circulation inside the stuffy, enclosed space. Up top, McDermott and Swanson sat on the outer hull on the back deck, facing out and pulling security. The rest of the infantry rode on the backs of the Abrams, split up between Lieutenant Baker and Staff Sergeant Kurtz's tanks.

The track came to a halt and bodies leaned forward and settled back into place again. Sleepy heads raised and eyes opened as the familiar clicks of the locks disengaged and the ramp lowered with a steady "weeeeeee" sound. Before it finished lowering, the people in the cramped troop compartment clicked off their restraints and began jumping off the back as the heavy metal door thunked on the ground. Seconds after that the engine shut down and heads popped up through the hatches atop the turret.

The company parked itself in a neat line-up, tucked into the rest of the battalion. All of those in formation lined up next to each other in columns and the soldiers wasted no time dismounting, finally getting a chance to stretch their legs. Officers called NCOs together for quick huddles, while the junior enlisted and civilians milled about, working the kinks out of muscles and getting the circulation going once again.

Organically the men and women of the platoon clustered together in a disorganized fashion, while Sergeant "Matthews" trudged off with the lieutenant to meet up with the battalion leadership. They found themselves in a grassy field with a treeline not far off in the distance. In the other direction they saw a tent city consisting of shelters of every description. There were hundreds of military shelters erected in neat rows, surrounded by civilian tents and shanties of every shape and size imaginable. The whole thing was massive. It quickly grew dark as the sun went down and pinpricks of light peeked out from some of the tents.

Burbey climbed out of the driver's hatch and found his large friend Donahue standing there, stretching his back, looking at the hobo village in the failing light. "God, I could go for a cigarette right about now."

"Why do you keep saying that? It just makes it worse. I wish you'd shut up about it." Donahue did some more stretches trying to get the feeling back into his limbs. As big as he was, being cramped inside the turret gradually evolved from discomfort to straight-up torture.

"I still wish I had one." Burbey pointed to the tent city. "What's that all about over there?"

"Beats me. Looks like some Beverly Hillbillies shit."

Harris came sauntering over and lit a Marlboro. "That's where they put the refugees. All the families and other civvies on Fort Riley. They've been here since shortly after the outbreak."

Burbey looked at the glowing cherry of the cigarette longingly. "You got another one of those?"

"Get fucked. I ain't got any to share, and if I catch you snooping around in my shit, I'll beat your ass." Harris took a long drag and blew out the smoke just to rub it in.

Over to their right Saxon walked around in a tight circle before squatting down and letting his bowels loose, taking a giant dump in the tall grass. He had the most sincere look of concentration on his face while he did so with Angie Carnegie looking on.

"I haven't heard from her in a while. News has been real spotty. You think Vanessa is in there somewhere?" Donahue turned his upper torso as far as he could to the left, making an audible crack with his back.

"Yeah, I'm sure she's fine." Burbey smirked. "I'm sure Candi's pole dancing for the entire camp over there as we speak. Though they're probably sticking MRE crackers in her g-string instead of dollar bills."

"Hey, fuck you, dude. I told you to stop talking about her like that!" Donahue faced off with his buddy. "And I told you her name's Vanessa, *not Candi!*"

Harris didn't say a word, electing to sit back and watch the show.

"Okay, okay. I'll stop calling her that." Burbey didn't sound convincing.

"Yeah, well you better."

"Anyway, do you think she's grown any of her teeth back? Meth is a hell of a drug."

Donahue slugged his buddy in the shoulder, sending Burbey rocking back on his heels. "Eat shit, asshole!"

The three of them didn't even notice when Mark walked up on them from behind in the fading light. "Are you ladies ready to get to work?"

They all turned to see the NCO standing there, looking unimpressed by the banter.

"Harris, get the platoon gathered up, I've got some information to put out." Mark's expression was completely neutral, the long drive from Kansas City having drained every ounce of emotion from him. He looked as if he were a thousand years old.

"Roger, Sarn't." Harris went to the other side of *BOHICA* and gathered up the others, bringing them around their sole remaining Non-Commissioned Officer. The civilians and sheriff's deputies came over as well, the entire motley group now identifying themselves as "2nd Platoon." They'd all been through a lot together over the previous couple of months and they all lived and worked together as a team.

Mark instinctively turned to the middle-aged former-banker in the group. "Is this everyone, Clay?"

"We're just missing Weber." Clay Roberts craned his neck to peer around the side of the platoon's sole, remaining Bradley Fighting Vehicle. "Ah, here he comes, he was off going to the bathroom."

"Hey, hurry the fuck up, jizz-lips. We're waiting on you!" shouted Private Devons. Clay gave him a stern look. He didn't like that kind of language in front of the girls. Devons met his gaze and wilted a bit. "Uh, sorry, sir."

Clay Roberts was by far the oldest member of the group and even though he had never served in uniform, he handled himself well over the last couple of months. He managed to keep his wife and daughter alive while integrating them into the platoon. He had grown to become Mark's confidant and essentially served as the small unit's de facto Platoon Sergeant. While he hadn't yet accompanied them on any combat patrols yet, he did take care of their day to day business in the FOB, freeing up precious time for Mark, so he could focus on other more pressing matters.

"Okay, listen up." Mark took a good look at the assembled group with Weber finally joining them. The five civilians and two sheriff's deputies all wore a mismatch of different clothing items. They'd scrounged some things that they found comfortable and augmented others with military uniform items. Every single one of them was armed, though most of that was military issue since the weapons were available and ammunition interchangeability was critical. Even so, Clay Roberts still carried that Mini-14 of his, even though the magazines were incompatible with military rifles. "We've got a few things we need to do before bedding down for the night. Clay, I need you to get a detail and link up with Staff Sergeant Packard near the One One Three. He'll take you over to the Brigade Support Area. I'm told they have hot chow for us."

"No problem. I'll take care of it, Mark."

"Also, they tell us we're in a secure FOB. Still, I want two personnel pulling security at all times. Clay, I'll need you to put together a guard roster before everyone beds down."

"It's already done." He held up a sheet of paper in the twilight before turning to the rest of the assembled platoon. "Everybody check this roster. Each of you have a shift." He looked to Angel and Consuela. Their English still wasn't very good, but proved themselves hard workers regardless. Clay made the mistake of putting the two of them on the same guard shift once in the middle of the night and found them off in a clump of bushes having sex instead of pulling guard like they were supposed to. Teenage hormones and young love clouded judgment, so he made it a point to split the two of them up on any work detail. They were far more productive that way. "¿Entender?"

The two of them nodded and responded in unison, "Sí."

"Okay, last thing. They don't have room in the tent city for us so we're sleeping out here. If you have a poncho or other shelter, set it up. Sleep under the stars for all I care, but don't stray far. Keep it tight. I don't want to have to go looking for anyone in the middle of the night. Also, Battalion says we got a lot of shit to do tomorrow, so get some rest. We will be busy. Any questions?" Mark scanned the lot of them and no one said a word. "Good, now let's get after it. Clay, you're in charge."

Mark tried to peel off from the group to work out the next day's work schedule but got intercepted by Donahue. "Sarn't, you got a minute?"

"Yeah, of course, Big Hoss. What's up?"

"Can we speak in private?"

"Yeah, sure. Come on over to my office." Mark led them up to the M-1 tank with the bumper number C12, which had the name "Cloud Nine" stenciled on the barrel. Once there, they were well out of earshot of the others. "What's up?"

"Sarn't you know my wife Vanessa is here, somewhere in that tent city over there right?"

Mark was well aware of that fact, since Donahue and Burbey constantly talked about it. Sometimes annoyingly on the track's intercom system while he was trying to listen to the radio command channel. "Yes, I know. I let the El-Tee know as well and he's working with Battalion to locate her. Once we find out where she's staying out there in that giant mess, I'll let you know right away."

"Does that mean I can go see her? I mean, I know we have a lot of work to do, but... well..."

"Don't worry, dude. I already got permission for you to get

a day pass to go see her. Burbey and I will pick up the slack doing maintenance on the track while you're gone. Don't worry." Mark smiled a bit, knowing this had been eating at his gunner the entire trip back and he didn't know how to broach the subject with him.

"Thanks, Sarn't."

"No sweat."

Before Mark could head back to *BOHICA*, Donahue piped up once again. "Uh, Sarn't. I have another question. Something that's been confusing me a bit."

Mark was taken aback, halting in his tracks. "Yeah, what is it?"

"Um, I know this is going to sound stupid, but…"

"It's okay, Big Hoss. We've been through a lot these last couple of months. You can ask me anything." Mark instantly felt a pang after uttering those words. The response came automatically from the leader inside of him. The escaped felon on the other hand, suddenly realized he'd said too much. *Oh, shit.* He had an idea of what Donahue had been meaning to ask him and it was a subject he'd been actively dodging for weeks.

Donahue took a deep breath before going on. "Sarn't, how is it that you know so much about the Bradley? Like, I know they don't teach Bradley Fighting Vehicle stuff at MP school, but you seem to know everything about them. I was just curious."

Mark had to take a second before responding. He'd known for a while that this question would come up and he'd carefully crafted his lie. He did want it to sound convincing when he delivered it though. "Oh, yeah. I guess I haven't told you guys much about my past. Anyway, I was infantry when I first enlisted. Did my first assignment at Fort Carson and then reclass'd later to Military Police when I re-enlisted. I don't, er… didn't… want to make the Army a career, so Military

Police gave me some good experience in law enforcement for when I got out. I wanted to be a cop back home." He felt at ease, knowing that the story came out just the way he'd rehearsed it in his head, sounding convincing enough. It should have been convincing, since that was partially the truth. He had in fact served at Fort Carson for his first duty station before being stationed at Fort Campbell, which is where he became familiar with the M-2 Bradley. So familiar, they nearly sent him to the Master Gunner school at Fort Benning.

"Oh, well I guess that explains it." Donahue nodded in understanding. "I couldn't figure out how you knew how to do everything in the turret and manage maintenance as well."

"Yup, that's the reason. I was a mechanized infantryman just like you before I became a douchebag MP." Mark smiled at Donahue, hoping the self-deprecating humor would end the conversation. "Anything else?"

"No. Thanks, Sarn't. I really appreciate it."

***

Mark slept soundly, better than he had in quite a long time. It might have been the quiet of not having trains running through around the clock, or maybe it was because they were so far from a city full of the dead, or it might have been the sweet smell of the fresh air, unviolated by the stink of rotting flesh. Whatever the reason, he fell into a slumber like he hadn't experienced in recent memory. Even the nightmares seemed to retreat for a time, finally allowing him some respite.

Then, someone shook him awake.

He groaned loudly before raising dirty fists to rub his eyes. "What… what is it?"

Clay leaned over him, gently pushing his shoulder. "The lieutenant wants to speak with you. Are you awake?"

Mark lay on his back on the bench seat in the back of the track. On the opposite side of the troop compartment Donahue occupied the other, snoring loudly. "Yeah, I'm good." He sat up and yawned before clumsily kicking his legs over, resting his feet on the diamond-plate flooring. "What time is it?"

"It's just after five."

The ramp rested in the lowered position and things were still very dark outside. It was overcast, making it almost impossible to see anything, though he could hear a gentle breeze blowing through the tall grass and several soldiers snoozing away. A faint conversation carried in the distance between a couple of sentries on their early morning shift. "Okay, give me a minute." Mark started pulling his boots on while Clay settled on the bench next to him, flicking on the hull-mounted light. "What are you doing up? Sunup ain't for a couple more hours."

"I was checking on the guards, making sure they were alert." Even in the blue glow of the light, the stubble on Clay's face stood out. As did the wrinkles. The man was on the downhill side of middle age, but didn't show any signs of slowing down, though he did look tired.

"Checking on the guards is my job. You don't need to do that." Mark pulled the laces tight on his boots before tying them, tucking the loops in.

"It's okay, you needed the rest." Clay produced a pack of chewing gum and offered him a piece.

"Where the hell did you get that?" Mark took a small stick and unwrapped it before popping it in his mouth. It was Dentyne, the same kind his grandma used to give him when he was a kid. The flavor elicited a ton of old memories that came flooding back. He chewed happily, careful to take his time and savor it.

"Our boy Jimmy Hong came across some. Don't ask me

how. That kid can sniff out anything."

"Yeah, he's the best scrounger I've ever seen."

"Just like Peter-san in *The Green Berets*."

Mark gave the older man a bemused look. "*You've* seen *The Green Berets*?"

"Just because I wasn't ever in the military doesn't mean I never watched the occasional war movie." He leaned back and stretched his legs before crossing his ankles. "Besides, I'm a big John Wayne fan."

"Well, alright then." He pulled his camouflage jacket on and zipped it before reaching for his FLC and rifle. He didn't bother with his body armor or helmet, but never went anywhere without spare magazines and water. The Army had conditioned him well. "You should go get some more sleep. The sun will be up soon."

"I'm okay. In fact, if you don't mind, I'd like to come with."

"You sure? These meetings are pretty boring." Mark made a sincere statement, while happy to have the company. He hoped Clay would insist on tagging along.

"It's okay. I'm learning a lot and I want to help out."

"Okay, suit yourself. Let's go."

***

When Mark and Clay approached, Lieutenant Baker stood there with a red-lens flashlight poring over a map. They were told that the area was secure so noise and light discipline weren't essential here, but old habits died hard. Standing on either side of him were Staff Sergeant Kurtz, the other tank commander and Staff Sergeant Pavolovski from 3rd Platoon. They were doing their best to get a look at something on the map as well.

Mark smelled the familiar scent of fine tobacco and watched the cherry of a Marlboro glow bright red when Baker took a drag. He'd quit smoking while in prison, electing to spend his money on other things at the commissary. He felt happy that he never picked it up again, particularly after watching so many soldiers go through serious withdrawals when cigarettes began to get scarce shortly after the outbreak. Still, the smoke held a pleasant fragrance for him which made him wonder where the lieutenant had managed to get them. They had become a pretty rare commodity these days with their barter value going through the stratosphere.

"Hey, sir. Were you looking for me?"

"Yeah, come on over and take a look at this." The cigarette dangled from Baker's lips while he spoke. "We got a Warning Order from Battalion about an hour ago."

Mark did a little mental math. If Battalion put out the Warning Order the hour beforehand, then they'd been working on the order for some time prior to that. That also meant that Brigade had issued their order sometime even earlier in the evening to Battalion. He figured that all those staff officers had been up all night churning on this thing and they'd still be up all day writing the formal Operations Order. Sleep wasn't something a staffer got an overabundance of.

Mark and Clay pulled in closer to get a good look at the map and Lieutenant Baker went on. "The word from Division is that we've got forty-eight hours to refit, then we roll out." He pointed to a spot on the map with an alcohol marker. "In an hour we're going to head to this location where they have a hot refuel point set up. We'll top off the vehicles and then get hot doing some maintenance. Bust out your dash-ten manuals and go through your vics with a fine-tooth comb. If anything is wrong, get one of the mechanics and start hanging parts. Any questions?"

Staff Sergeant Kurtz looked puzzled. "Yeah, El-Tee. You said we're rolling out in two days. Where are we going? Do we have another combat patrol planned or somethin'?"

"No. Battalion says we're un-assing Fort Riley and road marching the entire Division."

"Road marching the entire Division? Where are we going?" asked Pavolovski.

"We're headed to Washington state. That's where the government re-established itself." Baker took another drag and blew out the smoke before flicking the ash to the ground.

Mark ran a different set of numbers through his head this time, trying to figure out the mileage. "Sir, that's over a thousand miles from here."

Baker nodded. "More like seventeen hundred."

Mark shook his head. "Whoa."

"Whoa indeed." Baker turned off the flashlight and folded up the map. "Anyway, get your people up and get ready to link up with the refuelers. After that there should be hot chow waiting for us back here." He looked at his watch, pushing the illumination button. "Battalion is going to issue their Operations Order at noon to the company commanders. So meet me at 1800 tonight and I'll issue my Company Op-Order to you all. Clear?"

"Roger, sir."

"Good, let's get after it then."

***

The tanks and tracks parked neatly next to one another on the fringes of the tent city after topping off. The mechanics drove their tool trucks over and the whole field came alive with activity as the sun came up over the horizon.

A cargo Humvee pulled up to the platoon's makeshift

assembly area and Clay hopped out, waving to the others. "Come and get it! Breakfast has arrived!"

The soldiers immediately stopped what they were doing, picked up their weapons and lined up behind the truck. Clay and Jimmy Hong opened up the flap in the back and dropped the tailgate, revealing green metal containers. They were ancient insulated mermite cans used for transporting food and they looked like they'd seen better days.

"Before you get your food, make sure you grab one of these." Clay reached into a box next to the mermites and presented the platoon with a shiny mess tin. "I'm assuming you all know what these are." He opened one up in a clamshell fashion, revealing two large pieces with one of them attached to a folding handle. Inside were metal forks, knives and spoons.

"I've never seen one of those before," Gray said, giving it a skeptical eye.

"Oh, I assumed you all had used these before." Clay looked confused. He'd never served in the military himself, so he thought that this was something they were all quite familiar with.

Swanson pulled one out of the box and examined it carefully. "This looks like some old school shit right here."

Mark took one for himself. "It is. These were designed before World War II, but we haven't used the things in decades. Where'd you get 'em?"

Jimmy hopped down from the back of the bed of the cargo truck. "They were issuing them in the Brigade Support Area when we got the food from the cooks. They said there weren't any more paper plates or disposable flatware anymore. We're supposed to use these from now on."

"Old school indeed." Mark opened his up and inspected the contents inside. "Alright listen up. When you all get done eating off these things, make sure you thoroughly clean them or else you're going to get sick. That's one more thing I want the Team Leaders inspecting. Got it?" He heard a couple of them groan, but chose to ignore it. "Okay, dig in and scarf it down. We've got work to do." He wandered off to the side to watch the junior enlisted queue up and get their breakfast. Leaders always ate last.

Clay and Jimmy followed him over while the soldiers scooped out portions of powdered eggs and other lukewarm items. All of them hungry with no complaints to be heard. "Mark, you got a minute?"

"Yeah, of course. What's up."

Clay nodded over to Private Hong standing beside him. "Jimmy here heard some rumors while we were in the BSA this morning. I think you ought to hear this."

"Really? What is it?"

"I was talking to one of my boys over in the Distro Platoon and he told me about our upcoming deployment to Washington state." Jimmy looked over his shoulders to ensure no one else was listening. "The word coming down from Division is that we're only taking the bare minimum and that we don't have enough trucks to move our supplies. They haven't told anybody yet and they're trying to keep it quiet."

"I don't get it. Why the secrecy?"

"They said it's because we can only carry enough food and fuel to last us two or three days, and that's if we don't carry anything else. Plus, we're going to be taking all those civilians over there and they plan on feeding them too, somehow." Jimmy pointed at the tent city over in the distance. "They are going to cut everyone's rations again to stretch things further."

Mark took his hat off and scratched his head while the significance of this settled in. He looked over at Clay who stood there watching his reaction. "Two or three days? Is that it?"

"Roger, Sarn't."

"We've got to move seventeen hundred miles. That'll take at least eight or nine days. If we run out of food and fuel after a couple of days, we won't even be close." He shook his head. "Did they say what Division intends to do after we run out of everything?"

"They said they're is going to order us out on foraging parties along the way, but it's going to take a long time. It might take three or four weeks total to get to Washington state."

"Then we need to scrounge some additional food and other stuff for ourselves." Mark plopped the patrol cap back on his head.

"There's something else we need to consider," Clay interjected.

"You mean besides food, water and fuel?"

"Yeah. Three or four weeks puts us in the Rocky Mountains in late September. It's going to get cold and winter's right around the corner." He turned and pointed at the handful of bags and backpacks lashed to the side of *BOHICA*. "We don't exactly have a lot of equipment with us. We've been living off minimal supplies all summer. We need to find some proper cold-weather clothing, tents and other gear or else we're going to be completely at the mercy of the elements."

"Good point. What do you have in mind?"

Jimmy smirked. "Well, Sarn't. I suggest that before the rest of the Division figures this all out we need to send out a scavenging party while the pickings are still decent."

Mark nodded in understanding, stroking his chin. "We still have to carry out refit operations and maintenance."

Clay held up a hand. "Hear me out. We've only got one track left in the platoon which means the rest of us don't have much to do. You can spare a few people to go out foraging while the rest stay here and work."

"Okay, but how are you going to go and get the stuff?"

The two conspirators gave each other a knowing look before Clay faced Mark once again. "Don't you worry about that. The less you know the better. You'll have plausible deniability." He looked over at his wife Cynthia and daughter Bailey standing in line with the soldiers asking for help with their new mess tins, waiting for their breakfast like everyone else. "Trust me."

"Clay, you're beginning to sound like a seasoned NCO."

"Hey, what can I say? I learned from the best."

***

The company's supply sergeant was off taking care of some business when Jimmy and Clay "borrowed" his truck. The two of them rode in the cab of the Light Medium Tactical Vehicle, better known as the LMTV. It could carry a payload of 2.5 tons, which they hoped would be enough. To their front was the company commander's Humvee crewed by Weber and Devons, while to their rear was the First Sergeant's cargo Humvee with Swanson and McDermott. In the back of the truck rode Bags, Gray, Angie and Saxon. The rest of the platoon they left behind to turn wrenches and go off on work details. It wouldn't take long before the company headquarters element figured out that several of their wheeled vehicles had been taken, but they'd be well on their way before it would be discovered. At least they hoped so.

They didn't have authorization to leave the FOB, so they racked their brains trying to come up with a cover story for the gate guards. Luckily when they arrived there was already another convoy lined up, readying to leave the wire for a mission on the main post of Fort Riley. They simply fell in behind the rest and pretended to be part of the larger group of vehicles headed out. No one bothered to count the number of trucks or take notice of the bumper numbers to check if they were supposed to be there or not. They even waved to the guards on their way out, adding a nice touch.

After a short while the main column took a turn toward one of the large supply dumps on post, not noticing when 2nd Platoon's trucks peeled off, going the other way. McDermott manned the cupola of the command Humvee, leaning into the stock of the M240 Bravo machine gun, scanning for the dead. Meanwhile, the rest of them kept their eyes peeled as well. This wasn't their first rodeo and every single one of them was switched on. Clay hadn't gone on missions before, so this was a new experience for him. Moreover, the others looked to him for leadership and he felt very nervous about the whole thing. Still, he kept up a confident demeanor and the others seemed to be fine with him in charge.

"You know where you're going, Jimmy?"

"Yeah, I do. We're headed to Ellis Heights." The young soldier sat behind the wheel, maneuvering through side streets with ease. It was clear this wasn't the first time he'd driven the LMTV. "It's on the northeast side of Post. I told the other drivers before we left, so they're tracking too."

"Any particular reason we're headed that way? There's other housing areas that are closer."

"I got a buddy in S-2. He told me that the Division systematically cleared most of the neighborhoods on post and took whatever was useful, handing it out to the civilian refugees in the camp back at the FOB. Ellis Heights hasn't been touched yet, so there should be plenty of stuff still there."

"There might also be some zeds there as well." Clay nervously fingered his Mini-14 held between his legs.

"That's possible, but we've cleared houses before. It shouldn't be too dangerous."

"Can I ask you something?"

"Sure." Jimmy gave the older man a puzzled look.

"You're a private right?"

"That's right."

"How come you seem to know everyone and how things work? You're pretty junior but you seem to have things figured out, and you seem to have a supernatural ability to find the things we need."

Jimmy let out a short outburst. "Ha!" He slapped his knee and shook his head. "My rank is definitely junior, but I've been in the Army for a while."

"I don't understand. Why are you so junior then?"

"Clay, you crack me up. I used to be a Specialist, grade E-4. I even went in front of the promotion board for Sergeant." He gave the other man a wry smile. "That was, right up until the Army decided that I needed some remedial training and dropped me down two pay grades."

"I still don't get it."

"Let's just say, I wasn't real good with finances. I may have bounced a few checks. So they busted me down a couple of ranks."

"They took your rank away for bouncing a couple of checks? That's crazy!"

"Well... it may have been more than a couple of checks. Like I said, I wasn't real good with personal finance."

Clay's eyes narrowed a bit. "How many checks did you bounce, exactly?"

"I don't remember, but it was something like $30,000 worth." Jimmy's little smile began growing into a broad grin.

"Thirty thousand dollars? How in God's name did you bounce checks worth that much money? That's astounding!"

"I didn't know how else to pay off all the credit cards."

Clay had to take a minute to process that. His mouth hung open while he did the math. "Now, wait a minute. There's no way you needed $30,000 to make the minimum payments on credit cards. Even if they issued you a dozen of them, which they never would have, you wouldn't have needed that kind of cash. You're pulling my leg."

"There was some other stuff too. Like I said, I wasn't very good with budgets." Jimmy's smile then grew into a shit-eating grin. "Admittedly, I might have still been okay if I hadn't punched my friend's lights out in the barracks."

"Okay, I'll bite. Why did you do that?"

"He was mad that I wrecked his new car." Jimmy looked like a proud father on the day his first child was born before going on. "Of course I was drunk at the time. They said I had a blood alcohol level of .20 or something like that. Frankly, I don't remember. The details are a little fuzzy."

"Jesus, Jimmy."

"Yeah, so the Battalion Commander busted me in rank, took some pay and put me on extra duty for a while."

"Goodness." Clay stared at him in disbelief. "I hope you learned something from all that."

"I did." Jimmy sat up straight in the seat, keeping his hands at the ten and two o'clock position on the wheel. "In the future, steal someone else's checkbook and tell your buddy that his girlfriend was driving the car."

Clay had absolutely no response to any of that.

***

The three trucks pulled into the military housing district, which appeared like any suburban neighborhood you might find anywhere. The military went through great pains to make their housing areas appear like a normal slice of middle-class America, right down to the manicured lawns, the mailboxes and the identical single-family homes. Only now the lawns were overgrown and the houses stood dark, with weeds growing through cracks in the sidewalks.

They pulled into a cul-de-sac and circled around, facing out, in case they needed to beat a hasty retreat. It was always wise to keep an escape route open in the middle of the zombie apocalypse.

The brakes on the LMTV squeaked as they came to a halt and the soldiers dismounted the vehicles in an orderly manner, careful not to make any more noise than necessary. They even left the doors slightly ajar, not wanting to make any sounds slamming them shut. The area appeared clear, but they'd come to learn that the most innocent-looking places concealed all sorts of danger.

McDermott stayed on the gun, pulling watch while Swanson assisted him, since no person had eyes in the back of their heads. The rest gathered in close on a nearby sidewalk, never raising their voice above a whisper. The whole time Saxon worked his way in between people's legs, curiously looking up with tongue hanging out, observing the people acting strangely.

"Okay, where are we going first?" As usual, Angie Carnegie looked impatient. She only went out with the platoon when they cleared houses or other buildings and she made no secret that she didn't like it, but they always asked her to come along when they did, because she had the secret weapon. It was the German Shepherd that never left her side, who had a soft-spot for treats and belly-rubs.

Clay may have been the de facto leader of this patrol, but he sure didn't know what to do on an op like this, preferring to defer to one of the more experienced people huddled around.

Bags, the platoon medic, looked over and pointed to the nearest house. "Why not start with that one?"

There were several nods and no arguments, so Clay instinctively stepped in, reading the crowd. "It's as good as any. They all look the same to me."

"Okay, fine." Angie gently tugged on Saxon's leash. "Come." The two of them headed straight toward the nearest house, taking pains to quietly mount the front porch.

Clay watched Angie and the dog working as a team, unable to shake the thought that the sheriff's deputy bore an uncanny resemblance to Gina Carano, the MMA fighter. The young soldiers followed close behind, also doing their best to keep the noise down.

Up on the porch, Saxon moved up and sniffed the base of the front door. It didn't take long before the hair on his shoulders stood up, followed by a throaty growl. Angie turned around and nodded to the others.

Jimmy leaned in close to whisper in Clay's ear. "Looks like we've got Zulus inside. The dog is never wrong."

Clay's eyes darted from side to side, watching the relaxed demeanor of the squad. "Well, does that mean we pass this house up and move to the next one then?"

"No, not at all. If they got Zeds inside, that means the house hasn't been picked over yet. There's probably stuff in there untouched that we can use. We're definitely going in now."

"Won't that be more dangerous?"

"Nothing we haven't done a hundred times before. It's okay." Jimmy motioned to the others, pointing at the large picture window to their right. The curtains were closed, making it impossible to see inside.

Weber jogged over to the First Sergeant's Humvee and

pulled something out from the passenger-side seat. It was a military-issue machete and he deftly unsheathed it, then swung it around like a martial artist for good measure. He joined the others as they stacked up near the window, thumbs flicking off the safety catches on their rifles.

All of them checked ballistic glasses and goggles while pulling bandanas over their mouths and noses. A couple rolled their sleeves back down and a few pulled on gloves. Devons appeared from the back of the house, carrying a large, round, river rock someone had used for landscaping. They all moved in a coordinated manner, each of them well-practiced, knowing precisely where to stand and what to do.

Satisfied they were set, Devons tossed the rock through the large pane of glass, shattering it into hundreds of pieces. The noise made Clay flinch.

From inside the house came an animal howl, followed by the thumping of heavy footfalls. The curtains suddenly came alive, lunging forward and outward in the shape of a human. Only the thing covered by the light blue cloth was no longer human. It thrashed about wildly, unable to see through the material. It leaned so far forward it tore the curtains from the rod and the creature came spilling out into the yard onto the tall grass.

In a flash, Weber brought the machete down and severed the beast's spinal cord. Still covered in its new shroud, the body stopped moving, though the jaw kept working. Satisfied it was neutralized, he turned to face the open window frame, waiting for another to emerge.

McDermott leaned into his machine gun, scanning down the street. Nobody moved, everyone frozen in place. Even Saxon stood like a statue, ears perked up, staring at the now-open window. The seconds ticked by and no other sounds were heard.

"Psst!" Jimmy Hong pointed to Devons.

As if activated by remote control, Devons raised his weapon, looking through the optic, bringing it up over the windowsill, sweeping it inside across the living room. After a few seconds, he took his left hand from the foregrip of his M-4 and gave the rest a "thumbs-up."

Bags came forward and got down on hands and knees beneath the window while the others used her back as a stepping stool, climbing inside, into the house. Angie awkwardly picked Saxon up and pushed him up and over before following him in. When they were nearly all inside, Clay followed suit, entering into the darkened structure. Once in, Bags remained outside in the yard with McDermott and Swanson, guarding their escape route.

Plenty of ambient light from the windows lit the interior, so they didn't need their flashlights or night vision goggles. Using nothing more than hand signals, they communicated with each other, moving fluidly through the single-family home. The carpeted floors helped them keep quiet, still taking great pains to keep the noise down.

They moved into an inner hallway where the walls and floor were sprayed with blood. It had turned brown long ago and it stank in the enclosed space. Nearing the kitchen Saxon's throaty growl sounded once again and Weber posted himself near the front of the stack, machete in hand.

He scrolled in and found himself facing a child, no more than ten years old, standing in the center of the room. The only movement from it came from those awful red eyes that tracked Weber's movement. The soldier swallowed hard and brought the blade up as the kid lunged at him.

The blade flashed and Weber caught it in the neck and along the jaw. The blow did not take its head off, but the force sent the thing crashing into some cabinets. Without hesitation the soldier brought the weapon to bear and hit it as hard as he could, taking several chops to cut the head off. Like the other in the yard, the body lay motionless while the eyes and jaw continued to move.

The rest of the squad came in and continued on past, stepping over the small pile of fetid flesh on the floor. Clay came through as well, mimicking the movements of the others, learning as he went. He'd seen plenty of the dead over the last couple of months, but never got used to the children. It always gave him an unsettled feeling inside to see them.

They moved deliberately through the rest of the house, careful not to rush and bumble into something. It took nearly half an hour, but they only found the two infected, which appeared to have been a child and its mother. Once done they unlocked the front door and grabbed the empty duffel bags and rucksacks from the trucks outside, heading back in for the loot.

Chapter 7

"Jackpot." Jimmy Hong stood in the doorway of the pantry and tossed an empty duffel bag to the center of the floor. "Clay, take a look at this."

Clay worked his way past the island in the kitchen to see what Jimmy had found. He shined a flashlight into the darkened room to find a pantry packed with canned goods and other non-perishable items. When he caught sight of the cans of chili and soups his stomach began to grumble and his mouth watered. "Looks like a good haul to me. What do we grab?"

"Anything that ain't nailed down. If we can fit it in the trucks, we take it. What we can't use for ourselves, we can trade for something else later."

Weber squeezed in the doorway to get a look. "Spaghetti-O's? Shit yeah! And they got ramen too!"

"Okay, you start packing this stuff up. Just like the grocery store, try not to put the heavy canned shit in the duffel with the bags of potato chips. Oh, and grab the boxes of cereal too. Take it all." Jimmy pointed a finger at Weber to make his point. "You hear me?"

"Yeah, yeah. I don't know why you care so much about smashing up a few potato chips though." Weber never made eye contact with his buddy, he stood transfixed on the shelves full of food.

"Because, dumbshit, snacks like that are worth their weight in gold. I can barter those things for all kinds of stuff. So be fucking careful. Got it?"

"Hooah."

They'd been at this for hours now, moving methodically from one house to the next. There had only been the two infected in the first house, while the rest in the cul-de-sac were blissfully quiet and empty. Most of the homes had refrigerators and freezers full of rotting food, with not a whole lot they could use, so this pantry came as a welcome surprise.

Heavy-booted footfalls came running up a flight of carpeted stairs. "Guys, I think I found something." Gray had her Squad Automatic Weapon slung across her back with her helmet hanging off a canteen by the chinstrap.

Clay raised an eyebrow. "What did you find?"

"Oh, I think you're gonna like it." Gray turned on her heel and went back downstairs to the basement, pumping her short legs as fast as they could go.

Clay shrugged his shoulders. "Okay. Come on, Jimmy. Let's go see what she found."

They mounted the stairs to find Gray at the bottom, waving to them. It was dark down there and she had her massive Maglite flashlight switched on, an item that occasionally doubled as a club in a pinch. They both flicked on their lights and came down, still a bit wary about what might still be lurking around in the dark.

When they got to the base of the stairs, they swept their lights around in a quick scan. The previous owner had spent quite a bit of time and effort turning the basement into a "man cave" and it became immediately clear the previous owner had been an outdoorsman. It occurred to Clay that he should have figured that out already by all the taxidermy decorating nearly every other room of the house.

Off in a corner sat a weight bench with a barbell and plenty of free weights stacked neatly on a tree. Next to that sat half a dozen white 5-gallon pails with lids securely in place with small, clear, plastic devices sticking out the top, with spigots at their bases. Nearby were neatly-stacked crates filled with large brown beer bottles.

"Homebrewer," Clay said simply.

"My kind of man," Jimmy replied.

Against the far wall a homemade wooden workbench was erected, with a couple of stools next to it. It had a reloading press bolted to it, with various types of gunpowders lined up behind it. There were case trimmers, primers, bullets and reloading dies of various calibers. The whole operation appeared quite tidy and organized.

To the left were shelves containing all sorts of random pieces of suburban life. Boxes and plastic tubs with labels written in magic marker that read, "Christmas Decorations," or "Baby Clothes," another that said "Miscellaneous." These went from floor to ceiling, taking up nearly a third of the room.

Offset from that was another shelving unit, only this one held scores of canned goods. Unlike the pantry upstairs, this one dwarfed the smaller one located next to the kitchen. The cans contained here all had dates written on the lids and were set in chutes that gravity-fed them on an angle to a jerry-rigged dispenser. The newer cans were loaded on the left-hand side, the oldest would be retrieved on the right. The whole system kept the food supply in constant rotation, using the oldest stuff first.

In the center of the floor were more 5-gallon pails, only these didn't have spigots or airlocks for fermenting beer. These were sealed tight, piled up neatly several rows deep and standing at chest-level. They all bore labels which indicated they were full of survival foods of various types.

Clay whistled when he saw it. "Man, oh man. This guy was prepared."

"Not *that* prepared," Jimmy said.

"What do you mean?" Clay looked at him with a puzzled expression.

"Well, he ain't here using any of this shit. Dude's either chilling with his family in the refugee camp or dead. Either way, he doesn't have access to any of his stuff."

"I suppose."

"Wait, there's something else," Gray interjected. "Look over there." She shined her light on a couple of large, rectangular objects sitting off in the corner. It was a couple of gun safes, standing up against the wall. Next to them a dehumidifier sat silent with no electricity coming from the power outlet on the wall.

"Well, now. That is interesting." Clay ran his hand over the stubble growing on his chin. Each of those safes must have weighed 800 pounds empty and he felt a fleeting pang of sympathy for the movers who must have struggled to get the massive things down the stairs.

"Hell yes." Jimmy darted over and ran his flashlight between and along the backsides of the safes. "Clay, can you come over here for a sec?"

"What do you need?" Clay came over, curious as to what Jimmy was looking for.

"Help me see if we can move one of these."

"Are you serious? We'll never get one of these things up the stairs, even if we got everybody to help."

"If we're lucky, we won't have to. Gray, give us a hand, will ya?"

She shrugged and joined the other two, looking as confused as Clay did.

Jimmy got his hands behind the big metal container, putting his foot up against the wall for leverage. "Okay, let's all pull together on three."

Clay and Gray did as he asked and got set.

"One... two... *three!*"

All of them pulled in unison, straining and grunting under the exertion. Then, surprisingly, it moved. The corner of the safe came away from the cinderblock wall about an inch, scraping along the concrete floor, before coming to a stop.

"*Yes!*"

"What are you so excited for? We barely moved the thing," Clay said, his brow furrowed.

"It moved, so that means it's not bolted to the floor."

"I don't understand," Gray said, brushing the hair from forehead.

Jimmy inhaled deeply, gathering up some patience as if he were about to lecture a child. "Okay look, normally you're supposed to bolt a gun safe to the floor. Makes it harder to fuck with, but here on Fort Riley, the occupants of these homes aren't allowed to permanently alter their base housing. So they sit theirs on the floor and don't secure them."

"So what? We'll never carry these things out of the house. They're way too heavy." Clay felt a bit silly pointing out the obvious.

"Just wait, you'll see. Gray, go get Weber and Devons. I'll be right back." Jimmy ran up the stairs and they heard him run across the living room floor above their heads and head out through the front door.

"Do you have any idea what he's up to?"

"No clue." Gray shined the flashlight on the massive containers not knowing what to think. She didn't linger long and stomped back up the stairs, doing as she was asked.

A few minutes later Clay, Weber, Devons and Gray huddled around the steel boxes while Angie let Saxon sniff around the various items in the basement. He had the scent of something, probably some mice, and became completely distracted from the strangely-acting people.

Jimmy came barging back down the steps again, only this time he carried a five-foot long pry bar in one hand and a crowbar in the other.

"What're you going to do with those?" Weber shined a light in Jimmy's eyes, much to his annoyance.

"Get that thing out of my face, numb-nuts." He set the two steel bars on the floor and motioned everyone over to help him. "Okay everyone. We need to turn this thing around, then set it down on its back."

"That thing weighs a ton, we'll never move it," Devons said, shaking his head.

"It'll move, trust me. Now give me a hand." Jimmy picked up the heavy pry bar and stuck it behind the first safe, wedging it against the wall. Several of them got on the steel bar and the safe scraped across the floor, moving several feet this time. They grabbed it by hand and managed to get it turned around. "Okay, let's lower this thing. Be careful. Watch your hands and feet." The group got set once again and when ready, they slowly tipped it over, dropping it the last few inches with a loud "thud."

"What now?" Clay found himself no longer skeptical, but genuinely curious. The young man seemed to know exactly what to do and it was absolutely fascinating.

"I'm going to use the pry bar and lift up the edge of the door, once I get it open enough, stick the crowbar in there to hold it open. After that I'm going to move up a couple inches higher up the door and raise it. You slide the crow bar up. Then we'll repeat the process up the entire length of the door."

"That ain't going to work," Gray snorted.

"You'll see."

Jimmy stuck the flat end of the long steel rod into the corner of the door opposite the hinges, putting all his weight on it until the lip raised up just enough for Clay to insert the crowbar. Once he did, Jimmy worked his way up the seam and Clay followed it. To their amazement, the door gradually opened, bit by bit, fighting them every inch of the way, trying to slam shut again right up until the last bolt securing it in place gave way with a loud "pop."

Everyone stood there with looks of amazement. It took Jimmy less than three minutes to accomplish what they had believed impossible. They were completely speechless when he pulled the door open and aimed his flashlight inside, illuminating the contents.

"Hot damn!" Devons exclaimed. "Will you look at that?"

The inside was filled with guns of different shapes and sizes. Hunting rifles, shotguns, handguns and more. Some were designed for hunting, while others had a more tactical appearance for sport shooting. The soldiers had their issued weapons of course, carrying a variety of rifles and machine guns, but few of them had pistols or shotguns. Those two types of guns were in short supply and highly desirable in a post-infection world. In close quarters, shotguns and handguns were often much more practical than standard-issue carbines and crew-served weapons.

Without waiting for an invitation, they all started reaching inside and pulling the guns out. Their training had been well-conditioned and all of them pointed the things in safe directions, making sure to clear them first.

The only two who hadn't joined in were Angie and Saxon, who still busied himself sniffing along the base of the wall and around a darkened corner.

The group scooped up the guns and more than a few happy sounds were made when they all heard Angie call out from around the darkened corner of the basement. "Guys. Guys! You need to come over here!"

They all froze and gave each other an alarmed look. Clay didn't wait, bringing his Mini-14 to bear, shouldering it in the low-ready, charging around the corner fully expecting the worst. When he got there and saw what she was looking at he stopped in his tracks.

Jimmy came barreling around the corner and almost

knocked the older man over. It took him a second to process what he saw, not believing it at first. "Oh my sweet baby Jesus. *Score!*"

They had found shelves packed from bottom to top with liquor of every kind. Even better, off on the right-hand side were cartons of cigarettes, stacked several rows deep.

The rest came racing around the corner as well, suddenly halting to take in the majesty of it all.

"I think I died and went to Class VI heaven," Devons said.

Suddenly distracted from their newly acquired firearms, the group carefully began liberating bottles of booze.

Jimmy cradled a bottle of bourbon with a grin from ear to ear. "Well, it's official. This has definitely been a good day!"

***

"Is that them?" Lieutenant Baker's normally even-toned voice utterly boomed.

"Yes, sir. I believe it is," replied Sergeant Medina. He sounded as if he were savoring the fact someone else was about to get their ass chewed out.

"You tell them the minute they arrive I want to see them!"

"Roger, sir." Medina grabbed his rifle and moved out, not waiting to hear the rest of it. The lieutenant had been in a sour mood all day, ever since he found out his trucks had been "liberated." He jogged on over to 2nd Platoon, who they'd learned the perpetrators came from. When he got there he found Sergeant Matthews and Burbey securing some bolts to one of the sprockets on their Bradley. "Sarn't the El-Tee wants to see you and whoever's responsible for taking his vehicles without permission."

Mark was stooped over with a ratchet, trying to get a nut secured. He set the tools down and stood up, wiping filthy hands on the front of his trousers. He looked over and saw the small convoy in the distance, returning from their foraging operation. He suddenly felt the familiar feeling in his gut where he knew he was about to go face the music. It brought back a lot of bad memories. Not as bad as the time he got his court martial sentencing, but bad enough. "Yeah, yeah. Go tell the lieutenant I'll be with him shortly."

"Don't keep him waiting, dude. The El-Tee is pissed!"

"Yeah, whatever. Fuck off."

Medina took off and Matthews waved at the three vehicles steadily approaching through the tall grass. Without fanfare they pulled up beside *BOHICA,* the brakes squeaking as the LMTV and two Humvees rolled to a stop next the track. Once halted, they shut the engines down and the passengers immediately disembarked. Mark looked down at his watch and sighed. *It's after 1900 hours and they've been gone nearly all day*, he thought to himself, wondering just what had taken them so long.

The rest of the platoon stopped doing maintenance, to greet the rest of their teammates, all curious to learn what happened outside the wire that day. Doors opened almost at once along with the canvas back flap on the larger truck and soldiers came pouring out. Clay came around from the passenger side with a warm smile while Jimmy Hong hopped out from behind the wheel.

"You guys sure took your sweet time." Mark looked around doing a quick visual headcount. "Is everybody okay?"

Clay stretched out his back, reaching for the sky. "Yeah, yeah. We're all fine. Look, we have something to…"

"Sergeant Matthews! I need to speak with you!" Lieutenant Baker came stomping over, his jaw muscles clenching.

"Sir, if you want, I can meet you over in your Command

Post to explain." Mark's stomach started to twist in knots and he could feel the eyes of the entire platoon on him, none of them saying a word. He wanted to take this somewhere else and get his ass-chewing in private. This public stuff was humiliating.

"No, I don't want to take this over to the Command Post! You are going to tell me where your people took my trucks today! While they were off joy-riding, I had to go beg the Battalion XO for vehicles to move my parts for maintenance! I had to explain to the Battalion Commander how I lost positive control of my equipment, and now you're going to explain it to me... *right now*!" The more Lieutenant Baker spoke, the redder his face became. He looked like he might have an aneurism there on the spot.

"Lieutenant, allow me to explain." Clay physically interjected himself between the officer and Mark with hands raised shoulder-high, trying to placate him.

"You stay out of this Mr. Roberts, you are a civilian and shouldn't even be here!" Baker stuck a finger in Clay's face.

Clay's eyes narrowed to slits and his brow furrowed. "You're right, *Lieutenant*, I am a civilian. Therefore, I am well within my rights to tell you where to go!"

Before things escalated any further Jimmy Hong slipped in like a ghost and waved a carton of Marlboro Lights in front of Baker's face. The officer stopped before he could get another word out, his eyes tracking the cigarettes like a laser.

"Care for a smoke, sir?" Jimmy said with an angelic look on his face.

"Wuh... where did you get those?"

Jimmy delicately took the officer's hand, opened it and placed the carton in his palm. "If you'll follow me, sir."

With a dumbfounded look on his face, Baker followed the junior enlisted soldier to the back of the LMTV. Jimmy dropped the tailgate and pulled back the canvas flap revealing the fruits of their day's labor.

Baker dropped the cigarettes to the ground. "Holy shit."

Clay came up from behind and put a hand on his shoulder. "There's plenty more where that came from. We couldn't haul it all so we stashed most of it in a safe place. We got enough to share with the entire company."

Baker turned to look at the middle-aged banker. "I don't know what to say."

"How about, *'you're welcome.'*"

***

6 September, 2016
Fort Riley, Kansas
0600 Hours Local

"Short count, on my mark." The transmission crackled over headsets and speakers throughout the company's assembly area. "Three. Two. One. *Mark.*"

On the word "mark" every engine in the assembly area fired up all at once. Tanks, Bradley and trucks all synchronized, with engines turning over and coughing to life in the cool early morning hours.

The practice was something that mechanized units had employed ever since the first tanks were used on the battlefield. The idea was that if all of the vehicles in a unit started their engines at precisely the same time, then enemy scouts could not easily identify how many of them were out there by the sound of their starters. If each of them turned over their engines individually, then the enemy could ascertain the approximate size of your unit just by the sound. "Short counts" made that more difficult.

The practice was all the rage during the Cold War, particularly in Germany, but now was completely unnecessary and kind of silly, but it was kind of a tradition and the lieutenant loved that sort of stuff. So he made the company do it at least once a day, usually first thing in the morning. Eventually it grew into a sort of esprit de corps sort of deal with them all. At first some of the crews bitched about it and then after a time they grew to take it on as a symbol of pride. Bravo Company kept the old traditions alive while everyone else got slack. It was their thing.

After days of reset they were ready to go. The Division put out a movement order and then had to amend it several times. No matter what they did they could not seem to get things on schedule and they fell days behind. Finally, when they were ready to go the weather turned bad and grounded the Aviation Brigade, forcing yet another delay. Not that anyone in Bravo Company minded. It gave them more time to retrieve and pack up all the goods they managed to scavenge. The lieutenant may have been upset on the first day when 2nd Platoon "liberated" his trucks, but he became suddenly comfortable with their larceny the minute he tasted that first bottle of looted whiskey. After that, he became a member of the converted.

Units were already uncoiling from the massive base of operations with vehicles of every size and description falling into march serials at disciplined, predetermined time intervals. Everything had been worked out, as carefully planned as they could manage, limited by the experience of the staff planners and the number of hours in the day allocated to them. They dealt with any number of finite resources, with time being the most critical of them.

The tent city had been largely broken down and loaded up on every car, pickup truck, SUV and minivan available to move personal goods. Military Police worked in and among the civilians to organize and mostly keep them under control to prevent panic. The vast majority were military families, retirees and employees on Fort Riley before the outbreak. By and large they were orderly, organized and most importantly, compliant. The MPs didn't really have a difficult job keeping them under control, but there was an uneasiness out there among them.

Burbey had his drivers hatch open watching the Brigade's Cavalry Squadron move out with every vehicle covered in bags, rucks and tarps lashed to the sides of each and every vehicle. Even the most lean fighting unit looked like a gypsy caravan with gear hanging off every square inch of rolling stock. The Beverly Hillbillies rolling into California with their jalopy looked absolutely regal in comparison. Nobody wanted to leave anything behind, but there simply wasn't enough room to take the things they needed. The company assembly areas were littered with thousands of tons of abandoned gear, most of it perfectly serviceable. Leaders had to make tough choices and take what was essential while leaving rest behind. Bravo Company shoe-horned every bit of loot they'd found and stuffed it inside their vehicles, forcing the infantry to ride on top of the armored vehicles out in the open air, squeezing into any spot they could find.

Burbey keyed the intercom on his helmet. "I can't believe you brought her here to ride with us."

"Are you talking to me?" Donahue said, standing on his seat, looking out at the scene in front of them all from the Bradley's loaders hatch.

"Why couldn't she ride with the rest of the civilians? I mean, seriously?"

Donahue looked over at his wife, Vanessa, who sat on top of the turret next to him. He stroked her arm and she looked playfully at him with her dirty blonde hair blowing in the wind.

"You know why, retard. We don't have a working car. At least not good enough to make the trip. She's safer here with us." He smiled up at her lovingly.

"We ain't got no stripper poles for Candi to dance on. How's she going to earn her keep?" Burbey's words were especially bitter this time.

Donahue cupped the microphone around his hands so his wife couldn't see or hear what he said. "Listen, motherfucker. You say that again and I'll kick the living shit out of you!"

"Enough! Both of you idiots knock it off!" Mark spat. He'd been putting up with this back-and-forth since they woke up and he'd grown tired of it. Really tired of it. "I've had enough of this shit. Unless the both of you want to walk to Washington state, you *will* cease fire. Got it?"

The two junior enlisted acknowledged, sounding utterly dejected.

Mark spared a glance at Donahue and his young bride. When she felt sure her husband wasn't watching, she gave Mark a sultry wink. *Oh, for fuck's sake*, he thought to himself, *this is going to be one long trip*.

***

The Division Commander pored over his remote Command and Control station, looking as if he'd taken a giant bite out of a lemon. No matter how many times he looked at it, the situation appeared no clearer to him. He'd even sat with the chaplain to pray with him, hoping the answer would come, but it didn't. What presented itself to him were a number of unpalatable options, none of which filled him with any level of confidence.

Though he did put on a good act in front of his deputies and the staff. The only person he truly confided in, was his

Command Sergeant Major. That was the one person in the whole world he would open up to, relying on the man's experience and judgment to help guide his decision-making. At that moment, Command Sergeant Major Rick Gifford sat quietly, giving his commander a concerned look.

"I don't know, Rick. What do you think? Am I looking at this thing the right way?" Major General Bud Napier rubbed his eyes, doing little to alleviate the darkened circles beneath them.

"You know what I think. I have complete faith in you. You know I would follow you to Hell and back." The Sergeant Major locked gaze with him, his expression as somber as a State Funeral.

"Not looking for your confidence, Rick. I'm asking for your opinion."

There weren't any other soldiers around to hear their conversation, so as was their custom, the Sergeant Major and the General addressed each other by their first names. A practice they would never repeat in front of anyone else, even their spouses. "If you're asking my opinion, Bud, then I'll give it to you."

"Please."

"The quickest route is straight west, toward Denver. Then hook north to Cheyenne and then continue on." Gifford paused for his commander to respond.

"But we've got two problems. First, the shortest route has us crossing the length of Kansas. After that idiot Brigade Commander of mine shot his way through a sleepy Kansas town, the governor has ordered all of us federal troops out and we've already missed his deadline. Second, there are few places to stop for resupply in western Kansas." Napier trailed off, staring at the electronic image projected on his screen, hoping the answer would pop up at him.

"Then we stick with the plan then. Go straight north to Nebraska. It gets us out of Kansas faster and provides us more places to stop for resupply once we start heading west."

"That's going to add at least an additional 150 miles to our trip and at least a day of travel time. With the food and fuel situation, I'm not comfortable adding that kind of distance to our journey."

"Well, what choice do we have?"

The General looked up from his screen at his Command Sergeant Major. "None I guess."

"Then it's time to take our first bite of this shit sandwich and smile."

***

It took hours sitting in the assembly area before Lieutenant Baker got the green light to move Bravo Company. The Aviation Brigade had gone first conducting aerial recon, providing excellent reports back to headquarters. These reports were in turn used by the reconnaissance squadrons who ran screening operations to the front and flanks of the Division's primary route. After that, 1st Brigade took position as the lead maneuver formation, then the civilian convoys fell in after that. By the time 2nd Brigade got permission to move, it was already mid-afternoon. When they'd first lined up to move, the mood among them was electric, but after a couple of hours boredom settled in, and while it may have been September now, the oppressively hot and humid weather still managed to smother them like a heavy, wet blanket.

Things were proceeding in an orderly and disciplined manner, though incidents continued to occur that set them further and further behind their established timetables. The most significant of which was when they found that one of the bridges they intended to cross could not support the weight of their heavy tracked vehicles and they spent hours getting engineer assets forward to erect hasty ones, allowing them to proceed. Meanwhile the Division strung itself out over a distance of seventy miles from beginning to end, with the sudden starts and stops at the lead formations creating a massive accordion-effect in the rear. This did nothing to help already short tempers.

Out front, the aviators identified towns along the route heading north still populated by living people, those that appeared empty and some overrun by the dead. They dropped leaflets onto the towns with survivors in them, telling them that the Army was coming through and not to interfere. This worked well enough and those citizens still out there in their rural communities along the way watched quietly as the military passed through, doing absolutely nothing to interfere. In the small towns and villages consumed by the infected, the mechanized troops simply stayed mounted on their vehicles and passed them by, carefully conserving their ammunition, only shooting the creatures down when absolutely necessary.

Throughout it all, reports kept coming in of Kansas National Guard units shadowing them as the Divisions subordinate elements pushed north. The guardsmen stayed at a healthy distance away, following and presumably reporting the movements of the Division back to their state headquarters in Topeka. They offered no resistance while at the same time making no effort to directly communicate or help the federal troops. It was an uneasy truce, but a truce nonetheless.

Bravo Company finally started out sometime after 1500 hours, with at least 150 miles to cover. In a civilian automobile driving on the highway, one could cover that distance in two and-a-half hours easily. In a military convoy with tracked vehicles, that distance would be an eight-hour endeavor, assuming nothing went wrong. Which was always a bad assumption. Murphy's Law has great power in the military.

The company rolled out, moving along in the center of 2nd Battalion's formation. Once again they witnessed acre after acre of untended crops, passing through the occasional rural community. Along the way they saw few of the undead, at least none that posed any threat to them. A handful had come out to greet the lead elements only to get mashed under steel treads. Their flattened and smeared remains baked on the hot asphalt, drawing in the turkey vultures and the flies. Somehow the birds and other carrion feeders were immune to the virus, which was nice. Nobody felt interested in finding out what a zombie-buzzard was like.

After five hours the column passed a sign that read "Nebraska… the good life," indicating that they'd finally put Kansas behind them. Not that their surroundings appeared any different, it was still flat farm country as far as the eye could see.

Even though things looked pretty much the same, a certain level of tension dropped the minute they crossed over and everyone relaxed a bit. Even the air seemed to smell a little sweeter.

***

7 September, 2016
Tactical Assembly Area Dagger
Ten Miles South of Lincoln, Nebraska
0545 Hours Local

"Are you awake?" The disembodied voice tore Mark from his slumber. He'd been dreaming about his childhood home in Ohio and of his high school sweetheart he left behind. It was a happy dream with him and the girl whom he called Tish. He should have married her instead of the woman he ended up tying the knot with, but that was water under the bridge now. Still, he didn't want the dream to end, but some jerk insisted that he wake up.

"What is it?" He grumbled, not bothering to cover up his annoyance. When he opened his eyes he found himself looking up at Deputy Darin Jefferson. Dressed the way he was, you couldn't tell the difference between him or any of the actual soldiers in the platoon. Not that it mattered much these days.

"The lieutenant says he needs to speak with you. Over at his tank."

"So, what else is new?" Mark sat up and yawned, lowering the poncho liner into his lap. "Thanks, Jefferson."

"You bet." The former sheriff's deputy didn't linger, stepping back off into the pre-dawn gloom. There wasn't a star in the sky and it was fully overcast.

Mark stood up and tossed his field blanket on top of the air mattress he'd laid out on the ground. They'd pulled into the assembly area after midnight, the road march taking a brutally long time and he elected to curl up next to *BOHICA* to sleep under the stars rather than take the time to erect a tent. Most of the others had done the same. Though by the looks of things they got lucky they hadn't been rained on yet. He could smell it in the air though and knew they were in for some morning showers. A dull rumble of thunder in the distance seemed to confirm that.

They'd set up the Brigade assembly area in a massive cornfield and because the stalks were so tall one needed to be fully mounted to see over top. Luckily the company parked close and tight to each other, so it was simple to find the command post and the other platoons.

He yawned again and scratched the back of his neck,

trudging up the line toward the lieutenant's tank. He was particularly easy to find since he was smoking and Mark merely needed to zero in on the glowing cherry sticking out brightly in the dark.

"You needed to see me, sir?"

"Yeah, Sergeant Matthews, good morning." Baker's voice croaked. He sounded as if he'd not gotten any sleep at all the previous night, which might have been true. After they'd set in for the night he'd been called off to Battalion for a briefing. That was just over four hours ago. "We got a FRAGO from Brigade last night. There's a change of mission. We're going into the city to top up on supplies."

Mark fished a notebook out of a cargo pocket along with an ink pen. "I thought we were good for at least three days, sir. We've only traveled for one. We don't need to begin foraging yet. This will just slow us down."

"It's the weather." Baker pointed up to the sky. A brilliant flash lit up the clouds in the distance. "The entire Aviation Brigade is grounded until this storm front blows over. Division doesn't want to move without air recon out front and on the flanks, so since we're not going anywhere, we've been ordered to top up on fuel, water and food. Your platoon is getting sliced over to the Brigade Support Battalion to assist them today as they head into the city of Lincoln."

"The people of the great state of Kansas weren't so wild about us rolling into town and just taking shit, El-Tee. Is Brigade saying that Nebraska is different?" Mark was startled by the sound of a loud fart near his head. When he looked up, he realized it was Yokey, sound asleep on the back deck of the tank.

"Probably not, but our drones confirmed late yesterday that the city is one giant hot zone. The place is completely infected. So nobody's going to put up much of a fuss about us taking what we need."

"How do we plan to do this without air support? We learned a long time ago that it's unwise to do any sort of operations in the hot zones without the helicopters drawing the dead away with the noise and providing direct fire support. With the birds grounded, we'll be in there without any kind of support. Including emergency extraction." The more Mark thought about this, the worse the idea sounded. "I feel like we're rushing to failure. Why can't we wait until the weather blows over, then go in there properly?"

"Because time is against us. Transport trucks are the biggest weakness in the Division. They literally loaded every cargo truck up with JP-8 and food. Nothing else. We might be able to sit here and wait for the weather to blow over without burning any fuel, but I'm told from my buddy up at Brigade that we'll be out of food in thirty-six hours. Tops." Baker took a drag on his cigarette, drawing it down to the filter before dropping it to the ground and grinding it out with the heel of his boot. "That's why they're in a hurry. We gotta get moving right away. The longer we linger, the worse the food situation gets. The fact that we're bringing along thousands of hungry camp followers is *not* making the situation any better."

"Well, sir. I could be mistaken, but we seem to be surrounded by corn. I think we could eat some of this perhaps." Mark walked over a few feet and snapped off an ear.

"Yeah, we already thought of that. We could grab as much as we like, but without large-scale farming equipment it would take forever to harvest the stuff. We'd literally be doing it by hand. Then there's the storage issue. While we could use this to supplement our rations in the near term while we're here, this wouldn't be a solution for moving us down the road. No, we need the pre-packaged food and we need it in bulk."

"Okay, sir. I get it. When do we move out?"

"Two hours. Look, there's more."

"Yeah?"

"Every one of these trucks is precious. We can't afford to lose a single HEMMT fueler. Not one. Those things are our lifeline and without them, we're walking to Washington. I don't even want to think about that. Also, we're not getting resupplied on ammunition either, so don't be getting trigger-happy out there. Understood?"

"Yes, sir."

"Excellent. Good luck then. See you when you get back."

Chapter 8

7 September, 2016
Lincoln, Nebraska
0825 Hours Local

The small convoy consisted of 2nd Platoon's last-remaining Bradley Fighting Vehicle, an M88 recovery vehicle and two HEMMT fuel trucks. The dismounts mostly rode on top of the tracks which took the lead, while the fuelers brought up the rear. They'd been driving on US 77 North and were on the southwest side of the city when they spotted something of interest.

Mark toggled the intercom on his crewman's helmet. "Is that what I think it is?"

"Looks like it," Donahue responded.

Up ahead on the side of the highway stood an exit sign with Shell gas station marking on it. "Okay, Burbey, pull off up ahead." As they proceeded, he saw the giant sign over the service station looming up ahead.

They turned into the exit and the three trail vehicles followed them in, giving *BOHICA* some space. Cautiously, they pulled into the truck stop, parking off to the eastern side, careful not to get too close to the building. It was your standard setup with rows of pumps for cars and 18-wheelers, with the main building housing the store and a Subway sandwich shop.

Mark transmitted over the radio once they were set. "Okay, shut 'em down."

While the drivers turned off their engines, the grunts hopped down onto the ground and instinctively fanned out, quickly establishing a security perimeter around their precious vehicles. Mark ditched his crew helmet, swapping it out with a ballistic one, before climbing down from the turret himself.

The fuel-handlers wasted no time and began opening up the access covers to the underground fuel storage tanks. Each of the HEMMT refueler trucks was equipped with pumps to suck fuel out of tanks such as these, so they'd make short work of it once they got the equipment up and running.

They were still on the outer-ring road, sitting on the outer fringes of the city. They had no desire to go into that urban nightmare if they could avoid it, and finding a truck stop on the highway seemed like a tremendous stroke of luck.

Mark studied the main building, unable to see anything inside past the dust-covered windows. Overhead, the clouds got even darker and the first fat drops of rain began to patter on the ground around them.

Harris walked up to him, cradling a light machine gun. "You're not actually thinking about going in there are you?"

"I was." Mark continued studying the structure, seeing if he could identify all the entrances and exits.

"We're just here for the diesel, Sarn't. I don't think it's worth the risk of going inside for a bag of beef jerky or a can of Coke. Especially in broad daylight."

"That doesn't sound all bad. I could really go for some beef jerky right about now, but seriously, it'll be fine." He looked over and saw Angie petting Saxon right next to a couple of the others. "Johnson, Dubois, on me. Angie, you and Saxon too."

Angie wore a camouflaged poncho to try and keep dry. "Is this really necessary? I thought we were just here for the diesel."

Mark sighed, trying not to let himself get agitated. "Yes, it's necessary. Now get ready, please."

Johnson reached into his shirt and produced a Mjölnir pendant, kissing it before stuffing it back down his collar. Angie nodded and adjusted the dog's leash to a more appropriate length.

"Mark, I think you need to see something." From behind, Clay came walking over, with Mini-14 in hand. He had the hood of his rain jacket pulled up over his head, with the sides cinched down in anticipation of the inevitable rain.

"What's up?" he said simply, watching him approach.

"Look at that over there." Next to the truck stop was a small traffic circle, a common sight in the Midwest where power outages could knock out traffic lights for extended periods of time. They seemed particularly useful in the zombie apocalypse, if one desired to use the roads that is. On the opposite side of it no more than a few hundred yards away were giant fuel storage tanks, standing over ten meters high, with the sign "Phillips 66 Terminal" at the entrance.

"Now, how in the hell did we miss that driving up?"

"Don't know, you want me to check it out?" The heavy raindrops made a loud pattering sound on Clay's jacket and another dull crack of thunder resounded overhead.

"Yeah, take one of the fuelers over while we check out the inside of the truck stop."

"Will do."

"Okay," he said, turning to his hastily-assembled room clearance team. "Let's get this done."

They moved toward the front door of the blacked-out business, allowing Angie and Saxon to take the lead. Dubois executed an overly theatrical spin with the machete he borrowed from Weber, swishing it around as if he were Conan the Barbarian. Mark watched him with morbid curiosity, admiring the soldier's enthusiasm, which made up for any real martial talent with the edged weapon. Next to him Johnson stood holding a sledgehammer with both hands, rifle slung across his back. He could tell the two of them were already mentally checked out, totally in character, acting out one of their D&D fantasies. Not that anyone cared, the two role-playing nerds were particularly effective taking out Zulus when they were "in the zone." It just made everyone cringe when they started referring to each other by their character's names. It was just plain weird.

Angie brought the German Shepherd to the door and lowered his large snout to its base, giving it a good sniff. They all waited patiently, getting pelted with fat drops of rain while the dog did his business. After about a minute of this Saxon looked up at Angie, opening his maw and letting his tongue hang out. The hairy beast did not alert, so that was a good sign.

Mark signaled to Angie and she pulled the dog back and out of the way, making room for him. He pushed the glass door open with a loud scrape and he went inside, flicking on the flashlight mounted to the end of his recently-acquired shotgun. It was a police model Remington 11-87 semi-auto with an 18-inch barrel. Short enough for close-in work, but long enough to retain a decent magazine capacity.

Upon entering the gloom the stench of rotting meat hit him in the face like a freight train. It was so strong and concentrated he instantly retched, nearly voiding the contents of his stomach. The sound he made echoed off the walls and its volume caused Dubois and Johnson to pause for a moment before joining him inside. Reluctantly Angie and Saxon came in too, pulling up the rear.

"Oh my god. I got the stink in my mouth," Angie gagged.

Other flashlights flicked on and the beams swept the room from the outer walls, working their way in. The layout inside was typical of a facility such as this, with a convenience store section connected to the sandwich restaurant off to the side. The place was divided by aisles of display racks which still held an assortment of items, all covered in a layer of dust.

The automotive section still had racks filled with mundane items such as windshield wiper fluid, quarts of oil and air fresheners. Those sorts of items remained relatively untouched, while the racks set aside for fast food items were completely empty. Someone had gone through there already and cleaned out all the food, down to the last stick of chewing gum. The refrigerators were mostly empty too, except for containers full of spoiled milk and other perishable items.

Mark saw something on the floor and shined his light on, immediately wishing he hadn't. It was a human shape in the advanced stages of decay, swarming with maggots. He looked away only to spot another couple of others off in the corner, splayed out on the tile floor, leaking a terrible-looking liquid everywhere.

"Well, that explains the smell," Johnson said needlessly.

"Ya think?" Angie shot back, covering her nose and mouth with a rag.

"This place looks like it's been picked clean, Sarn't." Dubois looked at him hopefully.

"We need to check the back. They might have left something behind we can use." Mark didn't feel like investigating any further, but they sometimes found hidden gems in places they thought were already picked over. You never knew until you gave a place a thorough search. "Let's get to it. We're burning daylight."

***

The team emerged outside into the driving downpour, hammering the earth worse than it had when they'd entered the building. They all immediately dropped the rags and other face coverings, gulping in lungfuls of clean, unviolated air. They'd all been in places like this many times before and it never got any easier to deal with. Even the dog's mood seemed to perk up.

Clay greeted them outside, with the hood of his jacket cinched up as tight as it would go. The only thing visible were his two eyeballs inside. "Find anything useful in there?"

"We found some roadmaps which will come in handy. Other than that, all we found were a few quarts of 10W30. How about you guys?" Mark couldn't help noticing that the clouds seemed darker and more menacing than before.

"Nothing out here either. There's not a drop of gasoline or diesel left. Somebody came through here and emptied out these tanks awhile ago." Clay sounded crestfallen.

"We shouldn't be surprised. Everything outside of the city that's not overrun with the dead has probably been scavenged already by survivors. If we hope to find anything useful, we've got to go into the Hot Zone."

Clay paused before responding. "Mark, we can't go into the city by ourselves. That place is completely overrun. We need to go in with proper support. If we go in there foraging, we might get cut off and stuck without any help. We'd be as good as dead."

"Sergeant Matthews, the El-Tee needs to speak with you!" Donahue stood in the gunner's hatch of *BOHICA*, holding the radio hand mike in hand, waving it overhead. "He says it's urgent!"

"Be back in a minute." Mark jogged over and climbed up the side of the track, taking the handset from his gunner who looked as if he'd seen a ghost. "Battle Axe Six, this is White One Actual."

"White One, this is Six. We have a massive tornado inbound. You need to seek shelter immediately! You need to get your people in a basement right now! *Acknowledge!*"

Mark looked up at the sky that continued to dump on them by the bucketful. The skies were already dark, but the clouds approaching on the horizon appeared nearly black, except for the streaks of lightning that continued to illuminate the weather front like massive flashbulbs. It looked downright menacing and coming on entirely too fast. He looked around them and the truck stop sat in the middle of a cluster of small businesses, but none of them appeared to have anything like a basement.

They needed to get out of there. Right now.

He cupped his hands around his mouth before shouting to the others. "Everybody mount up! We're getting the hell out of here! *Follow me!*"

***

According to the road map, the southwest edge of Lincoln lay only a couple of miles away. There was a suburban neighborhood with dozens of houses and there were likely plenty of basements there. In the Midwest where tornadoes were a common occurrence, most homes had them and many even had reinforced safe rooms installed inside. That was what Mark was banking on as they raced along the road, all of them taking a look at the angry weather bearing down on them.

He pushed as fast he dared, knowing that the slowest vehicle in their small convoy was the M-88 recovery vehicle. It may have been powerful, but it couldn't manage to go very fast. He thought about leaving them behind and telling them to button up and ride this thing out, but he wasn't too keen on leaving people alone to fend for themselves. Plus, half his infantry rode in that beast and he'd have to take precious time to transfer them over or leave them too, and he sure wasn't excited about that idea either. Worse, the HEMMT refuelers were totally vulnerable in this weather and he needed to get those people to safety as well.

The rain came down in fat drops, pelting them relentlessly.

The lightning flashed and the thunder boomed while the sky grew darker and the wind began to pick up. As much as he wanted to, Mark fought the urge to tell Burbey to drive faster. Up ahead, houses came into view, all of them lined up in quiet, dark, rows. Eventually they made it to the nearest one as the wind began to howl like a wounded animal.

They came up from the backside, leaving the road and cutting cross-country. The yards were enclosed with tall wooden fences, which *BOHICA* flattened under its tracks with no effort at all. The M-88 bringing up the rear did the same, knocking down the wooden pickets in the adjacent yards as well.

Mark picked up his handset and keyed on their platoon internal frequency. "Everyone dismount, right now! Haul ass!"

He tore off his combat crewman's helmet and climbed out of the hatch, jumping off the side of the track, landing among the rest of the infantry who were doing the same. Men and women poured out of their vehicles and they scattered, headed toward the nearest row of houses.

Coming up to the closest residence, Mark stopped in front of a large sliding-glass door. He flinched when Johnson tossed a sledgehammer through it, reducing it to jagged shards that went crashing to the ground. Soldiers went dashing inside, running as fast as their feet could carry them. They fanned out and the disorganized group raced inside of the three nearest homes, in no particular order or organization. It was every man and woman for themselves.

Mark followed behind a disorganized mob, headed straight into the blackness. Instinctively, weapons lights flicked on, bobbing and weaving along the walls. Images of family photos and nicknacks flashed past intermixed with panicked voices calling out to each other. Men and women fled in different directions throughout the house, looking for the entrance to the basement. It didn't take long before a voice cried out, "It's here, this way!" followed up by the stomping of boots headed downstairs.

Right about then, Mark realized that he had completely lost control of the situation and was just along for the ride. He also figured out that he'd left his rifle and shotgun aboard the Bradley. He didn't have his night vision goggles or a flashlight either. All he could do was follow the others downstairs, barely able to see.

The moment the last of them got down inside the sound of the wind upstairs picked up even more until it sounded like a freight train, roaring overhead.

"Everybody down!" another voice called out, and the group of them hit the deck. Most of them buried their faces into the cold concrete floor, wrapping arms over their heads. No one said another word as the deafening sound rumbled overhead and the floor began to vibrate.

Not knowing what else to do, Mark said a prayer aloud, which nobody else heard with the sound of the wind howling in their ears.

***

Almost as quickly as it had consumed them, the sound of freight train—more like a dozen freight trains—completely subsided. Mark took a moment to collect himself, still on his belly and not sure whether or not to take his arms away from protecting his head, but he reluctantly did so, feeling his heart thumping in his chest. It became eerily silent until someone shrieked at the top of their lungs.

"Get it off! *Get it off!*"

Flashlight beams danced around the darkened room until

several of them settled on two figures in the corner. Jimmy Hong lay on the floor like the rest of them, but something else had fallen on him, something that used to be human. The stinking creature sat on the soldier's back, its jaws solidly clamped down on Jimmy's shoulder.

"Dear God!" someone shouted out, "Hang on, Jimmy!"

The two of them thrashed around on the cold, concrete floor while people picked themselves up and charged forward. Mark did too, drawing his pistol from its holster, following a few of the others with their weapon-mounted flashlights.

"Hold your fire!" Mark shouted, grabbing the shoulder of the nearest soldier with a weapon light. "Who's this?"

"It's me, Harris, Sarn't."

"Good, keep your light on them." Mark turned to face the other half-dozen beams of light, unable to make out faces in the dark. "The rest of you face about and watch our backs, in case there are more of these things in here with us." Without waiting for a response, he swallowed hard and ran forward, drawing his right leg back and letting fly like an NFL kicker, his boot connecting with the monster's temple.

The blow landed solidly and the jaws came loose from Jimmy's shoulder. The thing still held on tightly to the young soldier, but looked straight up at Mark with its glowing-red eyes and hissed at him. The sound made his blood run cold and he nearly froze in his tracks. He shook off the paralyzing fear and brought the 9mm semi-automatic up and started popping off rounds. The first bullets struck the beast in the chest, but he walked them up in rapid succession until one slammed into the thing's mouth, blowing out its brainstem and spattering it against the wall. It collapsed to the floor with a wet slap.

Mark held the weapon in his hand for a long few seconds, the smell of burnt gunpowder now discernable from that of rotting meat, if just barely. He took a deep breath, barely aware of the stink. "Jimmy, are you okay?"

He rolled away from the now, very dead corpse and jumped to his feet. "I don't know, holy shit, it hurts. God help me, please tell me I'm alright." Hong's voice trembled as he spoke.

Mark turned to the members of the team focused behind them. "How we looking back there? Any more of them?"

"No. We're clear, Sarn't," Burbey said.

"Fine. Watch the staircase in case something else decides to come down here and join us."

"Roger that."

"Harris, keep your light on Hong."

"Wilco."

Mark holstered the handgun and went forward, putting his hand on Jimmy's untouched shoulder. "Look at me, Jimmy." The soldier did as he was told, with tears welling up in his eyes. There seemed to be no contaminant bodily fluids on the kid's face, so the NCO went to the next logical thing. "Strip off your combat harness and your shirts."

Jimmy complied and stood there, half-naked. It was still relatively warm in there, but he shook like a leaf.

Upon inspection, the skin covering the muscle near the base of his neck on the left side was red. Thankfully the skin was intact and while there'd be one nasty bruise there, but he showed no evidence of any external wound.

Mark picked up the combat harness and put it up to the light. The infected creature had bitten down on the heavy, padded shoulder strap. There were teeth marks on it, and the kit had oily red goop smeared all over. If it had bitten Jimmy a few inches to the left, it would have cut through the thinner fabric of his shirt and left a fatal wound.

"Good news, Jimmy. It looks like it's your lucky day."

"I don't feel all that lucky, Sarn't."

"Trust me, you are. Now put your shit back on." Mark turned to the other blackened figures behind them, sweeping their lights from corner to corner in the basement. "Okay, who else is here? Sound off."

"Harris, Sarn't."

"Burbey here."

"Donahue is up."

"Devons, over here, Sarn't."

"It's Swanson, I'm up, Sarn't."

Mark did some mental math. There were seven of them there. With the fuelers and mechanics, he'd brought a total of twenty-four personnel and one mean dog. "We need to get accountability and we need to do it now. Did anyone see where the others went?"

"People jumped off the vehicles and scattered. I saw some go into the neighboring houses," Harris said, his light still shining on Jimmy.

"Okay, let's go police up the others." Burbey and Donahue, you take point. Harris you take up the rear." A cold lump formed in Mark's stomach as he thought about the rest of his people. He'd lost control of them up top and now they were scattered. It was his fault but he didn't have time to feel sorry for himself. There'd be plenty of time for that later.

They stacked up like they always did and went back up the stairs, weapons up and scanning their assigned sectors of fire. When they got to the top Burbey put his hand on the doorknob and looked at Donahue. His buddy nodded, signaling he was ready. The knob turned and the soldier leaned into the door but it did not budge. "Something's blocking the door from the other side."

"Well, that's the only way out, so do something about it." Mark didn't want to get frustrated, but his nerves were frayed and he struggled to keep his temper in check. "Put your back into it!"

"Move out of the way, skinny." Donahue gently pushed Burbey to the side and out of the way. "Watch how the big Irishman gets it done."

"No dogs, no Irish. That's what I always say," Burbey quipped, moving out of the way and giving his friend some room.

Donahue slung his weapon across his back and then prepared himself before crashing into the door with his shoulder. The six-foot two-inch, 220-pound soldier didn't even bother to turn the knob, electing to use brute force and ignorance, and when he made contact, he smashed through it, ripping it from its frame, sending him tumbling through.

He fell flat on his face after splintering the door and he put his palms on the ground, pushing himself up. When he did, he found himself staring at a pair of shoes in front of his face. He looked up to see someone standing there looking down at him and immediately did not like what he saw. One of the infected stood there looking down at him with its horrible red eyes, spider-webbed face and snarling teeth, cracked and oozing an oily saliva. It growled and then lunged at him before he could get up.

A loud crack thundered and the creature's head exploded, sending it falling flat on its back.

Burbey and the rest came stomping up the stairs and out of the basement, stepping over Donahue. They came out with weapons shouldered, fanning out in opposite directions. All except for Mark, who only possessed his handgun, which he held at the ready.

Emerging back into the light, they found the entire backside of the house completely gone, torn away in the storm. Bits of lumber, electrical wiring, insulation and other detritus hung limply like shreds of meat, still flapping in the wind.

They wasted no time getting out of the damaged house, running back outside. It still rained, but darkness began to subside and it became brighter. They could see the storm moving on from them, leaving a tortured and torn world in its wake.

In the yard they found everything littered with debris. Telephone poles were shattered and torn like matchsticks, while metal siding hung from drooping electrical lines. Homes in the neighborhood looked as if they'd be blown to smithereens by a succession of JDAMs. They found themselves on the edge of track, a trail of destruction left behind by the extraordinary power of nature.

Sitting there in front of them like monoliths were the Bradley Fighting Vehicle and the M-88. Conspicuously missing were the two HEMMT fuel trucks they had left in between the two.

"Where did the fuel trucks go?" asked Swanson, looking mesmerized, staring at the spot where the two large trucks once sat.

"Over there," Harris replied, pointing off to their right. Nearly a hundred yards away were both of them, laying on their sides, one folded in half as if its spine were cracked.

"Shit." Harris lowered his rifle in a dejected manner. "The tornado picked those big fuckers up and tossed them over there like newspapers in a wind tunnel."

"Except it couldn't move the tracked vehicles," Devons said, pointing at *BOHICA* and the recovery vehicle.

"Yeah, maybe it didn't blow them away, but everything strapped to the sides of them has been stripped off." Burbey pointed his carbine at the sides of the armored vehicles where their duffel bags and rucksacks once hung on the outer skin. Now all of it lay stripped bare.

"It's worse than that, brother," Donahue interjected. "Look

at the antennas."

Mark looked up at them and he shook his head. "The wind sheared them away. I guess we won't be calling Company or Battalion on the radio any time soon."

They all turned their heads in unison at the muffled sound of a dog barking. It came from underneath a pile of rubble that had once been the neighboring house.

"That's Saxon! Come on, give me a hand!" Mark dashed over to the crumpled pile of lumber, drywall, plywood and shingles. He began grabbing the wreckage and tossing it aside and the others watched him for a moment before jumping in and lending a hand, working at a feverish pace. "Devons, Swanson, you two pull security. Keep an eye out!"

The dog continued to bark beneath all the mess and the rain kept pattering down on them while they worked. It didn't take long before they heard the muted sounds of shouts from down below.

"We're coming for you, hang on!" Harris shouted back.

"Quiet, damn you. *Keep your voice down*," Mark hissed. His eyes burned at Harris before turning his attention back to the task at hand.

They tossed broken lumber and other ruined construction materials like mad, working in a frenzy. All the houses in this suburban sprawl were of similar design, so they had a good idea where the entrance to the basement was. They ignored the twisted nails and broken glass, focused on getting their comrades free, listening to their muted pleas for help.

"Umm... guys... we got a problem." Devons' voice squeaked at a higher pitch than normal.

"No shit, we're busy here." Mark was so focused on clearing the mess away, he couldn't think. It took him a moment to register what Devons was trying to say. "Wait, what is it?"

Devons pointed over a couple hundred yards away. "Over there, Sarn't."

They all looked up to see movement between the other single-family homes. Some of it seemed slow, while other shapes flashed past the gaps between the houses.

"Goddammit," Mark whispered to himself. "Where are the machetes and other melee weapons?"

Before anyone could answer, Swanson cracked off two shots, followed up by another.

"Dammit, Swanson! You're going to draw them in!" Mark felt his chest tighten.

Swanson squeezed off another couple of shots and a figure nearby crumpled to the ground. "Sorry, Sergeant, but they've seen us already."

Devons squeezed off a round. "We've got runners!"

"Shit!" Mark glanced up and saw movement all over the place. Most of it appeared slow, but there were enough fast-movers to raise the hairs on the back of his neck. The temptation to pull everyone off wreckage to engage the incoming threat flashed through his mind, but he resisted it. They needed to get their trapped people from underneath the wreckage. If he could do that, then they'd have more shooters and more options. If he stopped trying to free them, the handful of people he had with him would quickly be overwhelmed and they'd have to break contact, leaving the others behind, buried alive. That was simply not an option.

"Work faster you guys, get the lead out!" Saxon continued his frantic barking from underneath their feet while they struggled to get the mess cleared away. Devons and Swanson's rate of fire gradually began to pick up and it became impossible to ignore all of the dead that were drawn in by all the racket. The runners started getting so close that the two riflemen fired in bursts, now having to take turns covering for the other while he reloaded.

Mark noticed Swanson had his M320 grenade launcher affixed underneath the barrel of his M4 carbine. "Swanson, use the grenade launcher. Fire it behind the Zulus off in the distance!"

"Are you sure, Sarn't? The rounds will land somewhere in those houses. I can't see where the rounds will land and I'll just be wasting ammo."

"Just do it!"

"Roger." Swanson flipped the safety catch off and raised the launcher up to a forty-five degree angle, then let one fly with an audible "thump." The grenade arced high, sailing over the roofs of the nearest homes, landing outside their line of sight, detonating with a loud "crack."

"Good, keep doing it until you're out of rounds!" Mark grabbed hold of the kitchen's island that had been ripped out at its base with the intact stainless steel sink still inside, trying to drag it off the pile of junk. "Donahue, give me a hand with this."

Devons began laying the rifle fire on quick, snap-firing at the growing crowd of infected that continued coming on. Luckily most were only able to walk or shamble, but the few runners presented them with a terrifying problem. Still, with the number of walkers increasing, he wouldn't be able to hold them off for long either. "Sarn't I need some more help over here, there's too many for me to handle!"

Swanson let fly with another grenade, and then another after that. The steady stream of explosions behind the crowd of infected began to distract them and many turned around, headed to the sound of the small detonations. The grenadier figured out what was happening and fished another 40mm shell from his harness, popping it into the launcher's breach. "It's working, Sarn't. Some of them are getting distracted!"

Mark knew that it wouldn't fool all of them and even if it did, Swanson didn't have an unlimited supply of M320 ammo on hand, but it would buy them a little time.

Donahue grunted and the junk broke free, rolling off to the side onto the back patio, currently buried in crap. Then, some carpet and broken 2x4s bulged up like a magma bubble from below and flipped over. People immediately came up and out from below, emerging into the light rain. Gray, Weber and McDermott came boiling out, followed up by Angie and Saxon.

"Everybody up on the perimeter, let's go!" Mark pointed to Devons and Swanson who were holding back the tide. Only now Swanson kept feeling around his pouches in vain, looking for more grenades for his launcher.

They came running out of their subterranean prison and as each one emerged, Mark slapped them on the shoulder and counted them out. Some of them were his from 2nd Platoon, others were a mix of mechanics and fuel handlers. When the last of them came up he did the mental math. *That's only sixteen total, where are the rest?* He thought to himself. He saw the medic nearby, racking a round into the chamber of her weapon. "Bags, where's everyone else?"

She had the look of a cornered animal and without saying a word, simply pointed over to the next house along the line, totally flattened just as theirs had been.

There were eight still missing, buried underneath the rubble of the next house on the block. Then it hit Mark… Clay wasn't there. He must have been in that mess. "Where the fuck is Clay?"

Bags shrugged her shoulders. "I don't know, Sergeant. I have no idea."

The rifle shots really began to pick up and a couple of SAWs joined in. Without grenades to distract them, the dead came from everywhere, only coming into sight as they cleared the last row of houses across the street. The walkers and shamblers came through the open corridor the tornado had opened up, while the more intelligent runners used the still-standing structures for cover, only emerging when nearly on top of the soldiers.

"Harris, Hong, Burbey and Donahue—on me! The rest of you keep them back!"

The fire picked up while the five men darted off to the next mess along the line, immediately tossing away the loose stuff, digging into it as fast as they could. They hadn't cleared much away before a scream sounded from behind them. They looked over to see Devons on his back with a runner on top of him. The soldier pushed the thing's shoulders back to keep the snapping jaws away, but it clawed at the young man's face, causing him to cry out in pain.

Swanson pressed the muzzle of his carbine against the zombie's temple and pulled the trigger, sending chunks of skull and rotted brains flying into the tall, uncut grass. Mark watched him help his buddy back to his feet, handing over a rifle and the two of them went immediately back into action.

"Come on, faster!" Mark worked feverishly, egging on the others. Then he heard shouts from under their feet and they redoubled their efforts. Still, he kept glancing up at the growing crowd of the dead, drawing in closer and closer. The platoon members set up a hasty perimeter and the volume of fire continued to crescendo, dropping bodies left and right. It made little difference and they kept coming on in even greater numbers.

Bags fired her weapon until the bolt locked to the rear. She dropped the empty magazine and struggled to free a fresh one from her web gear. "Sergeant Matthews, we can't keep this up for much longer. We need to get out of here while we still can!"

Mark grunted and tossed away a shattered board. "Fuck this." He looked over to his crew. "Burbey, Donahue, on me!" He broke away from the flattened home and ran toward *BOHICA*, climbing up the front armored slope, then dropping himself into the turret. As instructed, the two other men followed close behind, taking their positions.

Burbey wasted no time firing up the engine while Donahue flipped the turret power on, illuminating the control panel. The driver's hatch came down with a loud "thunk" and Mark slipped on the combat crewman's helmet over his ears before toggling the intercom. "Driver, you up?"

"Roger, Sarn't."

He found the Remington 11-87 shotgun right where he'd left it. He pulled it up and worked the charging handle and racked a shell into the chamber. "Move out, head toward the Zulus and start running them down. Get the ones closest to our people."

"Wilco." Burbey put the vehicle into gear and slammed his foot down on the accelerator. He drove past the M-88 and then took a hard right, taking a wide loop around the thin perimeter of soldiers, desperately holding the line. Within moments they were on top of the nearest of the dead, rolling over them without slowing their pace. Most of them were coming down the corridor the funnel cloud had cleared through the suburban neighborhood, so the Bradley crew focused their efforts there, electing to leave the intact houses and fences alone, to provide some barrier protecting their friends.

While the Infantry Fighting Vehicle rolled through the corridor channeling the majority of the undead toward their people, the small arms fire slackened. The IFV rolled dozens of them under its steel tracks and this bought the dismounts some respite.

A few of the runners jumped up onto the engine compartment, clawing their way up. Mark brought the shotgun into action, knocking them off the vehicle, sending them tumbling back down. With each trigger pull he'd send another empty hull flying, ejected from the semi-auto's heavy bolt. With a seven-round tube magazine on the weapon, he found himself constantly stuffing fresh shells into the feed ramp, but he did so without complaint, satisfied with the result.

Several members of the platoon peeled off and lent a hand digging through the pile of junk, while a few remained to pick off the runners. Mark then gave orders to Burbey, running down the infected who came on with singular focus.

"You want me to light a few of them up?" asked Donahue?

"No, wait for my command. We don't need to waste any ammo." Mark fed a few more shells into the ramp of his shotgun, craning his neck to find more targets. When he looked back over his shoulder, he saw Angie and a few of the others frantically waving to him. They'd opened up the third basement and the last of their trapped comrades were coming out of the ground like an anthill that'd been kicked over. "Time to go boys, turn this beast around."

The Bradley whipped around and came barreling back toward the others who wasted no time getting out of the way. It came through their hasty perimeter and then stopped about twenty yards to the rear, with the ramp dropping to the ground.

Mark tried to count heads but things moved far too swiftly with people running around in every direction. The dead kept coming, their numbers rolling in like an unstoppable tide. Weapons barked and some of the creatures fell, but there were now hundreds where there had only been dozens a few minutes beforehand.

"Everybody load up!" He waved them on, hoping they'd move faster.

Harris took charge of a small group and kept them out there, covering their rear while the rest climbed aboard *BOHICA* and the M-88. With the HEMMT fuelers destroyed, they had even more people to cram on top of the two tracked vehicles, with people hanging off nearly every exposed square inch. It wasn't pretty, but it looked like they'd probably have enough room for everyone.

Probably.

"Raise the ramp!" Mark cupped his hands together, shouting at Harris and their ad hoc rearguard. "Harris, break contact! You're about to be a permanent resident here!" He toggled the intercom. "Gunner, coax, Zulus!"

"Identified!"

"Fire!"

"On the way!"

Donahue cut loose with the coax machine gun, firing it inches over the heads of their buddies who were now in full flight, retreating from a wave of the undead. Most of the 7.62 NATO slammed into torsos and limbs, not even slowing the creatures down, but a few found their mark, smashing through skulls and ending their suffering permanently.

"Come on, Harris. Bali, bali, ajushi!" Jimmy Hong called out.

Harris slapped the other soldiers with him on the shoulder, indicating it was time to go. They immediately stopped shooting, turned tail and ran toward the tracks.

Hands reached down and pulled up their buddies with Jimmy pulling Harris up onto the Bradley. "I can't leave my Asian brother from another mother behind." He strained to pull the other man up, planting his feet on the armored side panel for leverage.

Harris climbed up top and squeezed in next to Jimmy. "Thanks, Battle, but just because I'm Korean, doesn't mean I can speak the language."

"I'll teach you one of these days. We're practically family after all." Jimmy wore a big, goofy grin.

"Dude, I grew up adopted by white parents living in an affluent suburb just outside of Denver. You grew up in some south L.A. shithole stealing cars by the time you were old enough to see over the steering wheel. I don't think you and I have much in common. I wouldn't exactly call us 'practically family.'"

"All you gotta know is to call me 'hyung.' We'll get to the rest later."

"Whatever."

Engines belched dark exhaust and the two armored vehicles pulled away, crossing a field as fast as they dared, putting distance between themselves and the suburban neighborhood. They moved out at a good clip and even the runners were left behind after a very short while.

Mark's heart beat like mad and his hands trembled. He took deep breaths to get his breathing under control, doing his best to get ahold of himself. When he finally got his wits about him, he took a minute to once again try and count heads, to see if they had all of their people. That's when he saw one of them hanging on to one of the radio mounts, where the antenna would have been attached if it were still there. The man's head sagged, looking away from him. He realized it was Devons and that one of the zeds had scratched the man's face.

"Devons, look at me," Mark said, raising his voice over the noise of the engine.

He looked up at Mark, confused. "What's up, Sarn't?"

Mark gasped. Devons' face had the telltale blue spider-webbing and his eyes were already turning red. The scratches had done their awful work. "Get off the track!"

"For what? I'm okay, really." His hand went to the claw

marks on his cheeks. "These aren't deep. They barely even hurt. I'm totally fine."

He reached for the sidearm, drawing it and pointing it at the other man's nose. "You're not okay, buddy, and you can't stay with us."

The exchange drew the attention of men on either side of Devons and they recoiled in shock when they saw him. They tried to put some distance between themselves and their infected comrade, but the top of the vehicles was covered in people and there was nowhere else to go.

"Don't make me shoot, Devons. I don't want to do this." Mark swallowed hard and steadied the weapon. He locked his gaze on those horrible, red eyes and could see them turning translucent as they spoke.

Devons twitched, but otherwise did not move from his spot. "Sergeant Matthews, I feel fine. You can't leave me out here by myself. Please, don't do this to me!"

"Battle, you don't look so good. Just jump off. We'll come back to get you. I promise," Swanson pleaded, unable to get any more space between him and his buddy.

Devons trembled again, his nervous system giving an involuntary reaction to the virus. The soldier turned to his buddy, with thick, red blood beginning to ooze from his nostrils. "You promise to come back for me?"

Swanson's eyes grew wide, looking into the very face of death. "I... I... promise, Battle. I'll bring them back with me."

The infected man's glowing red eyes narrowed to slits. "I have a better idea. Why don't you stay with me?" He lunged at Swanson, wrapping both arms around his friend, then rolled off the top of the Bradley, sending them both tumbling to the ground.

The vehicle never stopped moving and the other members of the platoon watched in shocked horror as two of their teammates fell off, rolling around in the tall grass as they drove away, leaving them behind. Devons moved like a man possessed, while Swanson fought to keep the now-flashing teeth away from exposed flesh.

Johnson drew his M-4 and fired off a few rounds but missed completely

"Don't shoot, you'll hit Swanson!" Dubois cried out.

"Oh my god!" Mark said, watching the distance growing between them as BOHICA carried on, following the M-88 in front of them. "Burbey, turn around. We gotta go back."

"Why, what's going on, Sarn't?"

"There's no time to argue, turn around. Someone fell off!"

Donahue, now curious, popped his head up through the gunner's hatch and rubber-necked, trying to see what was going on.

Without working radios, they had no way to alert the M-88. As they whipped around, the recovery vehicle continued on, unaware they had lost anyone. They were hell-bent on getting back to the Company Assembly Area as fast as they could.

When the IFV came about, Mark toggled the intercom once again. "Driver, can you see them yet?"

"Roger, I see them."

"Pull up beside 'em."

Devons noticed the track turning around and let go of Swanson, getting back to his feet and running off like an Olympic sprinter.

When they pulled up beside Swanson, they found him lying on his back with a nasty bite on his neck. He held the wound with a gloved hand, but blood pumped through his fingers in jets, staining the ground red. He looked up at the others on the Bradley, not saying a word, the deathly look of fear etched on his face.

Bags tried to stand up. Her instincts told her to render aid, but Angie grabbed her by the combat harness and pulled her back down, sending her landing hard on the cargo hatch of the track, flat on her butt. "You can't help him, stupid. You stay put."

They all stared at their friend in silence while Devons continued to run away. None of them could move, or do anything to help, watching their friend slowly bleed out.

"Dammit." Mark unplugged the spaghetti cord of his CVC, climbed out of the turret and lowered himself to the ground. He stood over Swanson, wiping at his nose and swallowing the lump that grew in his throat. He shook his head. "I'm sorry, buddy. This is a shitty deal." He felt the eyes of the entire platoon on his back, none of them making a sound. He took a deep breath and drew his M9 pistol, letting it dangle at his side for a moment while giving the gravely wounded man a sympathetic look. Swanson closed his own eyes waiting for the inevitable while a single tear streaked down his temple and into the grass, intermixing with the arterial spray.

Mark raised the weapon pointing it at the man's forehead and gritted his teeth before pulling the trigger.

He holstered the weapon, then lowered his head and said the Lord's Prayer while some of the others joined him.

When finished, he climbed back up onto the track and lowered himself back into the turret, taking his position. He took a moment to compose himself before sliding the CVC back on over his ears.

"Are we going to go after Devons, Sarn't?" Donahue said meekly, finally breaking the silence.

"No. I've killed enough of my own men for one day." He toggled the intercom while adjusting his seat. "Driver, move out."

Chapter 9

8 September, 2016
Lincoln, Nebraska
0936 Hours Local

Major General Bud Napier made a detour through the refugee camp to see his wife before heading back to the Division Forward Command Post. He'd put out the order to have the commander's make arrangements for their subordinates to check in on their families. The tornado had ripped through the Division's footprint, wreaking utter havoc and there were casualties everywhere, both military and civilian, and while time continued to tick away while resources continued to dwindle, he made the conscious decision to take a tactical pause in order to regroup, reassess and figure out what to do next. That also allowed them the opportunity to check in on families, which were the glue that held the Division together.

His wife made it through the disaster just fine and she busied herself working at an ad hoc aid station caring for the injured. Most of the patients were dealing with minor cuts and scratches, though there were many with broken bones and other more serious issues. There were a smattering of civilian doctors and nurses in the camps who helped out. Military medical personnel assisted as well, but many of them were needed to tend to soldiers who had been hurt.

Bud's wife was a strong woman and she assured him that she didn't need him worrying about her. She spent some time talking with him and then ushered him off, telling him that she needed to get back to the aid station. That did wonders for his own personal morale and it gave him the strength he needed to go back to the headquarters element and figure out what to do.

When his Humvee pulled up to the Command Post he put the patented confident look on his face he was known for, before stepping out. The Chief of Staff met him outside and greeted him with a sharp salute, standing rigid as a statue. Bud returned it and offered a smile that never reached his eyes. "How are we doing Lorne? Is everyone here?"

"Yes, General. We've got the commanders and the staff assembled." The middle-age colonel relaxed his posture while addressing his commanding officer. He'd been with the Division for several years and had commanded an artillery brigade before relinquishing command and becoming the Chief of Staff.

"Did you get a chance to meet with your wife and kids?" Napier knew that the Chief worked himself to the brink of exhaustion routinely and rarely took time for himself. That included carving out time for his family. It was a habit he'd slipped into early in his career and was an unspoken sin among successful officers.

"Not yet, sir. I plan on seeing them later sometime today."

"I'm not kidding, you will check in on them today. Understand me? That's an order." Napier didn't raise his voice. He didn't have to. This statement meant there was no wiggle room for excuses.

"I understand, General. I will definitely take the time to check in on them."

"Good, then let's head on inside."

***

Normally, the daily Commander's Update Brief would be broadcast over a secure network with each of the Brigade Commanders checking in remotely. The practice of bringing dispersed commanders together in a central location for meetings was normally frowned upon as it dragged them away from their units, which was normally a bad idea, but this situation was extraordinary and General Napier felt he needed to have a conference in person with his senior leaders to go over their options.

"Okay, Dave. Let's get started." General Napier sat at the head of an improvised conference table, constructed from folding field tables. His commanders sat around the table with him, along with their Sergeants Major. Along the walls of the tent were the Division principal staff officers, who waited their turn to address the assembled group.

The Division Operations Officer, also known as the "G-3," stood at the opposite end of the conference table near a series of flatscreens, all of which were showing photographs and statistics listed on Powerpoint slides. He turned on a laser pointer and cleared his throat. "Sir, ladies and gentlemen, it's been a rough couple of days. We managed to get a single-day's road march behind us before 'Murphy's Law' kicked in."

"Kicked us in the nuts, you mean." The Division Command Sergeant Major didn't usually interrupt, and his comment caused heads to turn in his direction. The Division Commander didn't react at all to the outburst, and everyone turned their attention back to the G-3.

"I couldn't have said it better myself, Sergeant Major." The G-3 worked a remote control in his hand, advancing to the next slide. "As you all can see here, this is our current Battle Damage Assessment in the wake of the storm. The meteorologists report that this thing was an F5 tornado. It was unusually large, and also unusually late in the season. These things normally manifest in spring and early summer."

"I guess we got lucky then," Napier said dryly. He reached for the cup of coffee that wasn't there, remembering that they'd run out of the stuff the day beforehand. The "silver bullet" coffee maker sat idly over in the corner, cold and empty. "Let's get down to brass tacks. How bad was it for us?"

The G-3 pointed to a set of numbers on the screen nearest him, drawing everyone's attention. "We suffered a dozen killed and over two hundred injured in the Division. Double that for the civilian refugees in our camp. With no shelter, there just wasn't anywhere for them to run and we suffered awfully for it." He brought up the remote and clicked it, pulling up the next slide. "As far as equipment losses are concerned, it is critical. The Aviation Brigade took in on the nose, with approximately half our aircraft now no longer mission capable." He brought up photos of damaged Apaches, Blackhawks and Chinooks. Some flipped over, some with rotor blades torn off and some with obvious damage to the fuselage.

Napier had personally inspected most of it earlier, so none of the images came as a shock to him, though it still made him sick in the pit of his stomach to look at it. "Can we repair the aircraft?"

The Aviation Brigade commander leaned in from his position at the table, looking down the length of it to address the Division Commander. "Sir, we assess that most of the aircraft can be repaired. We'll need some time to do it, but my maintenance teams assure me that it can be done."

"Okay, good. How long will that take?"

"General, if I may." All heads turned to the back of the tent, where Lieutenant Colonel Rich Sullivan rose to his feet to speak to the assembled group. He had a clipboard in hand and pushed his glasses up the bridge of his nose with a single finger.

"Hold on, Rich. You'll get a chance to speak. We've got a slide in the presentation for you to brief later," interrupted the Chief of Staff, who tried to shut the Logistics Officer down. It wasn't the first time he had to rein in the man, who tended to speak out of turn.

"No, no. It's fine, Lorne. Let the G-4 say what he has to say." Napier held up a hand to the Chief of Staff and the man physically took a step back, his face turning a dark shade of crimson.

"Sir, it's not as simple as that. We can't fix a single aircraft in the Aviation Brigade right now because we didn't bring any spare parts with us. Nothing significant anyway. In fact, just about every piece of rolling stock in the Division carried nothing but fuel, food and water when we left Riley. We made the deliberate decision to do that, since we don't have the trucks and haul capacity to carry anything else." He walked over to the G-3 and motioned to the remote in his hand. "May I?"

"Be my guest." The G-3 handed the clicker over to the G-4 and backed up a few paces to allow the logistician to take center stage.

Rich took over and advanced the presentation to his portion, listing numbers and stats, along with a few graphs and charts. "Ladies and gentlemen, as you know, when we left Riley we had to take only the bare essentials since we are getting no external support to move ourselves. This is a situation no unit expects to face while carrying out combat or contingency operations. That being the case, we have precious few haul assets organic within the Division. To move the unprecedented distance of 1,700 miles to get to the *Cascadia Redoubt*, we were forced to focus on carrying the bare essentials. This gave us three days of supply moving in standard administrative road marches."

"Yeah, yeah, Rich. We know all of this. We briefed the CG on it before we left," interjected the Deputy Commanding General for Sustainment. She appeared agitated, being upstaged by her subordinate.

"Yes, ma'am. I'm getting to the point." He pulled up some more information, which caused a stir inside the tent once people at the table had a chance to read it. "I got an updated report less than an hour ago. The tornado took out a significant portion of our Combat Sustainment Support Battalion. Specifically, we lost nearly half the assets in the Petroleum, Oil and Lubricant Supply Company. The bottom line, with all of the camp followers in the refugee camp and the loss of many of our trucks, we've got less than a day's supply of food and fuel on hand."

There were audible groans in the room and the atmosphere grew frosty.

The Commanding General looked over at his Deputy in charge of Sustainment, giving her an icy stare. "Were you tracking this, Candice?"

"Yes, sir. I was going to give you a detailed rundown of this offline." She seemed to shrink in her seat under the commander's withering gaze. Some of the other senior officers shifted in their seats uncomfortably.

"You didn't think this was something I needed to know right away?" The volume of Napier's voice grew louder and his words more clipped. He stopped himself short of yelling at his subordinate General in front of the commanders, though the look on his face indicated that he could snap at any moment. He took a deep breath before turning back to the G-4. "You've got my attention now, Rich. So, what's the bad news?"

"If we want to repair the aircraft, we'll need to send a convoy back to Fort Riley to get repair parts. That in and of itself is a three-day operation. Then they'll need time to carry out the maintenance once the spares arrive. We could be here for the better part of a week. Meanwhile, people still have to eat, and we'll be out of food and water long before that." He lowered his clipboard and looked at Napier, pausing to let that settle in. The Commanding General looked as if he might have a stroke right then and there.

The general's withering gaze shifted to the G-3 who had backed into the dark corner, doing his best to disappear. "Dave, I suppose you were going to propose some Courses of Action to me at some point? Or were you intending for me to figure this out all on my own?"

The Division Operations Officer meekly came forward and cleared his throat. "Ah, yes, sir. We were going to sidebar with you after this to get your intent before gathering the staff together for a detailed planning session."

"Damnit, Three, that in and of itself could take a day or more! *We don't have time for this!*" Napier slammed his hand open hand down on the table with an audible "whack." An uncomfortable silence settled in the tent and no one dared make a sound or make eye contact with the commanding general. Then, he took a deep breath and composed himself before going on. "Does anyone here have a suggestion as to what we should do next?"

Rich raised his hand.

"Yes, Four. Since you seem to have my undivided attention now. Please go ahead." Napier interlaced his fingers and rested them on the table, leaning forward on his elbows.

"Sir, whether or not we repair the damaged aircraft makes little difference. The most pressing issue is that within the next seventy-two hours if we don't do something decisive, we will be literally starving to death here on the plains. This whole thing is a matter of logistics." Rich saw he had everyone's rapt attention now. Particularly that of the Deputy Commander for Sustainment, who appeared as if she were ready to leap from her seat and murder him at any moment.

The Sustainment Brigade Commander could no longer hold her tongue and interrupted the staff officer. "Listen, Rich. You're not telling us anything we don't already know. Now, my people may have limited equipment but we can work out…"

"Nadya, will you please shut the fuck up. I asked Rich to speak, now allow him to do so," Napier scolded. "Alright, Four. You were saying?"

"It all boils down to two choices. Either we abandon all of our heavy equipment, the tanks, Bradleys, helicopters and move out on light vehicles, or we acquire the haul assets we need to move ourselves." The G-4 focused his attention on the commander, doing his best to ignore the others so as not to be distracted by their icy and contemptuous stares.

"Well, Rich. If we leave behind our heavy equipment and weapons, then we're nothing more than a rag-tag collection of refugees streaming into the *Cascadia Redoubt*, which greatly reduces our capability and value to the surviving government. Right now all of it is priceless and irreplaceable. So, no, we're not leaving any of it behind. We're a Heavy Division and we will remain that way."

"Roger. Then we need to secure the haul assets and supplies we need to make the next leg of the journey. There are several warehouses and trucking hubs in Lincoln. There's even a Peterbilt facility on the northeast side of town. We should be able to secure plenty of trucks. An entire fleet of them without too much trouble."

The general nodded in understanding, now folding his arms across his chest. "I'm listening."

"We also need to plus up on large volumes of fuels and lubricants. The best place to source those is at the airport on the northwest side of the city." Rich flipped through a few slides and pulled up some maps with the locations highlighted on them.

"And what about the food? You mentioned that's the most pressing issue."

"There's likely plenty of it. There are grocery stores located all throughout Lincoln."

Napier scratched his chin while considering what he'd just been told. "Rich, the entire city is a hot zone overrun by the dead. Are you suggesting we go in? We'll have to shoot our way in and out of there. We've got a single basic load of ammunition with us and no way to replenish that once it's expended. Not unless we run back to Fort Riley, which puts us right back at Square One. We've still got another 1,500 miles to go before we get to our destination and winter will be on us before we know it. We have to get to Washington before the first snow flies or else we're camping out until springtime." He turned his attention back to the larger group. "Remind me again when we expect the first snowfall along our route?"

"We have to pass through Wyoming, Utah and Idaho. We could literally see the first snowfall of the season any day now. We're pretty much already on borrowed time," said the Aviation Brigade Commander.

"Understood," Rich said simply. "The problem we face is, every location that *isn't* already overrun by the dead has been picked clean like a plague of locusts passed through. The survivors have scavenged every scrap of food and every drop of fuel and there's nothing left. The only supplies available are in the areas completely consumed by the infected where the civilians and the ad hoc militias can't penetrate. It's a conundrum, but one we cannot ignore. We have the manpower and firepower to get what we need, but we have to wade into the worst places imaginable to get it.

"I propose we send a security element back to Riley with some of our trucks to get repair parts. While they are doing that, then the rest of our available maneuver forces should move into Lincoln to secure civilian trucks, fuel and most importantly, food. I believe it's our best and only option. If we don't, we should just head back to Kansas now and winter there while we still can."

Napier grimaced. "No, we can't send an element back to Riley for supplies or anything else. The governor of Kansas and the State Adjutant General made it clear that after the incident in Bremerton, the 1st Infantry Division is persona non grata unless we turn over the guilty parties—which we refused to do, since they'd unlikely get any sort of fair hearing." Napier intentionally avoided eye contact with Colonel Dane Williams, the man responsible for putting them all in that predicament. "Not only are we banished from ever entering Kansas again, we received reports that the Kansas National Guard rolled into Fort Riley right after we left. They have likely stripped every bit of equipment and all the supplies we left behind for their own use." He interlaced his fingers in front of him and sighed. "And in addition to that, our orders are clear, we must get to Washington state. We have no choice." He paused, looking thoughtful before looking back up at the G-4. "I understand the logic behind going into the city to replenish our depleted stocks, but if we roll into Lincoln with guns blazing, then what? After we've shot up most or all of our ammunition getting what we need, how do we proceed? We've got a long way to go and I suspect we're going to need bullets for force protection and to secure the civilian refugees. Besides, why don't we just secure the airport here in town and have TRANSCOM fly in some supplies. Surely, they can land some C-130s or C-17s."

General Candice Bucher shifted her weight uncomfortably, forcing herself to face her commander. "Sir, that's still not an option. The word from III Corps is that every available lift asset TRANSCOM has is tied up redeploying our troops and equipment from overseas."

"You can't be serious. It's been two months now. We should have gotten everyone home by now." Napier's cheeks flushed even more.

"Sir, we literally had over 100,000 troops stationed abroad, along with mountains of equipment. Add to that the fact that some of our air bases here in CONUS were overrun with the dead, consuming irreplaceable aircrews, which also exacerbated the problem, but, there's more."

"It's worse?"

"Yes, General. You see, we had to pull everything out of Hawaii too. Oahu is a total write-off. Nobody's sipping Mai Tais at the Hale Koa on Waikiki Beach anymore. Then, considering there's too many still left alive on the island to ship food to or support, the decision was made to evacuate all personnel and their families. The Pacific Fleet, Pacific Air Forces, Marine Forces Pacific, everything… is currently pulling out. The 25th Infantry Division is acting as rear guard while they pack up and ship everything that isn't nailed down out of Hickam and Pearl Harbor." Bucher appeared more confident now, assured her boss wasn't going to rip her head off in public again.

"I suppose the same thing is going on in Alaska then?"

"That's affirmative. There are flights running 24/7 out of Elmendorf while ships full of kit and personnel are steaming out of Anchorage. There haven't been any major outbreaks up there and NORTHCOM turned control over to the National Guard and the Alaska State Guard."

"No outbreaks up there? Why?"

"Because everyone in Alaska owns a gun it seems. The infections that did occur were dealt with rather quickly. The population in general weathered the initial storm fairly well, but they are in for one long, hungry winter. They doubt anybody outside of the remote villages has a chance of making it through until spring."

Napier shook his head, crossed his arms and leaned back in his chair. "How long before the redeployments are complete then?"

Bucher swallowed hard. "Weeks at best. Maybe another month or more according to the logistics planners at Corps headquarters." She looked over at the Sustainment Brigade commander and the G-4, looking for a little encouragement before going on. "There's more."

"You've got to be shitting me. What is it?"

"I.. I think the 'S' is referring to the refugee situation," said the Division Personnel Officer, doing his best to take the heat off the Deputy Commander. "You see, sir, we keep accumulating more of them."

"What the hell are you talking about? Didn't I give strict orders that we were to allow no more random people to tag along with us?"

"You did, General."

"Then how in blazes are we getting more refugees? Can someone please explain that to me?"

"Groups of people are showing up day and night. They heard there was protection and food so people are streaming in for miles. The longer we're stationary, the more we draw in. The word is out."

Napier slammed a fist on the table. "Have we completely lost control around here? *Why aren't my orders being obeyed*?"

An uncomfortable silence settled on them all and remained that way until the Command Sergeant Major decided to chime in. "It's really simple, sir. Our families in the camps won't turn away mothers with babies or families with small kids. Nobody has the heart to do it. So, they take them in and hide them in the tent city."

"I thought we had a system to keep track of people and keep this from happening," Napier growled.

"We did, sir," piped up the G-1. "Our block wardens were tasked with keeping up with the names and numbers of camp followers."

"*And?*"

"And then we ran low on fuel. Without enough JP-8 we had to run our generators less often. Without generators we couldn't run our computers. Without our computers we couldn't access the Excel spreadsheets with all the names to keep proper accountability." The G-1 Personnel Officer took off his glasses and rubbed his eyes before putting them back on again. "We tried going analog with clipboards and pencils but there's not enough block wardens and too many civilians. We left Fort Riley with over fifteen thousand of them. We've probably picked up another thousand since then and the number grows even more with each passing day. They keep coming out of the woodwork."

"I put out orders that the camps would receive no additional food or water for just this reason. Don't tell me that they are getting additional rations."

Rich took over, interrupting the G-1. "No, we haven't, but that hasn't made the situation any better. The civilians are burning through food and clean water at an alarming rate, even consuming only what we allotted for them, but now we're getting reports of violence in the camps, with people stealing from each other like crazy. We don't have the MPs to do much about it, since most of them are tasked with reconnaissance patrols and force protection. That being the case, I estimate we'll be out of food within the next twenty-four hours. We'll be out of potable water in forty-eight. The doc says we'll start losing people to sickness within a week due to dirty water and lack of sanitation. People will start dying of thirst soon after that."

"Jesus Christ." Napier pinched the bridge of his nose and squeezed his eyes shut, trying to focus on the answer. He spent a couple of minutes like that, concentrating as hard as he could while the rest stood quietly by, waiting for him to say something. When he looked back up at the G-4 he seemed more calm, almost serene. "Okay then, what's your recommendation?"

"General, our current situation is dire and time is a factor. I propose that we secure what we can here as quickly as possible and strike west. I've been in contact with III Corps who are currently consolidating at Fort Carson, Colorado. We can request that they send a logistical package to us near Denver. That would only require a small detour on our part and wouldn't slow us down too much." Rich surveyed the group to see if any of them were ready to argue the point. Instead, he found them whispering among themselves, discussing the feasibility of the move. "It's approximately four hundred and fifty miles from here to there and it's a bit of a drive for sure, but if we scrounge enough food, water, fuel and trucks, we should be able to make it. It'll take at least three days to make the drive to Denver, but there's not much between us here and there, so we could probably accept the risk of making that leg of the journey with depleted ammunition supplies on hand."

Napier rubbed his chin while studying his logistics officer. He didn't bother looking at the other more senior logisticians in the room, he just focused on Rich. While any other person might have wilted under that laser-like gaze, Rich did not, appearing totally at ease and confident of himself. Then the General's expression softened somewhat. "Alright, Four, you've sold me." He pointed at the G-3. "Dave, get the team together and I want a Course of Action decision brief in six hours. This is my intent and this is what I want. Is that clear?"

The G-3 straightened his posture, standing almost parade-like. "Yes, sir. We'll make it happen."

"General, if I may." All heads turned to face Colonel Dane Williams, commander of the 2nd "Dagger" Brigade. He held up a hand waiting for permission to speak, like a child in a classroom.

Napier fought back the urge to say something nasty to the man. After the debacle in Kansas City and then the incident on the road march headed back to Fort Riley, Dane Williams had managed to make a reputation for himself, and it wasn't a good one. It had gotten to the point where he didn't even want to look at the man's face anymore. "Yes, Dane. What is it?"

"Sir, with your permission. I'd like to volunteer 2nd Brigade to go into Lincoln to gather the critical supplies. It's a dangerous mission, but I'm confident we'll get it done."

Everyone in the room knew Williams had been looking for an excuse to rehabilitate his reputation and this appeared to be a convenient opportunity for him. Still, someone had to do it and was volunteering. Napier took a long moment to consider it before responding. "Fine, Dane, you've got the mission. Are there any other questions or comments?"

There were none.

"Good. I'll see you all in six. Dismissed."

***

9 September, 2016
Assembly Area Husker
1013 Hours Local

The officers and NCOs stood on the periphery of a massive terrain model, depicting the significant features of Lincoln, Nebraska. All sorts of odds and ends were used to replicate miniature versions of buildings, roads and bridges. Overlayed on top of that were strips of white cotton tape used to indicate control measures such as unit boundaries, phase lines and objectives. Standard practice dictated that they use something like this to brief subordinate leaders so they could easily visualize the operation while the staff officers briefed the plan, and while something like this at the platoon-level would be fairly small, the brigade's version spread itself out over dozens of square meters.

Mark stood on the eastern edge of the massive model, studying the various nuances of it while comparing it to one of the road maps he'd acquired earlier. A couple of NCOs from the other companies crowded around him, looking over his shoulder at the paper map, trying to do the same. He didn't mind them looking over his shoulders and would periodically pass it around so they could get a better look. The officers didn't do that, electing to pretend as though they didn't need to see the map, except for Lieutenant Baker, whom Mark had supplied with an additional copy earlier in the day.

Colonel Williams had briefed his subordinate commanders on their missions earlier and now the battalions took turns using the same terrain board to pitch the plan to their own people. It prevented duplicating efforts when time had become such a critical commodity.

Without fanfare the Battalion Commander strolled up with his Command Sergeant Major in tow. There were scores of leaders gathered around the massive sand table and they gave way as if the Red Sea were parting for Moses, allowing their commander to take his position up front near the southern edge of the model, where he could get the best view. Nobody mentioned aloud how Lieutenant Colonel Hamilton appeared to have aged a good fifteen years in the last month, but they all were thinking it. Even his gait had slowed to a shuffle, nearly dragging his feet on the ground.

Hamilton and Sergeant Major Yates settled into a couple of folding chairs that were set out there for them, while everyone else stood. The Battalion Commander grabbed the brim of his patrol cap and pushed it back, exposing his forehead before leaning forward, resting his elbows on his knees.

In the center of the terrain model Captain Gigatone, the Assistant Operations Officer, waited patiently with a radio antenna in hand, using it as an improvised pointer. The twenty-six year-old officer had been serving in the capacity of the actual Operations Officer ever since his boss had been killed back in Kansas City. There were a whole lot of junior leaders stepping up these days.

Hamilton spat on the ground, then looked up at his Ops Officer. "Alright, Alex. Let's kick this thing off."

Gigatone nodded then raised his voice loudly enough to be clearly heard by those gathered around. "Ladies and gentlemen, welcome to the Battalion Operations Order brief. Due to time constraints we had to run through a truncated planning process and on order of the commander, this briefing will be shortened as well, focusing on the most important details."

A couple of captains were having a sidebar conversation which drew the attention of the Battalion XO. When they noticed the major giving them the stink-eye, they ceased their conversation and began paying attention.

Gigatone raised his pointer and motioned to a series of routes and objectives, all with names assigned to them. "As you can see, the other battalions in the brigade will be rolling out early in the morning to secure Objectives *Marlin* and *Tuna*, located here and here." He pointed to an area on the northeast side of the city and to the airport on the west. "Our brigade's artillery battalion no longer has any howitzers after the fire back in KC, so their personnel have been reorganized into a transportation battalion. They will secure the trucks located at the Peterbilt facility and a few other locations. One Six Three Armor will take the airport while Five Four Cav conducts route security. While all of that is occurring, Two Seventieth Armor along with the Engineers, now designated as *Task Force Dagger*, will roll into Holmes Lake Park to conduct a feint, drawing the dead away from us, the Main Effort. On order, our battalion, One Eighteen Infantry will attack to secure the supplies located here, at Objective *Halibut*." He motioned to a large circle that surrounded two empty cardboard MRE boxes with the words *Costco* and *Walmart* written on them in black magic marker. "As we clear the objective, the newly-liberated eighteen-wheelers will link up with us and we'll load the supplies aboard. Once complete, we'll conduct a retrograde back here to the Brigade Assembly Area."

While Captain Gigatone carried on with the briefing, Mark stared at the area he and his platoon were tasked with. They'd have to roll in quickly, clear the facility, then start pushing supplies out to the loading docks in the back. Once the artillery battalion showed up with semis, they'd get more help, but they didn't have time to waste and they'd set to work right away, and while two battalions would be making quite a racket with their diversion, it would only be a matter of time before the infected noticed what they were up to and would be drawn in. So they had to move with a purpose.

He thought about Devons and Swanson, getting suddenly sick in the pit of his stomach. He was in no mood to lose any more people and he was bound and determined to get them all out of this one alive, one way or the other.

***

9 September, 2016
Lincoln, Nebraska
2207 Hours Local

Mark sat on a seat in the back of *BOHICA* all by himself, completely lost in thought. Burbey had lowered the ramp down and it rested on a wooden chock block, so the cool evening air wafted in unfettered. He'd switched on one of the dome lights in the back, with it turned over to a blue filter which gave the light a ghostly glow. The brigade located their assembly area in a corn field in the middle of nowhere, so noise and light discipline hadn't been strictly enforced. It left them all a bit on edge since a roaming walker or even the occasional civilian raider were always a concern. They'd nicknamed the civilian thieves "Slicky Boy" for their ability to infiltrate their perimeters and steal whatever wasn't nailed down. It began to happen with much greater frequency now that they were outside of the city or the secure confines of a military installation. So now they not only had to keep their eyes peeled for the undead, but they had to stay alert for people bent on stealing their kit. If it wasn't one thing, it was another.

He had a road atlas in hand, opened up to a map of the continental United States. They'd liberated it from the service station just before the tornado and he'd squirreled it away in the turret of the Bradley. He couldn't help thinking that they were going in the wrong direction and that they got further and further from his family in Ohio. His parents and his brother's family were there. Or at least they were before the outbreak.

Mark often wondered if they were okay, if they managed to survive when all hell broke loose. Unlike the others, he couldn't send word back home in the opening days when communications were still open. He was an escaped felon after all, pretending to be someone else under an assumed name. He just had to hope for the best while everyone else was able to send and receive messages to learn the fate of their loved ones. His dad and his brother had guns and they liked to hunt, so they possessed the means to survive, so he remained optimistic. They lived in suburbs and not in the middle of a major city so that gave him hope as well.

What really ate at him was the fact that sooner or later someone would find out who he really was. At some point, probably when they got to Washington state, they'd attempt to track down the family of "Sergeant Matthews" and maybe even gain access to his service record. Once that happened, the jig would be up. He could tell them the truth about how he escaped, but it's not entirely certain anyone would believe him. At best, he'd find himself behind bars again. At worst he might find himself up against a wall and shot.

No, he had to figure out a way to get out of there and get home.

Lincoln, Nebraska was farther away from southern Ohio than Kansas City was, but the distance could be covered in a reasonable amount of time. All he needed to do was get his hands on a vehicle and he'd be off and running. He could be home in a day or so, depending on conditions. He just needed to figure out a way to get away from the others.

Mark didn't really want to leave them, but there really wasn't much choice. They'd all vouch for him of course, but that'd make little difference once his true identity got revealed.

The other problem that presented itself was the mission they'd received from Battalion earlier in the evening. They'd gotten orders to head into Lincoln on a "Smash and Grab" operation. Bravo Company was tasked with securing as much non-perishable food as they could carry. The whole thing briefed well, but he knew from experience that they would be kicking over an anthill the minute they rolled in there. They drew the short stick on this one.

He couldn't walk away from the platoon before they headed out on one of the most challenging and dangerous jobs they'd ever been assigned. No, he figured he needed to stay and help, but the minute they were done he made up his mind to disappear, find some transportation and get the hell out of there for good. He needed to do it before it was too late.

"What are you looking at?"

Mark nearly jumped out of his skin, startled by the intrusion. He looked over to find Clay standing there next to the ramp, watching. "Jesus, you scared the shit out of me."

Without an invitation he climbed aboard, bending at the waist, careful not to hit his head on the ceiling of the troop compartment. He settled into a seat next to Mark and leaned his Mini-14 against the inside of the hull. "Is that an atlas?"

"Yeah," Mark said, closing it up. "I was just taking a look to see how much farther it is to Washington state." He set the book down on the diamond plate decking near his feet. "What are you doing?" he asked, trying to change the subject.

"I finished making sure that everyone got topped up on ammo and had fresh batteries for their NODs and radios. Now I'm checking up on you to see how you're doing." Clay gave the younger man the paternalistic look he'd come to expect when the others weren't around. He'd become the one confidant Mark could open up to, though he still had to lie to him about his past for obvious reasons.

"No, I'm good. I was thinking about turning in and getting some rest here shortly." Mark always said that so the others wouldn't worry about him. The truth was, he never slept the night before an op, he'd be too keyed up and stressed out, constantly running the following-day's mission through his mind.

"That'd be a first. You really should actually do that for a change. We need you to be sharp tomorrow." It was less of a criticism and more of a helpful suggestion.

"I'll try. I promise." He smiled before scratching the back of his neck. "So, how was Swanson's funeral today?"

"As good as could be expected, I suppose. The chaplain said some very nice words and a couple of the mechanics fabricated a pretty decent grave marker for him." Clay's expression got noticeably serious. "You should have been there, you know. The platoon were asking about you and why you didn't attend."

"You told them I was up at Battalion for a briefing, right?"

"Yes, I lied to them for you, but don't ever ask me to do that for you again."

Mark looked down at his boots, unable to make eye contact. "Yeah. It's just that I couldn't do it, you know? I barely kept my shit together after putting him out of his misery. I would have completely lost it in front of everyone."

"I'm sure it would have been okay. They would have understood."

"Yeah, maybe." He cleared the frog from his throat before going on, noticing that his eyes had grown watery all of a sudden. "How did the others take it?"

"Fine. The girls cried like babies. Well, except for Gray and Angie. The rest stood by quietly while the prayers were said and then helped fill in the grave when it was over."

"Well, his troubles are behind him now." He looked back up at Clay. "How're they doing otherwise? Everything else okay?"

"They're hungry. Ever since the entire brigade went to half-rations they've been griping about lack of food."

"You didn't let them dip into our reserve stocks we scrounged back at Riley, did you?"

Clay shook his head. "No, of course not. You were quite specific about that."

"Good, it's going to be a long trip to Washington and we're going to need those supplies. Nobody's starving yet, so they'll be fine."

Clay nodded in understanding. "There's something else I need to discuss with you." He ran dirty fingers through greasy hair before going on. "Angel wants to go out with us on the op."

"What? No way. The kid's not ready yet." Angel had long ago ditched his civilian attire and dressed like a soldier, mimicking the members of the platoon. He even copied some of the mannerisms and used much of their slang, even with his broken English, and while they felt comfortable enough tasking him with guard duty on the perimeter at night, they'd never taken him along outside of the wire on missions. Without training, Mark considered him more of a liability than an asset.

"I hear what you're saying, but he won't let it go. Besides, after losing Devons and Swanson, we need all the help we can get."

Just hearing those words made Mark cringe inside. He hadn't lost anybody on a mission since the outbreak and this wasn't sitting well with him. "I don't feel comfortable taking an untrained civilian on one of these missions. It's already dangerous as hell." He immediately felt stupid the moment the words left his mouth. Clay had broken that taboo and proved himself perfectly capable. If not as well trained on the others in basic tactics, he made up for it in other ways and he was learning fast.

"You're not going to make me point out the obvious, are you?"

"Okay, but you're different." Mark hoped Clay didn't pull the string any further. His argument was weak at best and he knew it.

"Listen, Mark. Angel is young, he's strong, and he's proved himself to be very bright. Some of the guys taught him how to shoot and they even zeroed his personal weapon. He might not speak English very well, but he understands hand-and-arm signals. I've seen him practicing battle drills with the others and he seems fine. On top of that, he's killing himself to impress Consuela. He wants her to feel like he's a real man and we aren't allowing him that opportunity."

"So, we should take him along so he can impress his girlfriend?"

"That's not my point. My point is, he's highly motivated and he'll do anything not to let us down."

Mark held his hand up, yielding to Clay's point. "Fine, he can come. I'll let him know right after this."

"No, don't bother yourself. I'll take care of it and get him ready. You need to get some rest."

"I'll try."

"Is that a promise?" Clay slapped him on the shoulder and got back up again. "I'll be by in a little while. I expect to see you curled up in your sleeping bag."

"Yes, Mom."

Chapter 10

The members of the platoon finished up the final inspections of their equipment, working in the pre-dawn gloom. There were plenty of stars in the sky and the half-moon cast enough light on them all, providing plenty of illumination to work with. They'd all lined up as if they were a single squad, which reflected a cruel reality. Before the outbreak there'd been over thirty men and women in the platoon, but now they were down to eleven soldiers, including Mark and their medic, Bags. To augment their depleted numbers they'd added Sheriff's Deputies, Darin Jefferson and Angie Carnegie, to their ranks. With Clay Roberts and now young Angel Ortiz, they had fifteen effectives. Sixteen, if you counted Saxon.

Mark went down the line and checked their gear, one by one. He ordered them all to pull out their ammunition, looking to see if it was clean and in sufficient supply. He spent a little extra time going over the machine gun belts to ensure the steel links weren't rusty and that everything had been secured properly. He also checked their personal water supplies to make sure that canteens and Camelbaks were topped off. They didn't get a resupply the previous day and the jerry cans were getting low, but they had enough on hand.

Lastly, he meticulously checked their night vision devices, laser illuminators and flashlights. He inspected to make sure they functioned properly and that the batteries were still good. He checked the batteries on the squad radios too, feeling uncomfortable after doing the commo checks. While they had plenty of AA batteries, mostly scrounged from houses, the proprietary military batteries were in extremely short supply. It would only be a matter of time before those were expended and then the dismount radios would be useless. Mark pushed the thought to the back of his mind, staying focused on the task at hand.

"Motherfucker, I should kick your ass," Dubois said, looming over his buddy Johnson who busied himself cinching up his rucksack.

"I told you, they're around here somewhere. I didn't lose them," Johnson responded, not bothering to look up at his friend.

"Well, if they ain't lost, then where are they?"

Harris, in no mood for the arguing so early in the morning, stepped in to intervene. "What's the problem with you two?"

"Nothing. Nothing's the problem," Dubois responded indignantly, still standing over his buddy.

"You two have been at it since last night. What the hell is it?" Harris said, planting his hands on his hips, not moving until he received a proper answer.

"Dubois thinks I lost something. That's all." Johnson finished securing the top flap on the backpack before standing up, glaring right back at his friend.

"Lost what? You didn't lose a sensitive item, did you?" The idea that one of them had misplaced a weapon or some other piece of critical equipment would have been bad enough under normal conditions, but under the current set of circumstances, it might put all their lives at risk.

"No, it's nothing like that." Johnson did not elaborate which began to visibly irritate Harris.

"Spill it. Tell me what this is all about."

Dubois rolled his eyes. "Fine, I'll tell you then. Johnson lost our only set of dice."

"Dice? What are you… wait, are you serious? You guys

are at each other's throats because you lost your Dungeons and Dragons dice?"

"I told you, I didn't lose them. I just misplaced them. They've got to be in one of the duffel bags somewhere."

"We already looked through all of them you dickhead!" Dubois balled his hands up into fists while clenching his teeth.

"I told you these two were idiots," Gray piled on.

"Mind your own business and butt out!" Dubois snapped back.

"Okay, knock it off. The both of you. We've got serious business to take care of and I don't need this shit right now. Got it?" Harris stabbed a finger at them.

"Roger," Johnson said, before hefting up his rucksack by the shoulder straps.

"Fine," Dubois added before turning away from his buddy.

"Look at you, falling right in on this new Squad Leader role. Before long they'll be pinning stripes on you." Gray wore a wicked little smirk on her face.

"Listen, Gray. If I wanted any shit out of you, I'd squeeze your head." Harris scowled at her, clearly in no mood to take any crap.

"Whatever," she said, slapping the feed tray cover of her SAW back into place.

Mark watched the whole exchange from a few feet away, disinterested in getting into the middle of another one of their petty arguments. They'd spent nearly every minute of every day with each other for over two months now and they were beginning to get sick of looking at each other's faces. Even the tiniest of nuisances would set one of them off. It was getting really old.

Off to the side Cynthia Roberts and her daughter Bailey lugged some mermite cans over. After setting them down, Consuela and Vanessa set to work opening them up and getting them ready for serving. Nobody called Vanessa by her stripper stage name anymore, not after her husband punched Jimmy Hong in the face for calling her "Candi" once. She didn't seem to mind, but Donahue was incensed.

The soldiers wasted no time in digging out their mess tins, anxious to get their breakfast. With short rations, they'd make short work of the contents once they dished it out. Mark wanted to knock out the inspections first before they ate, so most of them stood by impatiently, staring at the food.

He wandered over to the two sheriff's deputies who tended to stick together. They weren't soldiers and had worked together before the outbreak, so they had a tendency to pair up. "How's the leg feeling?"

Darin Jefferson looked down at it before responding. "The Army surgeon did a pretty good job with it and the wound has mostly healed up. It still hurts though."

"You've got a noticeable limp. You sure you're alright? You can sit this one out if you want to." Mark wasn't thrilled about the idea of leaving anyone behind since they were so short-handed, but he didn't want to take anyone out on a mission if they couldn't keep up either.

"I'm good. Don't worry about me."

Angie knelt next to Saxon, petting him on the head. "Seriously, Darin. If you're not ready then you should not go out."

"No, I'm fine. It just hurts a bit but I can walk. I can run too, if I need to."

"Well then, let's get this show on the road." Satisfied that everything was in order, Mark raised his voice. "Okay, line up for chow. Scarf that shit down quick. After that, get loaded up, we're REDCON 1 in twenty minutes!"

***

Task Force Dagger
Holmes Lake Park
Lincoln, Nebraska
0947 Hours Local

Colonel Dane Williams stood atop the turret of the M1 Abrams, raising a set of binoculars to his eyes, trying to get the best view he could. He found himself frustrated being on the ground and unable to see everything going on around. He'd been up in a Blackhawk for a while, but the damned things couldn't loiter when mortars and artillery were coming in, so he begrudgingly ordered the crew to set him down in the center of *Task Force Dagger*'s perimeter.

The engineers constructed some barrier materials to funnel the dead into prepared kill sacks, but it didn't look terribly impressive. They didn't have the amount of concertina wire and U-shaped pickets they'd enjoyed in previous operations, since the brigade only possessed what it could physically carry, strapped to the hulls of the combat vehicles. Luckily, the northern and western sides of the park were surrounded by a lake and the infected could only come at them from the east and the south. That allowed them to concentrate their obstacle effort in a smaller, 180-degree arc.

He scanned around, watching the flurry of activity. The tanks, infantry and engineers worked like mad, continuing to improve their positions while the Zulus trickled in. The noise and activity drew them in like moths to the flame, just as intended, but they weren't quite ready yet. The random pops and bursts of small arms fire rang out along the southern edge of the perimeter while picket-pounders clanged.

Williams lowered his binoculars and sucked at his teeth. A slight bit of distress nagged at him as he thought about his experience back at the World War I museum. It would have been a whole lot safer flying around in a helicopter, above all of this, but it was the best he could do. He rationalized that from the seat of a Blackhawk he'd be better able to command all of the dispersed maneuver forces and that's where he should be. He continued to deny the fact that he felt frightened to be there in the thick of it all, literally acting as bait to keep pressure off the main effort.

"Sir, 1st Brigade's artillery battalion is standing by. Should I have them fire their first concentration?"

Williams looked down at the officer in the commander's hatch of the tank. It was the battalion's operations officer, holding a radio handmike, awaiting orders. "Yes, Peter. Please have them initiate."

The major nodded before speaking into the handset. Williams took a deep breath and sighed, the smell of vehicle exhaust hanging in his nose. *We're off and running now*, he thought to himself.

***

BOHICA rolled down the highway headed north, careful to keep their speed at twenty-five miles per hour. They were capable of driving faster, but it wasn't a good idea. If one of the steel pins holding the track shoes in place snapped, they would violently throw track and if moving too fast, the vehicle would roll over and tumble. With nearly the entire top of the IFV covered in riders, they'd have a very bad day under that scenario. Not that the crew on the inside would come away much better.

They rolled as part of a massive convoy, with other platoons and companies both in front and behind them. Tucked into their rear were the company's light trucks driven by their supply sergeant and the NBC NCO. They also had some additional LMTVs as well, on loan from the battalion's Distribution Platoon. They'd need all the vehicles they could get their hands on to carry out the badly-needed supplies they were after.

Their battalion's objectives were in the suburb of Porter Ridge which sat on the southwest side of the city. They were after the Costco and the Walmart Supercenter. These two facilities were not located too deep inside the city, located nearly on its fringe. That made this a particularly desirable option, since the deeper they had to head into the Hot Zone, the more dangerous the mission became.

The few serviceable attack helicopters buzzed by just over their heads and peeled off, headed to the center of Lincoln. Behind them followed a few Blackhawks, with their crew chiefs leaning in behind their pintle-mounted machine guns. They were going to do what they always did on these large-scale ops. They were in support of the task force already committed deep inside the city, drawing pressure away from the other battalions. There weren't a whole lot of serviceable choppers available after the storm. The maintenance teams worked night and day to cannibalize the severely damaged birds for parts to get more of them up and running.

Mark looked up and saw a billboard on the side of the road advertising a local casino only a short distance up ahead. It instantly reminded him of their firefight with a group of desperate civilians back at that casino in Kansas City. The memory of that made him shudder. They'd lost a lot of good people that day.

Even with the headset on, he could hear the thundering booms of artillery landing on the far side of town. They'd been eavesdropping on the Brigade command net earlier in the day right up until they got the order to move out. As far as they could tell, everything was going according to plan and now it was their turn to get activated.

They passed through untended fields on both sides of the highway, while up ahead the battalion made its turn east, headed into the city. The column stretched for miles, with the tracks and trucks keeping a modest spacing between each of them. Mark's track followed just behind Lieutenant Baker's tank. Sergeant Yokey occupied the loader's hatch and turned around, waving at Donahue. Mark's gunner responded by flashing his middle finger. Yokey roared with laughter and turned back around, going back to annoying his lieutenant.

The lead elements of the battalion soon turned right, then crossed a creek before finally entering the suburbs. The neat little neighborhoods had once been nice places to live, but now were overgrown with uncut grass and weeds. Occasionally they'd pass an abandoned car here or there, but mostly the streets were empty. Every now and again the column would pass human remains on the sidewalks or in driveways, all in advanced stages of decomposition. It reminded them all of scenes they'd come across many times before.

They came upon a row of houses completely burned to the ground, with very little left besides the blackened timbers. Passing by, a runner came out of nowhere and pursued them, its bare feet slapping the pavement. The infantry riding atop the armored vehicles did nothing more than watch the creature out of curiosity, not bothering to shoot. One of the Bradleys suddenly swerved to the right and caught it, grinding it mercilessly into the asphalt without even slowing down.

Within minutes the other companies began peeling off, headed to their individual objectives. Bravo Company continued pushing forward, following a section from the battalion's scout platoon who had already done a thorough recon of the area. They didn't need the scouts to show them how to get to their objective, but they did need them to proof the route. All too often in the past they'd run into unexpected roadblocks which cost them precious time or even put them in physical danger. The recon elements made sure they got to their intended destinations as quickly and efficiently as possible.

Finally, they emerged from one of the suburban neighborhoods and pulled into the sprawling parking lot of Walmart. As planned, Lieutenant Baker went along with 3rd Platoon, setting up a perimeter around the area, doing the best they could with the limited number of people available. Even the two scout Humvees helped out, their gunners scanning from behind .50 caliber machine guns.

BOHICA pulled up near the main entrance before coming to a stop and dropping ramp. The people inside emerged into the sunlight while those riding up top immediately climbed down. Mark removed his CVC and replaced it with an ACH helmet before grabbing his shotgun. "Donahue, tell Burbey to shut her down and let's go."

He climbed down off the Bradley and watched the group organize themselves. They fell naturally into two different squads, clustering together while getting lined up to go inside. Angel looked at him, giving a big toothy grin and a "thumbs up." Mark gently squeezed the kid's shoulder with his right hand and reciprocated with a smile that didn't quite reach the eyes.

"Looks like somebody's already been inside." Weber pointed at the doors with his machete. They'd been completely smashed and glass covered the entranceway.

"Well, at least we won't have to make any noise going in." Mark looked over at Angie. "Okay, Deputy. You're up."

Angela Carnegie slung her rifle across her back and drew the Glock from her service holster before looking down at

Saxon. "Come on, Boy. Let's do this." Still holding him by the leash, she carefully approached the entrance, pointing the pistol inside. Gingerly, she stepped on the shards of glass while Saxon moved alongside her, his head held low, sniffing at the ground and the air. Then he stopped. The hair on his shoulders stood up and the dog began to growl.

Mark nodded and swallowed hard. "Okay, 1st Squad. Your turn."

"Roger," Harris said. "Johnson, you take the lead with Alpha Team."

Johnson and Dubois went in first. Johnson flicked on the weapon light and took the lead, while Dubois followed right behind him holding an axe. If they made contact with a walker, standard procedure dictated that they use a melee weapon to minimize the noise. They'd use the firearm if they ran into a runner. Or worse.

Gray came in next, carrying a Mossberg 500 with Harris behind her, sledgehammer in hand. Bags went in next holding an HK USP chambered in .45 with both hands. The weapon appeared particularly large for her, but she'd been training with it and preferred the magazine capacity and stopping power. She definitely preferred it in close quarters.

Mark fell in next, pulling the olive drab army-issue bandana over his nose and mouth, while checking to make sure his goggles were firmly in place. He shouldered his Remington 11-87, keeping it at the low ready while Burbey and Donahue followed.

Mercifully, the smashed front doors allowed plenty of fresh air inside. Still, the smell of death became nearly overwhelming and a few of them retched once they made it inside. It didn't matter how many times they'd been exposed to this, it never got any easier.

They moved in a tight formation, with weapons and lights

facing out in every direction. Burbey and Donahue took particular care to make sure nothing snuck up behind them. They'd been through that before too and it hadn't been pretty.

Mark swept his weapon light around and found the place in total disorder. Moving past the checkout lanes toward the grocery section, they saw racks toppled over and dried blood smeared all over the place. They took a wide berth around a rotted corpse sprawled out on the tiled floor, nearly covered in a cloud of flies and shimmering in a mass of maggots.

"Oh, dear God," Bags whispered loudly upon seeing the sight.

"Steady. We've all seen this before. Stay focused," Mark responded, doing his best to sooth her fraying nerves.

They moved swiftly and smoothly, like jungle cats, zeroing in on the aisles of food. Things were in disarray and items littered the ground. The stink of rot grew even more intense from the meat that had decayed once the coolers and freezers shut down.

Mark gave the hand signal to "halt," then waved Harris over.

"What's up, Sarn't," Harris whispered, looking around nervously.

"It looks like we weren't the first ones in this place." Mark pointed at the looted shelves.

"I guess we shouldn't be surprised, but there's plenty left. Whoever came through before us didn't get everything." Harris leaned over and picked up a packet of instant noodles off the floor, showing it to the NCO before shoving it in his cargo pocket.

"Let's head toward the storage in the back. We need to get the bay doors open at the loading dock anyway."

A loud hiss broke the silence and heads snapped to the left to find one of the dead making its way toward them, emerging from behind a display of stacked soda cans. The skin on its face drew tight and leathery over boney cheeks and away from those awful, red eyes. The black ooze they'd become all-too familiar with dripped from its mouth and down its chin, breaking off in oily drops onto the floor. It moved with great difficulty, dragging a broken leg, its upper body swinging violently at the hip, limping forward.

Dubois reacted instantly, lunging forward, swinging the axe high. When the creature saw him approach, it howled loudly, trembling in anticipation. It reached its hands out in a deathly embrace toward the soldier, only to have the steel bit land squarely on its cranium, caving in the top of the skull. The creature collapsed under the blow, folding in on itself and crumpling to the ground.

Pulling the tool free Dubois heard another loud noise and saw that there were many others coming from the same direction this one had just come. "Contact!" He backed off raising the weapon again, realizing there were too many to take out this way and they were only a few feet away, closing in fast. He swung again at another one that looked like it used to be a middle-aged woman, only to have the blade glance off the creature's cheek and smash into its collar bone.

Before he could bring the weapon to bear again the thing swiped at him with jagged nails, missing his face by mere inches. Howls erupted all around and many more hideous faces emerged from the dark.

The tower of precisely-arranged soda cans came crashing down, landing on top of Dubois, burying him. The others all reacted the same way and shined their flashlights in his direction, suddenly staring face to face with dozens of the things flooding around the corner of the potato chip aisle. Their luminescent eyes glowed horribly when the lights shined on them.

"Oh shit, oh shit, *oh shit!*" cried Gray. She brought her shotgun up and let fly with a thunderous boom that assaulted their eardrums. She cut loose without aiming but the things were so close it was hard to miss. She caught one in the side of its face, blowing its left cheekbone off, sending shards of bone and scraps of rotted meat splattering into its companions. One of the 00 buck pellets passed through the orbital cavity and into the brain, sending a ballistic shockwave through the soft fleshy contents of the skull, doing enough damage to drop it in its tracks.

"*Let's rock!*" screamed Bags, who popped off rounds in rapid succession with her USP, sending tiny ashtrays of .45 ACP toward the dead at 900 feet per second. A couple of them near the front snapped their heads back and fell to the ground while the others ignored the carnage and surged ahead toward the fresh meat.

An Aliens *reference at a time like this? Are you serious?* Mark thought to himself. "*Weapons free! Go kinetic!*" Mark shouted, bringing up his own scattergun, watching the things come out of nowhere. Pistols, rifles and shotguns all barked at once in a deafening symphony. The first row of them collapsed to their front, while many, many more emerged from the gloom.

They might not have been fast, but there sure were a lot of them and were coming out of the woodwork. The image of Sergeant Apone flashed in Mark's mind for some reason as he blasted away with his 12 gauge.

***

Colonel Dane Williams held the handmike to his right ear, while sticking his finger in the left to block out some of the noise. "Repeat. I say again, repeat. How copy? *Over!*"

Artillery shells came hurtling in, geysering dirt and debris all along their southern and eastern perimeter. Massive shell splinters from the 155mm shells scythed through the air, cutting the dead to ribbons as they writhed around in the concertina wire obstacles erected to the front of their fighting positions.

"Roger, Six. Repeat," crackled the disembodied voice over the radio, acknowledging the Brigade Commander's fire command.

More rounds came in, pummeling and smashing the surging tsunami of infected bodies, rushing toward the battalion. They continued firing every weapon system they had, cutting the animated bodies into chunks of blackened, stinking, flesh. When the wind changed direction, the smell of burnt powder was replaced by something that made many void their stomachs on the spot.

Dane brought the binoculars up and couldn't believe how many there were and the numbers continued to increase. *Where in the hell are they coming from?* he wondered.

"Six, this is Guns. Shot, over."

"Roger, shot, out." Dane looked at his watch and couldn't believe the time. He could have sworn they'd only been there a few minutes, but hours had gone by. They'd been at this for a while already. The dead trickled in at first and they made no attempt at stealth, doing their best to draw them in. Steadily, over time, the numbers coming in increased until it became something awful and unbelievable. Reports streamed in that commanders were becoming concerned about their on-hand supplies of ammunition. It hadn't become critical yet, but it was only a matter of time.

"Splash, over."

Another series of tooth-rattling explosions flashed to their front, the shockwaves washing over them. "Splash, out!" Dane winced involuntarily under the concussions. Those shells were already "danger close" and a few of their people reported shrapnel bouncing off the skins of their tracks and tanks. The boys and girls on the ground were hugging the earth and making themselves as small as they possibly could, crawling into any available depression for cover.

"Dagger Six, this is Guns. Rounds complete. Over."

"Guns, this is Dagger Six. Need you to fire another concentration. Same grid. Over." Nervously, he turned to look off to the north and west. Those flanks were covered by a lake and since the dead couldn't swim, they milled around on the far side, flowing around it and into their well-established kill zone.

"I'm sorry, Six. Orders from the Division Commander. We have to keep a few shells in reserve. We've shot everything we're allowed to shoot today. All we've got is Division Fires and you're too close for that. We can't bring it in any closer."

"Son of a bitch!" Dane cried out. Standing on the turret of the tank, the vehicle commander looked up at him after the outburst, careful to look away before the irate Brigade Commander saw him staring.

No sooner had the shells stopped falling than a pair of Apache gunships popped up from nearly a thousand yards distant, immediately blasting away with their 30mm chain guns. The rounds were far more precise than the artillery and worked like scalpels, slicing away the lead ranks of the dead getting caught up in the wire, but as good as those aviators were, there simply weren't enough of them and the horde kept coming, streaming in by the thousands.

Small arms fire picked up and the thunder of claymore mines boomed along the line. The Bradleys poured it on with their anti-personnel rounds while the Abrams filled their air with clouds of tungsten shot. Flesh and bone exploded, but the dead continued to press on, letting out their howls of ecstasy, quivering in anticipation of the impending feed.

Without warning the Apaches suddenly peeled off and Dane's mouth grew cottony. The surge at the wire along the east side grew at alarming speed. The meager wire obstacles they'd managed to emplace would last no more than a few seconds at best. It was obvious to anyone that they'd come crashing through at any moment and this thing would be hand-to-hand, and bayonets against the dead almost always ended badly.

Just then came a streaking roar as a pair of A-10s flew in at less than 200 feet. They dropped a few cylinders from the hardpoints on their wings before pulling up toward the sky. The oblong shapes tumbled to the ground in and among the infected, bursting into giant blossoms of jellied fire. The napalm engulfed hundreds of them in an instant, sending forth a blast-furnace of heat that made the soldiers nearest it turn away.

At first the damnable things coated in incendigel kept coming on, seemingly unaffected by the flames, but once the heat began to cook the rancid brains in their skulls, they began to drop, one by one, consumed in a massive funeral pyre.

The attack aircraft came swooping in for another pass, doing the same along the southern approach. Soldiers picked themselves off the ground, hooting and hollering in elation. They gave each other high-fives and fist bumps, while some embraced one another. Even the major in the commander's hatch of the tank spared a moment to give Dane Williams a big, toothy smile.

The Air Force was indeed bringing the heat.

Literally.

***

Five of the undead stood on the western shoreline of Holmes Lake watching the soldiers on the other side fighting off wave after wave of the infected. Walkers and shamblers milled around them, paralleling the waterline and following it toward the living. They couldn't resist the smells and the sounds of the men and women just a short distance away. Their ravenous hunger drove them with singular focus.

While the vast majority of them worked their way around, afraid to enter the water. When they emerged on the flanks of the park, soldiers with heavy machine guns blasted them into pulp. Still, they pressed on, undaunted. The dead did not feel fear and no concept of pain. At least the walkers and shamblers didn't.

These five were different from the others however. Three men and two women, wearing clothes matted in sticky, dried blood. The blue spiderwebs on their faces accentuated the glowing red eyes. Shoulder to shoulder they watched, studying the action a short distance away. The Alphas still possessed the ability to think, communicate and plan. They retained the intellectual capacity of dogs and stuck together in packs, hunting like them too.

On the western side of the lake the expanse of water grew narrow, almost like a canal. Across this spanned a single footbridge, erected as a shortcut to get to the park. The soldiers had piled a gnarled pile of razor wire in the center of and plugged it like a cork in a bottle. Many of the walkers and a few runners tried to get through only to get hopelessly entangled, whereupon a handful of soldiers guarding the bridge would dispatch them. That didn't stop others from trying, and the footbridge was packed with creatures, some crawling over the motionless bodies of their brethren.

The lead Alpha in their pack had been a man in his early

thirties before he'd been bitten and turned. He was bigger than the others and asserted his domination. The others had followed him now for weeks, and they'd taken dozens of the living down in that time, sneaking, stalking and ambushing their prey. They normally took the small and the weak, avoiding large armed parties of people, knowing they were incredibly dangerous, and normally they wouldn't dream of approaching soldiers, organized as they were, but this time was different. They hadn't fed on anything in days, and their hunger made them desperate.

So they remained steady and watched, looking for an opportunity, any opportunity to present itself.

They watched the airplanes come in and drop their bombs, incinerating hundreds of their animated companions. The fire consumed them without mercy and flames licked the sky, sending up clouds of thick, black, smoke roiling upward. They watched the planes come in time and time again, dropping bombs and strafing with their big guns, laying waste.

Then, a breeze picked up, blowing into their faces. The smoke along the eastern side of the perimeter wafted over the soldiers and their armored vehicles, obscuring everything. Eventually, it came across the canal and onto the western shore, engulfing them too.

The lead Alpha grunted in satisfaction, before turning to his pack. "*Come.*"

He took off at a jog headed straight toward the footbridge. The other four wasted no time and followed, not sure of what he intended to do, but trusting him implicitly.

The leader came upon the bridge but did not mount it like the scores of others trying to bull their way through the obstacle, instead he entered the water underneath it. He used the bridge as cover and concealment from the soldiers on the far shore who guarded it.

Most of the dead feared going in the water, but Alphas still retained basic skills. The five of them swam across the narrow expanse, following in a line behind the dominant one, careful to stay under the bridge and out of sight. With the thick smoke everywhere, they made their way across completely undetected.

They emerged from the water on the far side, keeping low and sneaking up the slope, moving like the predators they were. The leader had nearly climbed all the way to the top when he motioned to the others to stay back. He'd spotted one of the soldiers nearby and didn't want them bumbling into him.

He sniffed at the air and could tell there were others around too, but it was so difficult to see, the others were invisible. The wind shifted again and the leader crouched near some bushes patiently, waiting for his opportunity, and when it came, he signaled to the rest to follow him.

He darted from behind cover and raced into the smoke, toward where he'd last seen the soldier. In seconds he and the rest of the pack were on top of the unsuspecting combat engineer, claiming their first victim of the day.

Chapter 11

"*Contact right!*" Mark screamed over the small arms fire.

A group of the things worked their way around the pet food aisle and came up on the flank. Gray swung her Mossberg over and let fly with a spread of 00 buck, fluidly working the slide and racking another shell home before letting loose with another. She repeated the process again only to have the firing pin snap on an empty chamber. "Reloading!"

Harris had his night vision monocular positioned over his right eye and switched on, relying on the Infrared laser designator to aim. The beam danced into position settling on the forehead of one of the monsters. He pulled the trigger and popped off a round. He didn't wait for the Zulu to hit the floor before taking aim on the next one, dropping it too.

"*Contact Left!*" Bags yelled.

Left? How the hell did they get around us to the left? Mark thought to himself, sparing a moment to look. Sure enough, some of them had worked their way around the cash registers and were now standing between them and the way they'd just come in. They were now effectively cut off. "Everybody fall back! Head toward the deli!"

All at once the entire squad broke contact, hauling ass to their rear. They did not thin the line and bounded back by fire teams or pairs, instead they moved as a single unit at once. Moving as fast as their feet could carry them, running past neatly stacked bags of dry dog food and other pet items, headed for the glass showcases up ahead. The nearer they got to the coolers full of rotted meat, the more intense the smell, but with the adrenaline surging through their veins, they hardly noticed.

They pushed their way through the employee gate and lined up behind the glass, as if to service some rather surly customers. Gray reached into a pouch on her chest rig and came out with a handful of shells, stuffing them one by one into the feed ramp of her shotgun. While she did that, Donahue and Burbey checked the back to ensure they didn't have any unwanted company coming up from their rear.

"Bravo Team, this is White One. Bravo Team, this is White One. Answer me damnit!" Mark looked down at the squad radio attached to his MOLLE system when he noticed it wasn't switched on. *Jesus Christ, what a fucking rookie move!* He thought to himself while turning it on.

"*...this is White Two, over!*" the radio crackled to life.

"Here they come!" said Harris, as he opened up along with Johnson and Dubois on either side of him.

"White Two, this is White One. Need you to lend us a hand, we're in it deep. Over." Mark brought his Remington up, using the flashlight attached to the barrel to aim. The beam centered on the awful face of something that used to be a teenage girl. He pulled the trigger and its head disappeared in a shower of gore.

"*We've been trying to reach you. What's the situation? Over.*" Clay's voice came in clear in Mark's earphone, now that the radio was actually turned on.

"We ran into a large group of them and they've got us cut off. Need you to come in, hang a right and when you reach the end of the checkout lanes, get on line facing to your left, oriented on the pet food aisle. Over."

"*Okay, we'll be there in a sec!*"

Mark didn't acknowledge, instead sweeping his barrel to the right where one of the things attempted to climb over the glass showcase. He blasted it in the face, sending it tumbling backwards. "Everybody orient your fire to the right of the checkout lanes. We got help coming and I don't want you hitting any friendlies!"

Bags popped off a series of rounds with her USP, the large handgun bucking with each shot when the slide locked to the rear on an empty magazine. "Reloading!"

Burbey and Donahue came out from the back and began pouring on fire of their own. They knocked down a few, but the dead kept emerging from the inky darkness to the rear of the store. They couldn't get a good count and all they knew for sure is that the things were coming out of the woodwork.

Suddenly a hail of fire erupted from their left and they saw the familiar sight of flashlight beams and IR illuminators. The beams of those lights pointed lengthwise across to their front. It was Bravo Team and they'd managed to set up in a classic "L" shape, catching the dead in a perfect crossfire, knocking the creatures down like bowling pins.

The ones exposed out in the open went down quickly, while others worked their way behind cover in the various sections of the grocery annex. With more living soldiers joining the fray, the things lost focus, not solely concentrating on Alpha Team in the deli any longer and they began falling in heaps.

Mark's semi-automatic shotgun went dry and started to reload it while the others picked up the slack. "They ain't paying us enough for this shit, man."

Gray turned to him, "What did you say?"

"What? Me? Oh nothing. Never mind."

***

Task Force Dagger
Holmes Lake Park

The mortar platoon had their M1064 tracked carriers clustered together in the extreme northwest corner of the park.

In combat against an enemy who could shoot back, they'd have spread their vehicles out in case of counter-battery fire, but since their current foe couldn't operate firearms, or artillery for that matter, they elected to keep everything in tight for ease of control.

They set up as physically far to the rear as they could manage in order to be able to range the targets nearest to the battalion's kill zone. The mortars could lob their rounds at a distance of nearly five miles, but they didn't need nearly that much reach on their current mission, so they set the tubes at extreme angles and prepped the rounds with minimal propellant charges.

The platoon lingered around their four mortar carriers with the command element clustered around the Fire Direction Center track. They hadn't shot a fire mission in hours, ever since the dead made their first concerted rush at the perimeter wire. Ever since then the artillery, Apaches and now the Air Force kept them at bay, but they watched the A-10s make their final passes, expending the last of their ordnance before peeling off toward the horizon. Going back to wherever they'd come from.

Sergeant First Class Meadows coughed violently in the choking black smoke. Ever since the wind shifted, they struggled to breath and the tears streamed from their stinging eyes. It may have been unpleasant, but they still felt buoyed by the knowledge that they'd roasted hundreds of the creatures hung up in the wire.

"Sergeant Meadows, Battalion says that they will be processing fire missions shortly and that we should stand by." The Platoon Leader stood on the ramp of the FDC, handmike jammed up against his ear.

"Roger, sir. It's about damn time." Meadows didn't feel like standing around any longer, nervously pacing back and forth in front of his Humvee. He heard the distinct sound of the coax machine guns going into action again. Their high cyclic rate distinguished themselves from the dismounted variants.

He caught some movement about thirty yards distant and hacked up some phlegm, spitting it to the ground. He looked back up and blinked hard to clear his sight in the haze to see soldiers walking around aimlessly, almost strolling. Though difficult to see, some of them were wandering around without their weapons. Those that did, had their carbines hanging loosely by their slings.

Someone suddenly let out a high-pitched scream to his left.

Over on Gun Track Four he saw several people struggling and there were panicked shouts. Soldiers wrestled in the dirt and someone fell off the top of the track. Then, rifles cracked in rapid succession.

"What the fuck is going on over there?" Meadows called out, bringing his own weapon to bear. He set off in a trot toward the mayhem, hearing others near Gun One carrying on. He shouldered his weapon and peered down the holographic optic, through bleary eyes.

The lieutenant dropped his handset. "Sergeant Meadows, report!" A soldier came sprinting out of the haze and tackled the officer at full speed like a linebacker, taking him clean off his feet. The two of them tumbled in the dirt and the lieutenant let out a shriek.

When he reached Gun Four he found his men intermixed with other soldiers, grappling with one another, grunting and calling out for help. A few fired their weapons, shooting some of their comrades down. Someone opened up with a .50 cal on Gun Three, slinging slugs wildly, knocking soldiers down indiscriminately.

Someone came running straight at him, hands outreached.

It was a female clad in her camouflage uniform, ammo pouches bouncing in rhythm with each stride. Her helmet hung loosely on its straps, fully exposing her forehead. The varicose spider-webbing on her face accentuated by the dark blueness of her lips and the glowing redness of the eyes. She pulled those lips back, exposing snarling teeth.

He brought the barrel of his weapon up and snapped off a few rounds in rapid succession, the last one landing at the bridge of her nose, sending her sprawling at his feet.

Meadows stood there with chest heaving, looking down at her while chaos raged.

When he looked back up, something hit him hard in the back and he went flying forward, landing on top of the thing he'd just shot. He began to push himself up off the corpse when a set of teeth clamped down on his neck, slicing through the skin and into the flesh.

Sergeant First Class Ron Meadows let out yelp while the world came unglued all around him.

***

Captain Alfonse Caldwell found himself choking in the thick smoke before ordering his sappers to put on their gas masks. They hadn't been using them lately and most of the engineers had to run back in relays to their armored personnel carriers to dig them out of rucksacks and duffel bags. He watched his people scramble around trying to find their kit in total frustration. He wanted to lash out and start screaming at people but realized that would be counterproductive, so he opted to sit there stewing in silence.

The raging inferno on the perimeter held back waves of the dead and the small arms fire along the perimeter slacked off, but it would only be a matter of time before the napalm burned itself out and they'd be full on again.

He stood on one of the bench seats in the back of his M113 in the open troop hatch just behind his Track Commander, who kept vigilant behind the spade grips of his .50 caliber machine gun. Alfonse tore his attention away from the flames and smoke to his front, looking down at his map board and going over the withdrawal plan in his head. He flipped through some operational graphics taped to the plexiglass when some shots rang out to their rear.

He craned his neck, trying to see what was going on. There shouldn't have been anybody shooting behind them, the engagement areas were in the other direction. His agitation over the protective mask fiasco now elevated to frustration and anger at the thought of undisciplined fire potentially hitting some friendlies.

"Goddammit. What the hell is going on back there?" He said to himself, picking up his personal weapon, preparing to dismount and get a look for himself. He ducked down and descended the lowered ramp when the volume of fire to their rear picked up in a rapid crescendo.

Then he caught glimpses in the haze of soldiers running past to his left and right. Then he saw others hot on their heels.

Blood curdling screams punctuated the noise and Alfonse froze in his tracks, watching a soldier taking aim and shooting at some of the others, before getting mobbed and taken down to the ground. The infected wore camouflage uniforms and body armor, just like the rest of his engineers. They tore the flesh from his bones while he kicked and squirmed, trying to get free of them.

"Dear God." He turned and bolted back to his track, snatching up a handmike and broadcasting on the battalion command channel. "*Blue Babe Six, this is Rock Six. We've got dead inside the wire they're coming from the…*"

Before Alfonse could finish his transmission a group of runners emerged from the smoke and sprinted up the back ramp, pulling him down inside the troop compartment. He let out a shriek before his Track Commander could do anything. The enlisted man couldn't depress his machine gun into the back and had no pistol on his person. Instead, he climbed out of the hatch and jumped off the side of the vehicle, leaving his captain and driver behind to fend for themselves.

As he strained to breath through his gas mask while he ran, people flashed past him going in both directions while shouts, screams and gunshots crackled around him. Within seconds that entire section of the perimeter completely disintegrated with men and women running for their lives and the dead in hot pursuit.

***

Mark and the rest of the squad emerged back into the daylight after spending the better part of an hour clearing the last corners of the store. Clay came out with Bravo Team and gave a knowing look. They all took big gulps of fresh air the moment they made it back outside. Angel came stumbling out, pushing the lip of his helmet up so he could see.

"Fix your chin strap, Angel. It'll hold your brain-bucket in place properly," Weber said derisively, shaking his head. The kid had performed poorly inside, barely keeping up and constantly tripping over stuff. He kept flagging the rest of them with his weapon and they nearly took it away from him. He'd shot at some Zulus, but hadn't brought a single one down.

Out on the edge of the parking lot, members of the Scout Platoon busied themselves whacking walkers and shamblers that came at them in ones and twos. There'd been a lot of noise inside the Walmart, but it had only drawn a handful of Zulus from the surrounding houses, and none of those had been runners.

Lieutenant Baker came striding up and slapped Mark on the shoulder. "Good job, Matthews. Did you get them all?"

"As best as I can tell, sir. We can do another sweep if you like." Mark regretted saying those words the second they left his mouth. He sure as hell didn't want to go back in there.

"No time for that. Look over there." Baker pointed to the major intersection off to their east. From there, a column of eighteen-wheelers came rolling into the parking lot and then went around back to the loading docks.

"Are they going to need a hand?" Mark pointed over his shoulder with a thumb while the rest of the platoon looked on, watching the trucks pull in one by one.

"No, you and your people take a break. I'll call you when I need you."

"Lieutenant, Battalion's on the line. They said it's important." Yokey sat on the turret of his tank, *Carnage*, holding the handmike in the air, the spaghetti cord stretched nearly to its limit.

Mark watched the lieutenant jog over to his tank and felt a pang of discomfort. Something wasn't right. He took a look at his G-Shok and inhaled deeply. "Clay, Harris. I need to talk to the both of you."

The two of them broke off from the group with puzzled looks. "What's up, Boss? You look like something's wrong," Harris said, adjusting the sling on his weapon.

"Get everyone topped off on water and ammo. You've got ten minutes." Mark started stuffing more shells into the feed ramp of his Remington.

"Why? What's up?" Clay asked, raising an eyebrow.

Mark pointed over his shoulder to the lieutenant with his

thumb. "I got a feeling we are about to get a FRAGO. Get your people ready to move."

***

Holmes Lake Park
1245 Hours Local

As the thick pools of jellied gasoline burned itself out, the smoke began to clear and Dane could finally see how badly his rear-area had fallen apart. Men and women who had recently been under his command were now ravenous flesh-eaters, running amok, infecting their former comrades with merciless dispassion.

"Someone give me a report!" he demanded of the major, who spoke frantically into the radio handsets, doing his best to figure out what was happening. They'd received bits and pieces of panicked messages from every unit in their perimeter and none of it inspired any confidence.

The mass of dead along the east and southern approaches came surging through the dying flames, smashing the cinders of their companions underfoot, charging headlong into the blackened concertina wire. Bradley and tank crews opened up again, doing their best to hold back the oncoming waves of them, while dismounted infantry and engineers reoriented themselves, doing their best to contain the catastrophe in their rear. Harried officers and NCOs barked orders, yelling themselves hoarse while their voices remained muffled inside their gas masks.

The major pulled off his own protective mask in frustration, tossing it inside the tank. His face appeared beat red and covered in sweat. "Sir, my commander says he's working with the engineers to secure our rear."

Their tank sat idle next to the pro shop of the Holmes Golf Course, situated just on the east side of the park. The charred and cratered fairways to their east and south seemed to undulate with the dead. To their west, Dean saw dismounts taking up position, with their leaders putting them in place. Sometimes gathering up ad hoc groups to plug gaps all along the line.

The commanders on the ground thinned the lines to the east and south to create a line, oblong and almost cigar-shaped, but the thinning meant there were fewer guns aimed at the mob assaulting the wire and they were beginning to spill over top, breaching it with their very bodies.

"Where are my mortars? Where is the artillery?" Dean screeched, his eyes glued to the binoculars. He watched in horror as the wire began to fail to their front and groups of the dead fed on scores of his people from behind.

"Sir, our mortar platoons have been overrun. Division is working on getting us some support!"

Glassing the desperate fight in what had recently been his secured rear area, he caught sight of a half-dozen infected clad in uniforms mob a young female soldier. They set to work in seconds ripping flesh from bone. He dropped the binoculars, letting them hang loosely around his neck.

"If Division can't support us, then we need to pull out." Dane watched a platoon of engineers organize themselves nearly 200 meters distant. One squad laid down a hail of fire while the others bounded forward, doing their best to re-establish some sort of control.

"The G-3 called down and said that they need two more hours. The supplies in the city and out at the airport aren't secure yet. Our diversion is working, but we need to keep it up to buy them some more time." The major looked apologetic, not wanting his commander to kill the messenger.

"That's crazy! If we pull out, they can just send us back out here again tomorrow to finish the job!"

"Sir, Division says there's not nearly enough artillery or ordnance left for the aircraft to attempt this again. The Division Commander himself said that if we don't pull this off, there won't be another chance. This is it!"

Thoughts ran through his head like a freight train. The loss of Kansas City. The eviction from the state, and now this. It dawned on him that this was his last chance to redeem himself. This was his chance to rise to the occasion and become the hero-leader he was meant to be. The urge to run dissipated. Frustration built up in his chest and he refused to acquiesce. Failure wasn't an option and he was either going to prevail, or go down fighting.

He crouched down and grabbed the handmike from the major's grasp. "Guidons, guidons. This is Dagger Six. You will hold your positions at all costs. There will be no retreat from the field. You will hold your ground or you will die trying. This is our moment when posterity will look back upon us at the critical moment when we turned the tide and snatched victory from the jaws of defeat!"

***

Holmes Lake Park
1332 Hours Local

In a center section of the perimeter wire the infected kept piling up on top until the weight of their bodies finally flattened it. Hundreds of them came up from behind, trampling those caught in the razor wire and simply walking over top of the others. They held no sympathy for those they trod upon, crushing their cracking bones beneath their feet.

One of the tank crews saw the breach first and fired a blast of canister their way, tearing dozens of them to ribbons, but hundreds more came pouring through and the loaders couldn't keep up. Within minutes the dead were everywhere, intermixed with the vehicles and their crews, who shot desperately from the protection of their armored vehicles. The dismounted infantry and engineers on the other hand, were caught out in the open with nowhere to go.

A general panic broke out in the ranks and those on foot scattered in every direction. Officers and NCOs did everything in their power to exert control, but to no avail. The fear became contagious and nearly as deadly as the virus, washing over all of them, sending many into flight. Some even dropped their weapons, out of their minds with terror.

The tank and Bradley crews began closing their hatches, buttoning up, before putting their armored beasts into gear and launching themselves forward. They drove straight into the fray, mashing the infected under their tracks, grinding their bodies into the unkempt golf course fairways. They drove up and down the line, stopping the breaches by running the infiltrators over, mashing them into pulp.

Some of the dead swarmed the Abrams and Bradleys, only to have the others "scratch their backs," peppering the other armored vehicles with coax machine gun fire, sending the dead cartwheeling to the ground. Before long, the hulls of the tanks and tracks became coated, slick with thick, dark blood and viscera. The smell of it grew ever worse causing soldiers to vomit all up and down the line.

Dane watched with great apprehension as the men and women under his command fought for their very lives. Losses continued to mount and the perimeter continued to shrink in the face of valiant, suicidal efforts. Some fired their rifles while others swung mattock handles, shovels and axes taken from their vehicles. They used any tool available to fight back the advancing horde.

A grenadier fired his M320, sending a grenade arcing into a cluster of advancing walkers. It detonated in the center of the group and took off one of their legs just below the knee, while peppering the others with shrapnel. The slightly wounded ones carried on as if nothing had occurred and their maimed companion crawled along on the tortured ground, still headed straight for the living.

A lieutenant gathered up a random group of infantrymen and charged into a mass of the dead, cutting them down with small arms fire. They did it to cover the retreat of dozens of others who were in the process of re-establishing a defensive line a few meters to their rear. The lieutenant and his scratch team died horribly, doing their best to save their comrades, giving their last full measure.

In the center, things completely collapsed and the cigar-shaped perimeter suddenly split into two, like a cell dividing. The soldiers tried their best not to fire into and hit their friends on the opposite side of the field, but it couldn't be helped. People began to fall from friendly fire nearly as often as from the dead.

"What is the status of my support?" Dane demanded of the harried major, who crouched over his map board, clutching a radio transmitter in each hand.

"It's still a ways off, sir. There is precious little artillery ammunition left and they won't fire it anyway, since it'll land on top of us. They are reloading the handful of attack helicopters that are still able to fly and they said a sortie of F-15s is on the way from Peterson Air Force Base, but it'll be a while before they're on station." The major didn't even bother to look up at the colonel while he delivered his update.

A stray bullet smacked the turret of the tank and Dane

reflexively crouched down low. A burst of tracer flew overhead, missing him by inches, the super-sonic crack of the rounds snapping in his ears.

"We've got another, more pressing problem, sir." The major flipped through a set of operational graphics and spit out some orders to one of the companies. His battalion commander had fallen to the dead a half hour earlier and nobody could find the Battalion XO. He'd been forced to assume command and the stress mounted with each passing minute.

"What is it?" Dane's eyes darted to and fro. Tanks and Brads ran circles around the ad hoc formations of dismounted engineers and infantry, running down the infected, doing their best to establish a sort of motorized force field. They were an unstoppable force, but there weren't enough of them and the dead continued to leak through. While the walkers and shamblers fell scores at a time, the handful of runners took their toll.

"Reports are coming in from across the board. We're Red and nearly Black on ammunition." Finally, the major looked up at his Brigade Commander to emphasize the point, his eyes ablaze with emotion.

Dane clenched his fists and tried to find a solution. They still needed to hold out for another hour at least to take the pressure off the other battalions. If they retired from the field, they'd fail their mission and that wasn't an option at this point. There was no artillery. No air support, and no ammunition for the tanks, tracks or dismounts.

Think, damnit. Think!

It hit him like a lightning bolt. He thought back to his time in Iraq, back when he served as a Battalion Operations officer back in 2003. He remembered one operation in particular that drove a stake through the hearts of their enemies, and a similar tactic would serve them just as well this time.

He reached down and snatched a handmike from the major's hand. "Guidons, guidons. This is Dagger Six. Effective immediately I want all personnel to load up. We are headed out of here ASAP. Since our position here is untenable and we still need to take the heat off the rest of the brigade, we are going to execute a 'Thunder Run' through the center of Lincoln and draw the infected away. I will push the route to you in five mikes. All stations report when REDCON ONE. Acknowledge, Over!"

***

The infantry and engineers scrambled aboard their armored vehicles, packing into the backs of the troop compartments, many jumping in while ramps were still lifting. Under normal conditions, elements would have covered the moves of their buddies, laying down covering fire, allowing the others to move. This didn't play out that way and the moment the order was given to load up, they all abandoned the line at once, every man for himself.

Once the armored personnel carriers and Bradleys loaded their dismounts, the crews buttoned up their hatches tight. Within seconds the infected covered the outer hulls, some of them possessing the presence of mind to try and pull the doors and hatches open. To their frustration, they were all combat locked from the inside, where the surviving soldiers found refuge.

Reports went over the command frequencies stating they were ready to move and Dane Williams, stuffed uncomfortably inside the command tank with its crew, gave the order to move. The lead platoons used the flattened sections of wire for their exit, mashing the squirming undead beneath their treads. The companies uncoiled from the defensive position and drove out from behind their hasty fortifications across the fairways of the golf course and back out onto the streets.

Upon reaching South 70th Street they turned north. Dane intentionally headed that direction which would take them through some densely-populated neighborhoods. It would also take them further away from his other battalions who were still in the process of securing food and fuel. He still had to keep up the diversion for another hour at least, according to his XO who manned the brigade command post, tucked safely in the Division's main Assembly Area just southwest of the city.

The major relinquished his seat to Dane, giving up the commander's position in the tank. This allowed him access to the periscopes up top and the commander's optics and backup weapons control station. He took over at that point, using the gun's optics to see outside of the vehicle and their surroundings, giving the occasional order to their driver over the intercom, who could see even less than they could, buttoned up inside armored vehicles gave one excellent protection, but lousy visibility outside.

On his instruction, the lead elements drove at a crawl, going no more than five miles per hour. He didn't want to outrun the dead, he wanted to lead them away. The battalions acted like one giant Pied Piper, and the creatures came from every direction, following the howls and screeches of their brothers and sisters. Still, even at this pace, they left many of the shamblers and walkers behind, dragging themselves along, reaching out toward the living with decomposing hands.

In the back of one of the Bradley Fighting Vehicles, a sergeant turned after getting splashed in the eyes with fetid body fluids. He attacked his companions in an animalistic rage, biting and clawing nearly all of them before someone put a pistol in his mouth and pulled the trigger. The vehicle continued down the road for a time with the commander and gunner secured safely in the turret, trying to figure out what to do, when more of them turned and squeezed through the tight space between the turret wall and the inner hull, grabbing the driver and dragging him back into a hellish abattoir of snapping jaws. The vehicle eased out of the column and came to a halt on a nearby sidewalk. The commander and gunner cried out for help on the radio, but no one stopped. The rest of the column passed on by, unabated.

"Dagger Six, this is Dagger Five. Over." The Brigade Executive Officer's voice came in somewhat broken over Dane's headset. Even with the retrans repeaters set up across the city to keep the communications network up, they were still at the extreme edge of their communication range. Added to that, the vehicles operated in and among houses and other structures which helped break up radio signals.

Dane keyed the transmitter. "Five, this is Six. Send your traffic. Over."

"Roger, sir. Our scavenging operations are nearly complete. You should be good to return now. Over."

Dane smiled. This was it. He'd successfully secured the supplies the Division desperately needed to make the next leg of their journey west. Now he'd finally redeemed himself and could hold his head up high among his peers. If he was lucky, he'd even get a commendation from the Division Commander for this. For the first time in recent memory, he actually felt optimistic and happy.

Once we get to the Cascadia Redoubt and things get reorganized, maybe I'll even get that promotion to Brigadier General, he thought to himself. The idea of it sent a shiver up his spine.

"Dagger Six, this is Bulldog Six. We've got a problem. Two of my tanks just ran out of fuel and fell out of formation. I've

got several more that are running on fumes as well. How copy? Over."

Dane's smile suddenly melted away.

"Sir, we're in bad shape on fuel too. I don't know how much further we're going to make it," said his own driver over the intercom.

Just then, the turbine engine made an awful sound as it sputtered and died, bringing them to a grinding halt.

Chapter 12

Lincoln, Nebraska
1445 Hours Local

The column pushed northbound along South 27th Street, moving as fast as they could manage. The scouts left them in the dust, driving their Humvees as swiftly as they dared through the streets littered with debris and rotting carcasses. The armored vehicles fell far behind, limited by the speed of the M-88 recovery vehicles they elected to put in the front to clear obstructions out of the way. The big monstrosities moved maddeningly slow, but there was nothing to be done about it. They all gritted their teeth and pressed on, listening to the desperate cries for help on the brigade command frequency.

Interspersed throughout the convoy were the big military refueler trucks known as HEMTTs. They'd been topped off and linked up with the combat troops shortly before moving out. The drivers and crews in those trucks arrived and did their duty, with the looks of fear and determination etched on their faces.

They passed hundreds of single-family homes along the way, most standing vacant. Along the way they'd pass walkers and shamblers who tried to approach, arms and hands outstretched. Occasionally a runner would burst from a door or driveway, snarling and howling only to be ignored by the crews and the infantry covering the tops of the armored vehicles like a second skin.

Charlie Company led the way and hooked a right-hand turn on Old Cheney Road, headed east. They held up the entire battalion for a few precious minutes while the '88s cleared some wrecks that blocked the road. The scouts reported it earlier and bypassed, but they didn't have the luxury, so they lowered their blades and pushed the smashed cars out of the way, clearing a path for the rest.

While the column waited with engines idling, the dead took advantage and descended on them from all sides. Within moments rifles and machine guns crackled all up and down the line, dropping them by the dozens, their bodies laying in heaps alongside the road. The noise created the expected result, only drawing them in even faster and in greater numbers. About the time the dead got uncomfortably close, the convoy began moving again, pulling away from their pursuers.

Mark stuffed as many red shotgun shells as he could fit into his ammo pouches. Listening to the lieutenant relay updates to them over the company net. *BOHICA* fell in behind the tank section, trailing bumper number "Charlie 1-2." On the back deck of the tank rode Jimmy Hong, McDermott, Weber and Bags. None of them looked terribly thrilled to be there. From the commander's position on the tank, Staff Sergeant Danny Kurtz swung the .50 caliber off to the right, while his loader, an Australian named Stuart Brown scanned off to the left with the Two-Forty Bravo.

In the back of the Bradley in the troop compartment, Angie Carnegie rode holding and stroking Saxon's head. The dog kept trying to stick his head out of the cargo hatch, but lost his mind every time he spotted one of the infected, barking and snarling like crazy. Darin Jefferson sat buckled in next to them both, rubbing his aching leg that still hadn't fully recovered from the gunshot wound he got back in Kansas City on the day his friend Martin White died saving his life. The three of them were crammed inside next to Angel, Dubois and Harris while the rest held on tight up top.

Clay had a death grip on the bustle-rack attached to the back of the turret, leaning in closer and shouting over the noise of the engine. "Have you heard any updates?"

Mark turned with a puzzled look. "Yeah, and it ain't good." He pulled one of the earphones of his CVC away, while squinting. "Most of the tanks with the Brigade Commander's task force are out of fuel. Those that aren't, shut down their engines to conserve what they've got remaining. If an M1 Abrams runs out of fuel, it takes a hell of a lot of effort to get them started again, so the ones that still have a little are saving it so they can turn the engines over again once relief arrives."

Clay nodded. "You're right, that ain't good."

"It gets worse." Mark lowered the earphone and adjusted the cravat covering his mouth and nose. "They're spread out over hell's half-acre and it's going to be a bitch recovering them. I have no idea how we're going to get them out of there with the dead literally swarming on top of every stationary piece of rolling stock. We'll be lucky if we get half of them out alive."

"Well, that's encouraging. Once again, you're a ray of sunshine."

Mark smirked from beneath his bandana. "Since when have I ever been known for my optimism?"

"Good point." Clay shook his head before checking to see if his weapon was loaded.

***

The battalion rolled into the parking of the Gateway Mall located on the northeast side of the city and immediately set to work establishing a perimeter around the place. While the combat troops busied themselves with that, the fuel handlers parked their HEMTTs in neat rows. They began pounding grounding rods into the asphalt as best they could, while unraveling yards of hose from their spools. They set up the "hot refuel point" like they'd done countless times before, only this time they moved much faster.

BOHICA followed Lieutenant Baker's tank section and set up between the two of them, spread out by a hundred meters or so. The dismounts climbed off the Abrams and disgorged from the Bradley, taking up position under the direction of Clay and Harris. Mark elected to stay on the track so he could monitor the radios.

Donahue squeezed his giant torso through the gunner's hatch and took a moment to size up their situation. "That's ironic don't you think?

Mark flipped up a sheet of plexiglass covered in operational graphics so he could more clearly see his map. "What are you talking about?"

He pointed to the massive structure behind them on the other side of the parking lot. "We ended up at a mall. Isn't that how every zombie scenario plays out?"

Mark pulled his attention from the map and looked at the darkened building with the occasional abandoned car dotting the parking area. He scowled at his gunner. "Very funny, now get back to work."

"Roger, sarn't." With a sardonic smirk, Donahue lowered himself back inside and began scanning through his optics looking for targets.

They hadn't been there five minutes before the dead appeared from the surrounding area, making their way toward the battalion. Luckily, they were few in number and there weren't any runners yet.

Lieutenant Baker leapt down from his tank and jogged over to *BOHICA*, climbing up and standing next to Mark. "The Brigade XO gave the order to every vehicle in *Task Force Dagger* that still had enough fuel left to meet us here. They're hauling ass and should be linking up in a few minutes. It's mostly APCs, Bradleys and a handful of tanks. They'll top off and then head out of the city, straight back to *Assembly Area Husker*. They'll take the fuel trucks with them."

Mark watched his infantry set up positions around the tanks, preparing their small arms and melee weapons, as a small group of walkers approached. "Then what?"

"Then, we go in further and evacuate the survivors that are stuck out there. Which includes Colonel Williams."

"The Brigade Commander got us all into this mess, perhaps he should get out and walk back to the assembly area." Mark's eyes were hard. The casualty reports that came over the radio were awful. In fact, they'd been the worst losses the Brigade had experienced since the outbreak. This day had not been pretty.

"I'm not even going to dignify that comment with a response."

"Roger, sir." He thought about saying something else, but kept it inside. Off, about a hundred yards distant, Johnson and Dubois charged into a group of undead, swinging axes and crushing skulls. The two D&D nerds reveled in the action. Mark figured they were both disappointed they didn't have swords at the moment.

Then, coming southbound along North 66th Street, the first vehicles from *Task Force Dagger* came into view. They drove at unsafe speeds and came on without any semblance of tactical order or formation. They were in full retreat, doing their best to get the hell out of Dodge.

The leading vehicles were M113 armored personnel carriers loaded full of combat engineers. Without fanfare, they pulled into the parking lot, taking directions from ground guides who motioned them over to the fuel HEMTTs. They happily complied and lined up next to the trucks while soldiers clad in fire retardant Nomex uniforms passed hoses and nozzles up to the crews. As they filled up, more tracks and

Bradleys came racing in.

***

"*Vanguard Six, this is Battle Axe Six. We are moving. Time, now. Over.*"

"Roger, Battle Axe. That's a good copy. Over." Lieutenant Colonel Jerry Hamilton stood in the turret of his Bradley with the wind blowing in his face. He tried to ignore the smell of rot and decay, staying focused on the task at hand. He'd successfully gathered up the remnants of *Task Force Dagger* who could still move under their own power and sent them on their way, back to Division and safety. Now, he had to go after the rest of the survivors and extricate them. It would be no easy task with them spread out the way they were, left behind one vehicle at a time as their fuel tanks ran dry.

There were hundreds of men and women stranded along the task force's marching route, buttoned up tight inside their vehicles, helpless to do anything. With almost no ammunition left among them, they'd been left with little option other than to wait for rescue, since they couldn't fight their way out.

What made the situation even more critical was that without fuel, the stranded vehicles couldn't recharge their batteries. That meant that the only way to find many of them was by their radio calls, and once the batteries ran out, then they'd have an even more difficult time locating the crews. They could retrace their route of course, but that would be time consuming and time was something they didn't have a lot of. Particularly since their own fuel supplies would eventually run out.

The Brigade Commander himself was out there, calling him constantly on the command net, demanding an update. Jerry assured Colonel Williams that they were on their way, but the man grew increasingly impatient. Speed was a critical consideration, but bumbling along blindly with no plan or organization would get a whole bunch of them killed, so he moved his battalion deliberately. They weren't moving slow by any means, but they weren't going to rush to failure either. Too many people had already been killed this day and he had no intention of contributing to the butcher's bill.

"*Vanguard Six, this is Dagger Six. SITREP. Over!*" Williams' voice had an edge to it. This must have been the fifth time he asked for an update in the last ten minutes alone and he sounded more exasperated with each call.

Jerry sighed before picking up the transmitter. "Dagger Six, this is Vanguard Six. We are approximately two klicks out from the first vehicle. We will begin the evacuations shortly. Over." He tossed the handset down in disgust, catching sight of a runner out of the corner of his eye.

This was turning into a very long day.

***

The M1 tank up ahead sat quietly in the middle of the street, its turret and barrel oriented off to its 3 o'clock position, flanked on both sides by rows of single-family homes. Long grass grew from the cracks in the sidewalks on either side of the road, trampled by the dozens of infected climbing up and over the armored beast.

Staff Sergeant Pavolovski ordered his lead section forward, driving up along either side of the immobile tank. They crushed the walkers and shamblers like bugs, while the dismounted infantry riding atop picked off the others. The dead came streaming in from alleys, driveways and unkempt yards, taking face shots from marksmen perched up high off the ground, taking time to steady themselves between shots.

While they did this a single Bradley with an empty troop compartment backed up to the front of the Abrams, bumping its back end up against the tank's front glacis, smashing the sponson boxes affixed to the rear of the IFV.

Without waiting, the heavy hatches of the tank popped open and the crew boiled out. They leapt onto the back deck of the Bradley, jumping down inside through the open cargo hatch on the roof. The Bradley Commander gave the order to move just as the dead closed in on them, pulling away before they had a chance to crawl up onto the vehicle. They too did a lap, crushing a few of the less agile ones before closing back into formation.

"Blue One, we got 'em. Let's get the fuck out of here. Over."

And with that, the four Infantry Fighting Vehicles fell back into a column and trundled down the road.

***

Dane Williams leaned back into his seat, biting his fingernails and sweating profusely. He'd stopped looking out of the periscope or the commander's sight, horrified by the scene outside. The creatures were everywhere and they were trapped, left behind by his own people. He could scarcely believe it. He at least expected someone to stop and try to lend assistance to their Brigade Commander, but they hadn't. When he ran out of fuel they just kept on going, leaving him behind like all the others.

The good news was that he was still in contact with the rest of the brigade and managed to get a relief column to head their way. Jerry Hamilton had become a shell of a man since the outbreak, but he continued to carry on. He required a bit more motivation than he'd needed in the past, but he could still get the job done. Besides, his battalion was the closest and stood the best chance of rescuing Dane and the rest of his stranded people.

"Vanguard Six, this is Dagger Six. SITREP. Over!" Dane's knee bobbed up and down in a steady rhythm, though he didn't notice it. The rest of the men trapped inside the tank with him did though, but they kept any comments they might have to themselves.

"Dagger Six, this is Vanguard Six. Recovery operations are now underway. We've retrieved a half dozen crews along with some dismounts. I estimate we should have all personnel recovered within the next couple of hours. Over."

Relief washed over him at the thought of escaping this place. He'd seen a pair of gnashing teeth snapping at one of the periscopes earlier and he nearly voided his bowels. Now, it seemed as if his salvation were finally at hand. Once they recovered their personnel and equipment, they'd be back on the road and everything would be fine. This unfortunate hiccup would be forgotten in light of the mission's overall success. "Vanguard, this is Dagger. That's outstanding. How much longer until you reach my location? Over."

"Roger, Dagger. I estimate we'll be at your position in about an hour. Our team will clear your vehicle and temporarily secure it. We'll only have a minute or less, so get ready to dismount your tank and climb aboard one of our tracks. How copy? Over."

Dane's elation suddenly melted away. "Wait, are you saying that we need to leave our vehicles behind? Is that what you've been doing with the other crews? Over."

"Affirmative, Dagger. We've got to leave your equipment behind. We don't have enough time to hook up tow bars or refuel. There's just too many Zulus and we can't hold them off long enough. We'll clear just enough of them away and then

you climb on one of our vics and we'll get you and the rest of your people out. Over."

"Wait! No! That's not my intent! We need to recover all the vehicles along with the people. The whole point of this operation was to get the necessary supplies to get all personnel, weapons and equipment to the *Cascadia Redoubt*. This equipment is too valuable. We cannot leave it behind. You *will* recover all the vehicles as well as the personnel. Acknowledge! Over."

An uncomfortable silence settled over the radio net.

"Vanguard Six, this is Dagger Six. I say again, do you understand me? Over!"

"Dagger Six, roger, message received. If we do this, it will take significantly more time, and we don't have the support or the resources to do this properly. We will be hard-pressed just to evacuate the people. I'm not sure we can recover the equipment too. Over."

Rage bubbled up inside of Dane's gut. He did not like to be questioned, and having his orders questioned over the radio was the equivalent to having a subordinate back-talk him in front of the entire Brigade. Especially since he was fairly certain every person with a radio was tuned in to their frequency, eavesdropping on this very conversation. "Colonel Hamilton, I will not say this again. You will carry out my orders, or I will have you relieved and find someone who can. *Do you understand me?* Over!"

There was another lengthy pause before Hamilton came back. *"Sir, I will execute as you've ordered. Vanguard Six. Out.*"

A subordinate never "Outs" his commander and the breach in protocol was deliberate. Dane resisted the urge to chew the man out right then and there, but got hold of himself, electing to grit his teeth and fume in silence. He would be sure to take care of Jerry Hamilton later once they got back to the Assembly Area. Once he got done with the Battalion Commander, that man would never disrespect him again. That much he was certain of.

***

The sun sank beneath the horizon and the battalion found itself struggling to claw its way forward, inch by inch, block by block. The Brigade Commander's orders were clear and the operation to rescue those stranded crews slowed to a crawl.

The M-88 recovery vehicles possessed the ability to refuel other vehicles with their built-in pumps, hoses and nozzles, but that limited them to what JP-8 they held in their fuel cells. When they initially found Bradleys or M113s, they would clear the dead away, pump ten or twenty gallons into the stranded vehicle, then let them fire up their engines and race off to safety. The Abrams tanks on the other hand were a very different matter. It was too complicated and too time consuming to get them running after running dry. Plus, it took an enormous amount just to get them started again, so it was decided to hook up the tow bars and drag them out. This too consumed an enormous amount of time, which required a security force to fight off the Zulus to buy time, and the further they got into the city, the thicker they got, making the task more difficult as they went.

It didn't take long before 2nd Battalion began losing people in the rescue operation, and as ammunition supplies began to get tight, and the number of the dead increased, their casualties steadily climbed.

Lieutenant Colonel Hamilton rotated the companies going forward to give his people a break after each recovery operation, which allowed them to rest and redistribute the dwindling supply of ammo. They kept it going, well into the night even as the first stranded crews went silent out there in the city, their batteries finally having died and their radios going off the air.

So, when the latest casualty report came in, Jerry Hamilton could take it no longer. "Battle Axe Six, this is Vanguard Six. You're up next. What's your status? Over."

"*Vanguard Six, Axe Six. We're REDCON One. I've got my company standing by, ready to execute. Over.*" Lieutenant Baker sounded tired but confident. He'd been at it just as hard as everyone else and the lack of rest along with the soul-crushing stress began to take its toll on all of them.

Jerry Hamilton thought back to the first days of the outbreak. He remembered sending his people on relief columns into Kansas City and then later trying to seize the bridges over the Missouri River. Most of all he remembered giving the orders to hold their fire and only to shoot in self-defense. He'd believed at the time that whatever disease the poor victims had been infected with, that the medical professionals would find a cure. So he did his best to limit civilian deaths, truly committed to the idea that he was saving lives. That decision and his naïve conviction got dozens of his people killed needlessly, in the most awful ways imaginable. Later, he realized how very wrong he'd been, but by then the damage had been done. He'd led his people to slaughter and it was all his fault.

On that day a bit of him died inside. He'd been a shell of a man ever since, going over the events of the day trying to rationalize his decision and find a way to reconcile the terrible mistake he'd made, but no matter how hard he tried, he could not find that answer and he felt even more lost. Since then, he had issued orders that kept losses to a minimum, to the point that he'd grown completely risk averse.

Now the casualty counts started to roll in and it made his stomach turn, and with each passing hour they continued to get worse. Colonel Williams' orders to retrieve the vehicles along with the crews had resulted in a bloodbath. It finally got to the point where they were losing more people than they were saving, and not by a small margin either. They'd crossed the point of diminishing returns a long time ago.

On top of it all, Colonel Williams continued demanding updates on the operation. His calls became more clipped, more shrill with each transmission. It was obvious to anyone listening that the Brigade Commander was afraid for his own life and less concerned about the well-being of the soldiers in his command.

It was simply too much to bear anymore.

"Battle Axe Six, this Vanguard Six. Have your people link up with me at my location. I will push deep past the next two recovery targets and go straight for the Brigade Commander. I will lead this one personally. Over." Jerry felt the eyes of his gunner staring at him when he finished the transmission. He didn't bother to meet the man's gaze.

"Sir, may I ask what you have in mind?" His gunner asked. Never one to question orders, the sergeant posed the question out of curiosity.

He turned to his gunner with a sad smile. "I intend to get the Brigade Commander out of here right away and have him and his crew evacuated to the rear."

"I suppose that means, with him out of the picture, you will have the latitude to finish the rescue operation any way that you see fit. Is that right, sir?"

"You are very clever, Tim, but don't ask too many questions. The less you know about what I'm doing, the less likely they'll end up court martialing you along with me. It's best that you maintain plausible deniability. Understand?"

"Yes, sir. I think I do."

"Good. One other thing. I'll need a good character witness during sentencing and I'm counting on you to say something nice about me."

"That's easy, sir. You know I'd follow you to Hell and back."

"Well, Tim. I'm afraid that tonight, that's exactly what I intend for you to do."

Chapter 13

Six Bradley Fighting Vehicles along with two M1 Abrams raced through one neighborhood after another, using speed as security. They dodged wrecks on the streets, oftentimes having to smash their way through the occasional obstruction. They did everything they could to move fast, to outpace the undead in order to buy them time. They'd left the rest of the battalion behind to continue their mission while the Battalion Commander took a depleted company-team deep into the suburbs to retrieve their Brigade Commander, Colonel Dane Williams.

Lieutenant Baker brought his entire command to support Jerry Hamilton and his ride into the abyss. The 3rd Platoon Leader, Staff Sergeant Pavolovski, took point for a time, but he wasn't going very fast and he took a couple of wrong turns along the way. In frustration, the Battalion Commander told 3rd Platoon to follow him and try to keep up.

Lieutenant Colonel Jerry Hamilton had his driver mash the accelerator to the floor and they took off like a shot. Pavolovski and the others raced behind, doing their best to maintain visual contact with their Battalion Commander. The drivers struggled to see with the night vision blocks mounted in their driver's periscopes, compounding the problem. They could have switched on their headlights, but it would have drawn flocks of the dead, so they used night vision instead. Though it made it much more difficult to navigate through the littered streets at night.

"There they are, right up there!" called out Colonel Hamilton over the radio.

Sitting there, all by itself was a single, solitary tank. It rested in darkness on a major thoroughfare, on the corner of North 84th Street and Leighton Avenue. It was just on the fringes of two neighborhoods, sandwiched in between a taco joint and a fried chicken restaurant. There was very little ambient illumination with significant cloud cover, blotting out the moon and stars, but still they could see the infected milling about, some on top of the Brigade Commander's vehicle.

"Sir, I recommend you hang back in an overwatch position. I'll bring the infantry platoons up and secure the site. Then we'll get the tanks up to hook up a tow bar." Lieutenant Baker's voice sounded more animated than usual.

"Negative, I'm going in with them." Hamilton was in no mood to argue. He flipped back up to the Brigade command frequency. *"Dagger Six, this is Vanguard Six. We have arrived. We will secure the position momentarily, then we'll hook you up and drag you out of here. Over."*

"Roger, Vanguard. It's about time. Let's be quick about it. Over." Even at close range the radio transmission came in broken and weak, the batteries in the tank being nearly spent.

Hamilton's Bradley moved out with Baker's 3rd Platoon in tow. The two remaining tanks hung back, along with *BOHICA* in a nearby overwatch position.

Up in the loader's hatch of Baker's tank, the unmistakable silhouette of Sergeant Yokey emerged. He turned to face Mark's track. He wore a set of NVG's hanging over his brow on the front of his helmet. Curiously he started flashing the Infrared illuminator in their direction. It seemed to flash in random patterns.

Mark couldn't help but be distracted by the flashing. "What the hell is that all about?"

"It's just Yokey, sarn't. Ignore him," Donahue grumbled.

"Seriously, what the fuck is he doing?"

"It's morse code, sarn't. Don't worry about it."

"What's his message then? Is it important?"

Donahue sighed. "He's repeating a message over and over

again."

"What's he saying then?"

"He keeps flashing 'Eat a bag of dicks.' Told you it wasn't important."

Mark grimaced. "I'm sorry I asked."

From the neighboring tank, the other loader, Stuart popped his head up like a prairie dog and stuck out his middle finger at Yokey who immediately reciprocated in kind.

The five IFVs spread out and got roughly on line once they were able, utilizing the more open terrain. Once they got near the Brigade Commander's tank, they began running circuits around it, rolling over the nearly two-dozen infected flocking around the immobilized vehicle. It was a fairly easy task, as the noisy Bradleys drew in the dead like moths to a flame. Once they'd mashed the last one into the pavement, they set up a perimeter and signaled to Lieutenant Baker to come forward.

The M1 Abrams weighed in at well over 70 tons, more than twice as much as the Bradley. For that reason the Infantry Fighting Vehicles could not reliably drag an M1. The engines and transmissions were simply not stout enough to handle the extra weight, so in absence of a proper recovery vehicle, standard practice was to use a tank to drag another tank.

"*Axe Six, this is Vanguard Six. Execute. Over.*"

Baker nodded and gave a "thumbs" up. "*Roger, Vanguard. Moving.*"

Baker's tank lurched forward while leaving the other in a supporting role next to *BOHICA*. It moved down the road with its turbine gently whining, while the track pads clopped loudly on the asphalt. Lieutenant Colonel Hamilton moved his track out of the way so Baker could get into position. Once he got near enough, the driver did a neutral steer, swinging the back end of the vehicle toward the rear of the Brigade Commander's vehicle with each facing exhaust grate to exhaust grate. Then they slowly backed up, getting within a few meters.

Once close enough, they stopped.

Mark watched from a distance while people quickly dismounted and began unlimbering a massive tow bar. It took several people to do it and the piece of equipment was clumsy even under ideal conditions. The group of people wrestling with it now were clearly not practiced and struggled with it in the dark. He felt sweat beading up on his upper lip and brushed it away, then took a moment to hit the illumination switch on his G-Shok. The time read "23:47."

"Those guys look like a monkey fucking a football bat," Donahue said unnecessarily.

"You want to get out and give them a hand?" Mark adjusted his bandana, then reached back, feeling for his shotgun to ensure it was still there.

"Not unless you make me."

Something caught Mark's eye. The grainy, green image in his night vision goggles made it difficult to see. Particularly in low illumination on nights like this. "Wait, you see that?"

"See what?"

"Off to the two o'clock position."

Donahue slowly rotated the turret to the right, peering through his sight, with his head resting against the brow-pad. "Oh yeah, I see it. Zulus. Lots of them. They must have heard us pull up. I estimate the range at just over eight hundred meters. Should I engage?"

"Negative. Stand by." Mark keyed the radio transmitter. "Battle Axe Six, this is White One. We've got Zulus coming out of the neighborhood to your east. How copy? Over."

"*Battle Axe Six, this is Vanguard Six Golf. Actual is on the ground with the recovery crew. Over.*"

"The Battalion Commander is dismounted? Is he nuts?"

Donahue kept his reticle on the advancing dead, scanning slowly from side to side, doing a mental count of targets.

Mark ignored his gunner. "Shit." He keyed the transmitter once again. "Battle Axe Six, this is White One. Did you monitor? Over."

Yokey responded. *"White One, the El-Tee is on the ground with the BC helping him out. Over."*

"Oh for fuck's sake," Mark said out loud before composing himself. "Roger, you need to tell the officers that there are at least a couple hundred Zulus emerging from the houses to your east. You may have five minutes before they reach you. How copy? Over!"

Just then a rifle shot rang out, immediately followed up by several others. Within seconds, Staff Sergeant Pavolovski's Bradleys opened up with their coax machine guns, sending streams of bright, red tracers into the advancing line of the dead. Once that happened, all of the dismounted infantry of 3rd Platoon joined in, pouring fire on thick, sending forth a wall of lead.

One of the tracks cut loose with its auto-cannon, and the distinct sound of the 25mm Bushmaster thundered away, sending its ordnance downrange in rapid-fire, three-round bursts. They used the high-explosive anti-personnel rounds, which landed in and among the horde.

Hit like a buzzsaw, the infected tumbled and fell to the ground. Between the small arms fire and the auto-cannons, they were cut to pieces. Body parts went flying and many dropped to the grass, never to move again.

"Fuck yeah!" Donahue called out in glee.

"Dear God, no!" Mark exclaimed. The muzzles sparkled and the tracers zipped along, some ricocheting upon impact, flying off in every direction. In the darkness the light show was dazzling, something that could not be ignored.

Donahue's exuberance suddenly cooled. "What's wrong, sarn't?"

"Those fucking idiots just rang the dinner bell!" He pulled up the Remington 11-87 and set it next to his map board. "You better get ready."

***

Jerry Hamilton finally got the straps free and the group of them man-handled the massive tow-bar down from the hull. It was terribly heavy and there were four of them working together, trying to get it down without dropping it onto their feet. The system itself was simple, consisting of a scissor-style hinge at the head with three attachment points. A proper crew of mechanics would have this drill down to a science, but none of them there on the ground had hooked one of these up in a long time.

Jerry grunted under the weight and looked to the man on his left to ensure he had a good grip on it. He couldn't believe his eyes when he saw the chaplain right next to him, fighting with the huge piece of steel. "Chaplain, is that you? What in the hell are you doing here?"

"I was a stow-away in the back of your track this entire time. I heard you needed some help, so here I am." Chaplain Mulvaney strained under the weight, but held his own. He'd always been where the fighting was thickest, usually against the wishes of the Battalion Commander, always asking forgiveness rather than permission, just like now.

"Damnit, Chaplain, this isn't where I need you right now." Jerry had to give the man a dressing-down through gritted teeth, trying not to lose his grip.

"It looks like you do. Besides, that which does not kill us, only makes us stronger."

"That sounds like Nietzsche. Not terribly biblical if you ask me."

"Actually, Nietzsche stole it from the Bible. Romans 5… look it up sometime."

Hamilton couldn't help but smile and shake his head. "Okay, Chaplain, you win. Now, help me set this tow hook."

Lieutenant Baker stood off to the side of the vehicle giving hand signals to his gunner who stood at the front of his tank on the ground, mirroring those same signals to the driver. They gently moved the tank from left to right, inches at a time to get the tow hooks lined up properly, just as one would do lining up a truck with a trailer hitch.

Then, as they got the first of the three points set, the world seemed to explode around them. The Bradleys and infantry on the hasty perimeter around them suddenly opened fire, hammering away at something off to their east, invisible in the inky darkness. They didn't need to guess what everyone was shooting at, that much seemed obvious, and it motivated them all to work even faster.

***

The noise and flashing lights signaled everything within miles that soldiers were in the area. The dead let out howls and screeches, calling out to the others in an instinctive response. Deep within their corrupted DNA, the undead were driven by the virus which needed to spread itself to more victims. It tapped into the cerebral cortex and took over the host, driving it to infect as many others as possible. Of this it was single-minded, driving the infected through the physical pangs of hunger, which most efficiently spread bodily fluids through gnashing teeth and thick saliva.

There'd been thousands of them spread out along the

streets and roads who'd followed the armored column earlier in the day, but they'd wandered aimlessly when it sped off, leaving them behind, but they hadn't wandered far, lingering wherever they'd given up the chase, which meant that there were still an enormous number of them concentrated in the immediate area just out of sight when 2nd Battalion began their recovery op.

Now that there were new sights and sounds to key in on, they came in from every direction. Descending on the one place that offered them the best opportunity to feed.

***

With gargantuan effort they managed to get the second tow-hook set, with only one more to go. Small arms fire picked up all along the outer ring while a couple of the Bradleys swung their turrets around, desperately trying to reload their Bushmaster auto-cannons.

"El-Tee, look out!" Yokey screamed over the din. He depressed his M-240 Bravo machine gun as low as he could, tearing off a long burst, smacking the pavement in front of his lieutenant. The stream of full-metal jackets raced up and caught a runner mid-stride, sending it sailing back. It pounced back to its feet before Yokey pulled the trigger again, this time scoring a head shot, the body landing flat in front of the young officer.

The runners came streaming in by the score, dodging past their slower cousins, using the darkness to their advantage. All along the line the dismounted grunts did their best to push back the tide. The screams of the unfortunate sending chills down the spines of the others who desperately held on as best they could.

Baker instantly stayed focused giving hand signals to their

gunner, Gomez, right up until a pack of runners slipped through in between two of the Bradleys and took him to the ground, devouring him.

"Gomez, *no!*" Baker snatched the sidearm from its holster and charged at them, firing the pistol the entire way, landing hits on the dead with no effect. He stopped short of them, unable to block out the sounds of the visceral growling as the beasts ate his man. The lieutenant dropped his empty magazine and loaded another when he was hit from the side with the force of a small automobile.

Yokey tried to get a shot at the creatures who slammed into Baker, but couldn't get the weapon to depress that low, being so close to the side of the tank. Without pause, he climbed out of the loader's hatch and jumped off the side, landing on a couple of the creatures attacking his officer.

Yokey said nothing, using his massive, muscled frame to snatch the first one off Baker, tossing it aside like a rag doll. He leaned in to get the second one when he himself got overtaken from behind by half a dozen creatures. He fought wildly trying to get them off, throwing punches and kicks, doing whatever he could to get them off but to no avail. There were simply too many and the mob of them tore Yokey and his lieutenant to pieces.

***

Jerry, the chaplain and a couple other guys tried to get the single-point hitch set on the back of Baker's tank. The thing was mis-aligned by a couple of inches and they needed it to shift to the left. Then they could hook it up and get the bolts in place. He was shouting instructions over the booming gunfire to the lieutenant when he heard him call out, followed up by a rapid succession of pistol shots.

Jerry knew exactly what that meant.

"Everybody stop what you're doing and get on my Bradley. *Right now!*" He pulled his own sidearm free with his right hand, while pushing the other soldiers with his left, shepherding them in the right direction.

Before they made it five feet, a half dozen figures emerged from around the corner of the Brigade Commander's tank, dressed in frayed civilian clothes and covered in dried blood. Even as dark as it was, they could make out the distinct spider web pattern on their faces and those evil, red eyes.

"*Shit!*" Hamilton's Beretta barked, firing it single-handed while trying to pull the others back and away from the awful predators. He connected with two head shots before the rest were on him, knocking him down and quickly rendering him into a sickening pile of shredded meat.

The others turned to go in the other direction, only to be met on the other side by more of the beasts.

The chaplain tried to say a prayer but was silenced before they were all taken down.

***

Mark watched through the thermal sights as dozens of runners stormed the position, darting in and between 3rd Platoon's tracks, where they were firing with reckless abandon. He couldn't see what was happening very well, but by the sounds of the panicked fire, it couldn't have been good.

"Blue One, this is White One. What's the situation? Over." Mark could already feel the blood pumping in his ears while his mouth went dry.

No response.

"Blue One, this White One. I say again. What's going on over there? Do you need assistance? Over!"

"White One, this is Blue One Golf. Actual is on the ground with the dismounts. Things have completely fallen apart over here. There's zeds all over the place. I can't raise any of the officers on the radio and nobody knows what's going on. We need help! Over!"

"Um, sarn't. I think you need to take a look at this," Donahue said, interrupting the exchange over the radio.

"What is it? I'm kinda busy right now."

"Look through your commander's sight."

Mark lowered down to look through the commander's sight unit and his jaw dropped open. There were walkers coming up the road from the south and more of them than he could count. They were headed straight for 3rd Platoon and they were getting close. "Well, this keeps getting better."

Mark looked over to the remaining Abrams sitting next to him in the overwatch position with a few of his people sitting impatiently on top. The Tank Commander was looking at him, waiting for him to call. "Charlie One Two, this is White One. Did you monitor that last transmission?"

Staff Sergeant Danny Kurtz raised a thumb in the air. *"Roger, White One. I did. What's our next move? Over."*

"Move out. There's a shitload of zeds inbound and we've got to get our people out of there!"

BOHICA launched forward followed close behind by the tank with the bumper number "C-12." It looked like all the other tanks in the Brigade except for that individualized number stenciled on the front and rear, along with the name *Cloud Nine* spray-painted on the barrel.

When they got close enough to the cluster of vehicles around the Brigade Commander's tank, Sergeant Kurtz began running circles around them, squashing as many infected as he could. The dismounts up top held on tight, holding their fire and conserving their ammunition while the driver did all the killing.

Mark yelled over the side of the turret to the others, "Everybody stay on the track! Nobody dismount! It's a fucking shitshow out here!"

"You don't have to tell me twice," Angie hollered back.

The dismounted infantry of 3rd Platoon were still on the ground, shooting in every direction. It became immediately clear that there weren't a whole lot of them left at this point and they were hanging on by the skin of their teeth.

The dismounts riding on top of *BOHICA* began picking off the runners who managed to make it through the outer cordon. It ended up being an easier task than usual since most of them were engaged in a feeding frenzy near the tow bar in between the two tanks.

While the sharpshooters from 2nd Platoon busied themselves dropping the distracted zeds, the crew of *Cloud Nine* bought the others some breathing room. Mark shouted to those still on the ground. "If you ain't bit, get your asses mounted back up. *Do it now!*" He picked up the handset and keyed the transmitter. "Blue One Golf, once you get your people loaded, pull back to our overwatch position, we'll rally up there. Break." He took a deep breath before going on. "Is there anyone left on Lieutenant Baker's tank?"

"White One, this is Battle Axe Six Delta. I'm Lieutenant Baker's driver. I don't know where everyone else is. They dismounted and I haven't heard from any of them since. What should I do? Over."

Mark clenched his fists and squeezed his eyes shut. He took a moment to compose himself before replying. "Roger, Battle Axe Six Delta. We will recover your crew. Need you to get your tank out of there. Link up at the rally point with everyone else. Acknowledge. Over."

"Roger, sarn't." Without waiting any longer, Lieutenant

Baker's tank *Carnage*, bolted forward, peeling off back to the west.

The tracks of 3rd Platoon followed behind, but the Battalion Commander's Bradley still sat in place, idling. *"White One, this is Vanguard Six Golf. Do you have eyes on Colonel Hamilton? He isn't back yet. Over."*

"Six Golf, White One. We'll get him too. You just need to pull out with the rest. Over."

"Roger." There was a pause before he went on. *"Before we go, I've got the Brigade Command frequency punched up and the Brigade Commander is demanding a SITREP. Over."*

Donahue fired off a burst after burst from the coax, hammering a beaten zone off to the south, where thousands of lonely figures advanced toward them in the dark. When the bolt slammed home on an empty chamber, he switched over to the Bushmaster, laying it on as thick as he could.

"Fine. Everyone back to the rally point at the overwatch position and for the love of God, hold your fire. Get everyone inside an armored vehicle and button up tight. Then stand by for my orders." Mark opened up the access panel to the coax machine gun and cracked open another green ammo can of linked 7.62 before running it into the feed chute. Once he got the coax reloaded, he turned around and switched his radio to the brigade command frequency.

"...I say again, someone out there give me a SITREP goddammit!" Colonel Williams screamed, but his batteries were so weak that he still came in broken, even with BOHICA sitting nearly twenty meters away.

Donahue started engaging with the machine gun once again, laying waste to everything in front of him. The mob was so close now he couldn't possibly miss.

"Dagger Six, this is White One. I am the Bradley parked near you. You have maybe thirty seconds before it's too late.

Dismount your tank and jump on my track. We'll get you out of here. *Over!"* Mark wiped a bead of sweat from the tip of his nose, watching the dead draw in even closer. There were already runners all over the place, but the main mass hadn't arrived yet. Though they were only fifty yards away at the most. The crew could hear the howls and snarls even buttoned up inside the track.

"White One, this is Dagger Six. Negative! We will not be abandoning this tank! Recall your force and bring them back. You will hook us up and tow us out of here. Acknowledge! Over!"

"Switch over to HE, we're nearly dry on coax again. I need to reload," Mark said over the intercom.

"Almost out of HE, sarn't."

"Do it anyway."

"Roger."

Mark cracked open another can and began connecting the steel links to the remaining belt still hanging from the feed chute. Whenever the gunner touched off a burst from the 25mm, they could scarcely hear anything else. Even with the headphones on the noise was deafening.

There was an audible "chunk" as the Bushmaster went dry. "Out of HE, sarn't."

"You're up on coax."

"On the way!"

They poured on all the fire they could, but it did little to stop the advance and they seemed to come in even faster now, as if they could anticipate a kill.

"Do you read me, White One? You will recall your team and pull us out of here! Answer me damn you!"

Mark's mind flashed. He tried to think of a way to comply, but the solution did not come. They'd been unsuccessful before when there were far fewer of the dead to contend with, but the undulating mass coming at them was a much larger group by an order of magnitude. They could make another attempt, but it would be ugly, and then suddenly the stress dissipated.

"Fuck this." He turned to Donahue. "Cease fire."

"Sarn't?"

"You heard me." He inhaled deeply, then toggled the intercom. "Okay, Burbey. Take us out of here. Back to the rally point with the rest of the company."

"Roger, moving!"

BOHICA pulled out, grinding several of the dead out in front before veering off to the right, headed to the western edge of the open area overwatching the intersection.

"White One, this is Dagger Six! Where are you going? Come back here this instant! That is an…"

Mark switched off the brigade command net, going back down to the company command channel.

Donahue waited a moment before speaking. "Uh, Sergeant Matthews, are we going back to get the colonel?"

"We just lost some good officers, NCOs, and soldiers back there. All for nothing. I'm not in the mood to lose any more tonight. We're leaving. Is that clear?"

"Crystal."

"Good." Mark brought the boom mike to his lips. "Guidons, guidons. This is White One. Colonel Hamilton and Lieutenant Baker are gone. I am assuming command. We are pulling out. All elements fall in behind me. We will link up with the rest of the battalion and await orders. All stations acknowledge. Over."

Within seconds they all responded in the affirmative and the column headed back off to the west, into the night.

As they did so, an army of the dead swarmed over Colonel Williams' tank, trapping them all inside and leaving them to their fate.

Chapter 14

12 September, 2016
Assembly Area Meadowlark
Southwest of Lincoln, Nebraska
0826 Hours Local

Mark looked over the roadmap once again, sitting on the bench seat with the ramp down. He drew in another lungful of sweet, fresh air slightly accented by diesel exhaust, and savored it. It was good not to have the smell of rot hanging in his nose and he still hadn't gotten over the novelty of it.

Surrounding him was a whirlwind of activity as soldiers prepared and loaded up their gear to move out. Nobody paid much attention to him, sitting there by himself, while everyone focused on the task at hand. Light trucks and other prime movers came and went, as orders were shouted over the din. He paid no attention to any of it, completely blocking out the rest of the world around him.

They'd made him give a statement after they got back the previous day, trying to learn what happened out there. The Division Commander himself was demanding a report on what happened to his brigade commander and they'd sent down some officers from G-3 to get sworn affidavits from him and some of the others.

Mark found it amusing to sign sworn statements with his new false identity, going on the record with a completely fabricated report. It didn't bother him one bit to lie his ass off about it, since so many good people died out there on Williams' screwed up mission.

The report itself was kind of thin and wouldn't survive much scrutiny. It really hinged upon the surviving NCOs and soldiers who were out there on the ground that night sticking to their story. Since there were only a handful of people who really knew Mark left Colonel Williams behind, there weren't a whole lot of stories to keep straight. Most of the people out there didn't hear the radio calls and didn't have the big picture anyway.

The only wild card was the battalion commander's crew. They heard everything on their command radios and knew precisely what occurred, but they loved Lieutenant Colonel Hamilton and hated Colonel Williams, so they went along with the cover-up. They even embellished the tale a little and made it even more colorful for the investigators.

But if there were any serious investigation into this incident, the whole thing would fall apart like a house of cards. Not that Mark cared. He'd given the orders and in twelve hours he fully intended to be on his way to Ohio, headed back to meet up with his parents and his brother.

It was always in the back of his mind that he was an escaped felon, wearing the uniform of a dead man and that his current existence was a lie. Things were a total mess right now but someday they'd figure out who he really was and they'd likely lock him up again. Or worse.

He couldn't stay with them for that reason. No, he needed to get the hell out of there as soon as possible.

He'd become fond of the men and women in his newly-adopted platoon, but now that he'd seen them through the worst of it, he figured they could make it on their own without him. Clay and Harris would take care of them after all. They would carry on without him just fine.

After the initial inquiry, Mark jumped in one of the Humvees and took off on his own, conducting his own little recon. He'd seen enough of the outskirts of Lincoln the last couple of days, that he noted the location of several cars and trucks, left behind all over the place. It took him half the day, but he found an old Dodge Durango with keys still in the ignition. The battery was dead, but that was no big deal. He could work with that.

Overnight while the entire division was packing up and getting ready to move west, he procured four five-gallon cans of gasoline and got his hands on some jumper cables along with a spare battery. What he couldn't trade for, he stole. They all sat in the back of the company commander's Humvee and Mark had the only key for the cable lock wrapped around the steering column.

The entire division was already moving out in march serials. Based upon how big the unit was, it would take all day just to get the entire monstrosity on the road and their battalion wasn't scheduled to move out until later that evening. Mark was going to be long gone by then, headed in the opposite direction.

"Looking at that atlas again? That seems to be your favorite bit of reading material."

Mark jumped. "Jesus, Clay. Are you trying to give me a heart attack?"

"No, but you seem to have a guilty conscience. Is there something you need to tell me?"

He sighed. "You remember what I told you about plausible deniability?"

Clay gave him a very serious look, staring hard. "Anyway, the battalion commander is asking for you and Harris."

"You mean, Major Denney?"

"Yeah. After we lost Colonel Hamilton, Major Denney assumed command."

"When does he want to see us?" Mark looked at his watch again, seeing how much time he had left before he made a break for it.

"Right away. He said it's important."

"Fine, I'll be right there." Mark stuffed the road atlas back into his rucksack and grabbed his Remington, dearly wanting this meeting to be over as soon as humanly possible.

***

"Sir, Sergeant Matthews and Specialist Harris, reporting as ordered." Mark and Harris stood at the rigid positions of "attention" while rendering parade-ground salutes. Mark felt particularly ridiculous, but had hoped no one else was picking up on it.

Major Denney sat behind a field desk in the open air next to his Humvee. He preferred to work outside of the tent command center whenever he could. He spent far too much time in the "TOC" and liked to escape it whenever he could. He casually returned the salutes and leaned back in his folding chair. "At ease, both of you."

The both of them immediately relaxed, spreading their feet shoulder-width apart and clasping their hands behind their backs. They quickly gave each other a quizzical glance before directing their attention back to the officer.

"It's been a rough couple of days. How's morale holding up?" Denney studied Mark, cocking his head to the side a bit while crossing his arms across his chest. One of the enlisted men came up and placed a steaming canteen cup of coffee on the field desk in front of the major and moved on without saying a word. In the background, there was a flurry of activity as men and women finished packing up the last of their gear.

"I'd say with everything that's occurred, everyone is holding up pretty well I guess." Mark wasn't sure what the officer wanted to hear, so he kept his response guarded.

"That's good. Are your people ready to move out?" He reached down and retrieved the cup, blowing on it before taking a sip. He smacked his lips and grunted before carefully placing it back down next some random paperwork he was working on.

"Yes, sir. Everything is topped off, loaded up and squared away. We look like a gypsy caravan, but we're ready to move."

"Good. That's good." He shifted in his folding chair and leaned forward, resting his elbows on the desk. "Do you know why I've summoned you here?"

Mark swallowed the lump growing in his throat. There was never a good reason to get called in front of the battalion commander and the only thing he could think of was that he'd been found out. Someone must have either blown the whistle on them leaving the brigade commander out there to die, or worse, they knew he was an escaped felon from Leavenworth. Either one was bad. "No, sir. No idea."

"Well, we took an ass-whoopin' the other day. We lost more people than I care to think about. Overall, Division is calling the operation a success since we secured all the food and fuel we needed, but it cost us. Big time." He leaned back and spit on the ground before going on. "We've been short on officers since the outbreak and things have recently gotten a lot worse in that regard. Everybody's being forced to step and take additional responsibilities. Yours Truly included."

A clerk came over with a sheaf of papers and whispered something into Denney's ear before handing them to him. The major nodded in understanding and shooed the man away.

"Anyway, the reason I called you both here is to inform you that I am approving some battlefield promotions." He looked up at Mark. "Sergeant Matthews, I am told that you're a hell of a leader and that you got your people out of some tight scrapes on numerous occasions. Is that true?"

"I uh… I don't know about all that, sir. I just do what needs to get done," Mark answered, looking down at his boots.

"Well, if I had it my way, I'd be promoting you today, but I can't. You're not assigned to the 1st Infantry Division, so you're not in our chain of command. No matter how hard I tried, those dickheads up in G-1 wouldn't approve it, saying I need to get you formally transferred to us or some bullshit like that, and then they couldn't tell me how to make that happen. Typical bureaucratic chickenshit. In any event, I did put you in for a Bronze Star with a 'V' device for valor. I heard the Division Commander himself signed off on it this morning. I don't have a medal to pin on your chest yet, but I'm happy to shake your hand." The officer stood and came around the table and extended his hand.

Mark took Denney's hand and shook it with a baffled look on his face. "Uh, thank you, sir. I don't know what to say."

"You don't need to say anything. Well done, soldier." He went back and plopped back down in his folding chair and shifted his gaze to Harris, who at this point looked like a cat in a room full of rocking chairs. "Harris, they tell me you've been acting squad leader. Is that true?"

"Yes, sir. That's correct."

"I read the reports from Lieutenant Baker and Sergeant Matthews. They've had nothing but good things to say about you." He looked through the paperwork recently handed to him and he flipped through some of it. "It says here you're a college graduate too."

"Yes, sir."

"That's good. I just wanted to let you know that my nomination for your battlefield commission was approved a couple of hours ago. You're no longer a member of the E-4 mafia. You're now a Second Lieutenant and my new Bravo Company commander." Denney rose again and grabbed the former enlisted man's hand. "Congratulations, Lieutenant

Harris."

Harris looked like was about to faint. "Thank you, sir. It's an honor."

"I don't know how much of an honor it is, but it sure will be a lot of work, and I expect you to not let me down. Understood?"

"Yes, sir."

"I don't have a Bronze Star handy, but I do have one of these." Denney took out a pocket knife and stripped the "Shield of Sham" from Harris' jacket. He then reached into a pocket and pinned on a brand-new 2nd lieutenant bar in its place. "It's official and you're street-legal now."

Once again, the major sat down. "Listen, for the time being, Matthews you'll still have 2nd Platoon. I'm also keeping the two tanks with you attached to Bravo Company. We're cross-leveling personnel from across the brigade, so after we settle into our next assembly area on the way to Denver, you will get some replacements. Until then, get your personnel and equipment ready to move. Any questions?"

There weren't any.

"Okay then, you're dismissed."

Bewildered, they both saluted and moved out smartly.

***

The two of them meandered back through the assembly area, nearly getting run over by a LMTV on their way back to the company area. Harris shouted at the driver as he drove by, completely oblivious to them. Mark on the other didn't react at all, completely lost in his thoughts.

"Sarn't Matthews. Before we get back to the company, can I speak with you?" Harris looked as if he were about take an exam he hadn't studied for.

Mark almost kept walking, but sighed deeply, his shoulders sagging a tiny bit. "Yes, Harris. What is it?"

"I really need to ask you something." The worry lines on his forehead were deeply pronounced and his voice trembled some.

"You probably ought to spit it out. We don't have all day."

"I... I can't believe they just made me an officer."

"Yeah, me neither. The miracles never cease." Mark didn't have the patience for this. The clock was ticking and he had to get out of there soon if he had any chance of slipping away without being noticed. He kept thinking about the Humvee, loaded with his supplies and the keys to the Durango sitting in his pocket. "Do you have a question or are we going to continue standing here, gazing deeply into each other's eyes?"

"Sarn't, I'm not cut out to be an officer. I'm no leader, and not only did they make me a lieutenant, but they made me the company commander. I don't know the first thing about that. They can't be serious about this. I'm going to get everyone killed." Tears welled up in his eyes.

Mark's jaw muscles bulged and he pursed his lips. He didn't want to deal with this right now. He took a moment before saying anything, fighting back the urge to say something mean-spirited and hurtful. So many sharp comments flashed in his mind, but he fought the urge to blurt them out and tamped all that down. It would do no good to lash out at the kid, it would have been like kicking a puppy. Finally, with much effort, he composed himself before responding. "Get a hold of yourself, Harris. Don't fall to pieces on me. You're a leader now, whether you like it or not, so it's best that you start to accept that. For better or worse, people will now look to you for the answers and there's no turning back from that. You may not have been looking for it, but it found you. Do you understand?"

"Roger, sarn't."

"Now, wipe those tears away. Hold your head up and march on over to the company command post, like you own the place. You're in command. Act like it. If you show weakness in front of the rest of them, they'll lose faith in you right away and we can't afford that. Show confidence, even if you don't feel it. Got it?"

"Roger, sarn't."

"And don't say that to me anymore. You're an officer for God's sake. Act like the pompous ass that everyone expects you to be. Understood?"

"Yes, I think so." Harris sniffled and wiped the tears away with the sleeve of his camouflage jacket. He held his shoulders back and lifted his chin a bit higher, almost imperceptibly so.

"That's better." Mark squared his shoulders, locked his heels together and rendered his third salute of the day. Using customs and courtesies that had grown rusty through lack of practice over the last several years. "By your leave. *Sir.*"

Harris looked around to see if anyone was watching, with a look of bewilderment on his face. After a second, he snapped out of it and returned the salute. "Uh… yeah. Carry on."

***

He'd dog-eared the pages of the atlas so he could easily find the right page and he opened it up once again, studying the route. He reached down and pulled out the keys to the Durango in a fit of obsessive-compulsive behavior, ensuring that they were still there. He stuffed them back in his pocket and went through his mental checklist again before looking at his G-Shok. He really needed to get moving soon.

Over in the field nearby, Donahue kissed his wife before she climbed in the NBC NCO's truck. She'd become one of the helpers in the headquarters element, assisting the Supply Sergeant and a few of the others along with the rest of the civilian women.

Angie filled a metal bowl with water and gave it to Saxon while Jefferson cinched down some gear. Angel stood, totally focused on McDermott, who tried to explain how to check track tension on the Bradley. Jimmy Hong and Weber went around topping off canteens and water bladders with a five-gallon jerry can while Bags packed up the last of her kit.

He heard Bailey Roberts patiently explaining something in English to Consuela while her mother, Cynthia punched frequencies into the radios in the First Sergeant's M113. Burbey was off digging through a duffle bag looking for his dash-ten maintenance manual as Dubois and Johnson settled into the turret of *Carnage*, getting some last-minute instruction from its driver, Volks.

While the rest did that, Gray pulled the guts out of *BOHICA*'s coax machine gun, wiping down the freshly cleaned components with an oily rag. Then she carefully reassembled them once again before performing a functions check.

Everybody worked hard, getting ready to move out.

"I wonder what is so interesting about that thing."

Mark jumped once again. "Jesus, Clay. Will you stop doing that?"

"Doing what?"

"Scaring the living shit out of me."

"Sorry. Anyway, I thought you should know that I couldn't find Harris for the longest time and then I found out he's been hanging out in the company CP. Sergeant Packard told me to come and get you. He said Harris must have fallen on his head or something because he's claiming to be an officer and trying to take over command of the company. He wanted you to come get your boy."

Mark snorted. "Yeah, I probably should have told Top what's going on. That's my bad."

"I don't understand."

"Yeah, well I barely understand it myself."

"You're not making any sense."

"Please go tell Top Packard to assemble the company, because there's some news."

"Seriously, Mark. We've got less than an hour before we're supposed to move out. I don't know that we've got time for this."

"Trust me. We do. Now please go."

"Okay, I'll have Packard gather everyone up." Clay didn't linger, cradling his Mini-14 and heading off.

Mark paid no attention while Clay left, instead looking back down at the road map, tracing the route back to Ohio with his finger. He filled both of his lungs before slowly exhaling, then closed up the atlas and stuffed it into his rucksack before climbing back down the ramp of *BOHICA,* surveying the controlled chaos all around him.

He pulled out the car keys one last time and stared at them as if they were an alien object.

Then, as if possessed by a force outside of his control he pitched the keys as far away as he could, throwing them off into the nearby field, filled with active vehicle traffic. A moment later an M-88 ran them over, grinding them into the dirt.

"I guess I'll make that road trip to Ohio later. Besides, I've never been to Washington before. It couldn't be much worse than this," he said to himself.

And with that, he marched off to tell the rest of the company they had a new commander.

To be continued ...

Cannon has dozens of great books in multiple genres. If you're interested in learning more, please visit our website!

www.cannonpublishing.us

Follow Shane on Amazon!

www.ingramcontent.com/pod-product-compliance
Lightning Source LLC
Chambersburg PA
CBHW070633260626
47161CB00007B/2687